ONE HAPPY SUMMER

BECKY MONSON

One Happy Summer

Cover art by Melody Jeffries

ALSO BY BECKY MONSON

The Spinster Series

Speak Now or Forever Hold Your Peace

Taking a Chance

Once Again in Christmas Falls

Just a Name

Just a Girl

The Accidental Text

The Love Potion

How to Ruin the Holidays

Pumpkin Spice and Not So Nice

Love Songs Suck

The Wedding Jinx

Not Boyfriend Material

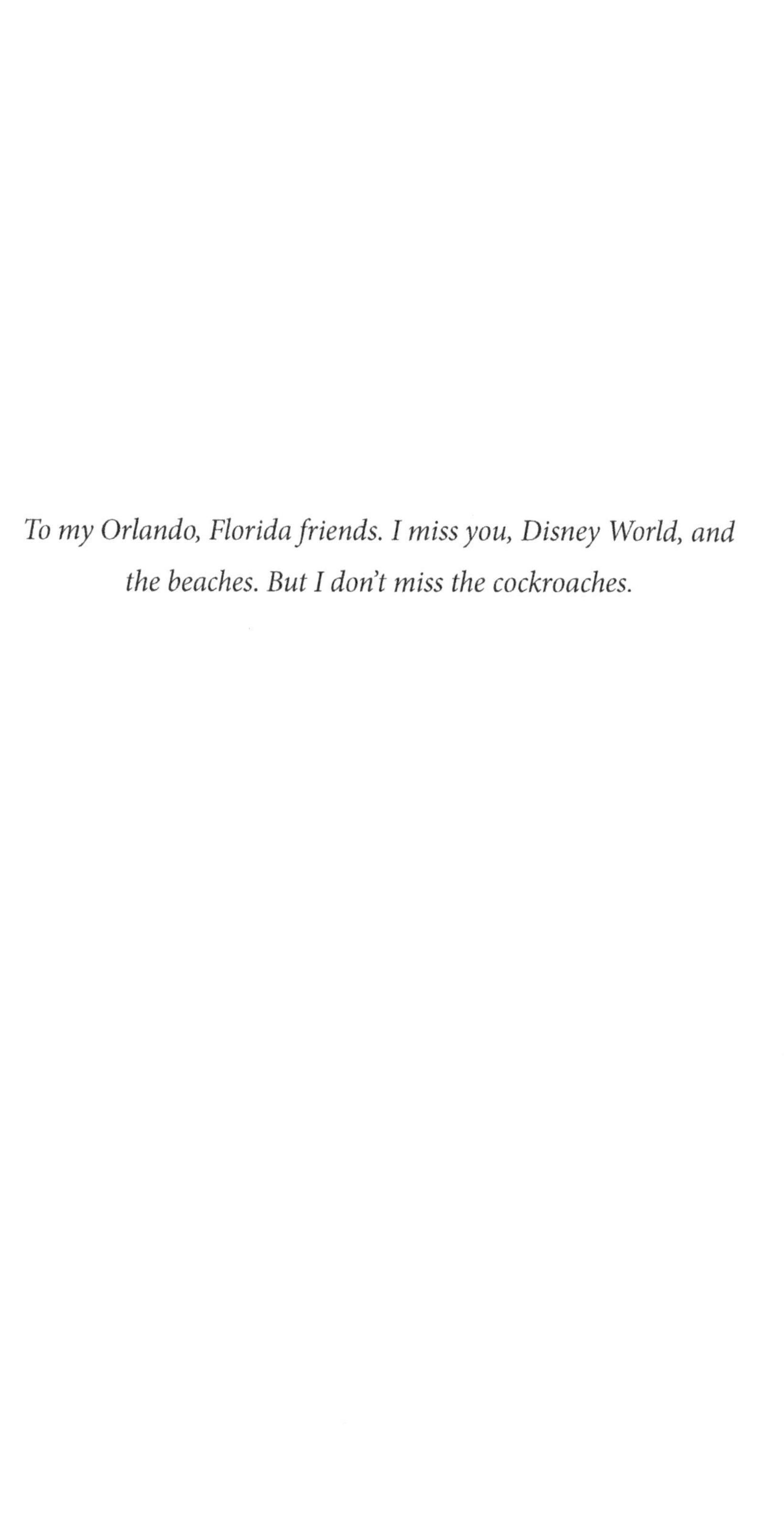

To my Orlando, Florida friends. I miss you, Disney World, and the beaches. But I don't miss the cockroaches.

WELCOME TO SUNSET HARBOR

SUNSET HARBOR IS a fictional island set off the west coast of Florida. Each book in the Falling for Summer series is set in this dreamy town and uses crossover characters and events, creating fun connections throughout the series. Be sure to read all seven books so you can fully experience the magic of Sunset Harbor!

WELCOME TO

SUNSET HARBOR

CHAPTER 1

Presley

OF ALL THE stupid, idiotic, ridiculous things I've ever done, this has to be the worst.

Presley James, you moron.

I laugh to myself as I sit on the plush leather chair of a private jet I hired to get me out of California as quickly and discreetly as possible.

It's not a real laugh; it's a what-the-heck-have-you-done kind of laugh. It's also mixed with some tears because I'm feeling very up and down right now, sort of like Jekyll and Hyde. Only, I'm not as crazed as Hyde. I hope.

Whatever the metaphor, it's all because of the dumpster fire my life has suddenly become. It's all my fault, of course. I have no one to blame but myself. I'd like to fault others—and I have. I've mentally pointed fingers at every person I can think of, trying to put the responsibility on someone else. But at the end of the day, it all comes back to me. Just me.

"Miss James, can I get you a drink?" asks a woman dressed in a tailored, plum-colored blazer and matching skirt. Her blonde hair is pulled up into a chignon and her lips, currently forming a soft, fake-looking smile, are coated in similarly plum lipstick.

I've never met this woman until today, but I'm fairly confident she hates me. I've gotten pretty good at reading people, because you have to in this business, and I can tell she's not at all happy to be here serving me drinks. It's in the forced smile, the way her eyebrows are pulled down just slightly, and the faint tic in her jaw. She's probably seen the leaked video and thinks I'm one of those spoiled celebrities, someone who thinks the world revolves around her, rather than the overworked actor who hasn't had a break in years and was at the end of her rope.

Not that it excuses my actions, but maybe if people knew the truth, they might not be so quick to judge. Somehow, I doubt that. Everyone loves a good fall-from-grace story.

Should I apologize to her? Maybe explain what happened? I haven't really been able to talk to anyone who would actually listen. All the people I thought were my friends apparently aren't, and everyone else is paid to be there. That includes my own mother.

No. It would be stupid to offer an apology to the flight attendant. She probably doesn't want to hear my sob story. Or she does and would sell it to the highest bidder. It's best to just keep quiet through this five-and-a-half-hour flight. Plus, it's possible I've got it wrong, and she hasn't seen anything. I could just be projecting. But just in case, I give her my best please-don't-hate-me smile. It's toothy, and my cheeks instantly burn with the exaggerated way they are pulling upward.

"Um, yes, please," I say to her in my sweetest voice. "Some sparkling water would be great."

With a simple nod, the woman walks toward the galley at the front of the plane and I drop my ridiculous grin.

Maybe I should have ordered something stronger. Something to take the edge off or at least to mask all the crappy feelings I'm having right now. It's probably not a good idea. I need a clear mind, especially if I'm going to figure out how to get to my destination, which isn't all that cut-and-dried. There's the transport from the airport to the ferry and then the ferry to the island, and then once I'm there, I guess I'm supposed to walk to the resort because there aren't any cars at my intended destination. Or, rather, my escape. I also need to do all of it without being seen or recognized. It will take a miracle.

I didn't actually have to walk. Noah, an acquaintance of mine and the person who offered me this refuge, said he could pick me up in a golf cart, but I declined. It was the idea of small talk on the way to the resort that had me saying no. The stilted conversation. Having to skirt around the big, bad, terrible thing I had done. At least Noah didn't think it was horrible enough to take back his offer allowing me to stay at his family resort whenever needed. And boy, do I need it now.

Okay, that's great. The tears are back. No crazy laughter this time. I couldn't possibly laugh with the instant snot-nosed crying fest that's just begun.

"Here you go," the flight attendant says with absolutely perfect timing. And by that, I really mean the worst timing ever.

I mutter a barely audible thank you, keeping my head down so she doesn't see me weeping. Not that I'm hiding anything, not with my hunched posture and my obvious shaking shoulders. Oh, and I just made a very audible hiccupping noise. She doesn't ask if I'm okay or try to offer any comforting words, not even a pat on the arm or anything; she just turns and walks back to the galley.

It's fine; I don't need comfort right now, especially from a stranger. I'm not the kind of person who enjoys being comforted, to be honest. Not that I've gotten much anyway. It's mostly been stern looks and words like "How could you let this happen?" and "What the hell were you thinking?" The latter was from my dear mother.

The truth is, I wasn't thinking. That's the real answer. I had a big, fat brain fart. Or really, I jumped on the crazy train and went for a joyride.

It wasn't like I woke up three days ago and chose violence. It was more like a myriad of things, a combination of frustrations that were a long time coming, and it all came bursting out of me in a verbal tirade over set lighting, of all things. I'd been standing there for what felt like an eternity, waiting for the gaffer to get the lighting right, my mind awhirl about how ridiculous my life had become, how everything I did was for show, and I just lost it.

Of course, someone recorded the whole thing and it was immediately put on social media for all the world to see, spreading like wildfire and taking me from A-list status to crap-list status in just a few short days.

I know why. I've seen the video myself. I'll forever be able to hear the shrillness in my voice and picture the redness of my face as I spit out phrases like "you people," "unprofessional," and "Do you even know who I am?"

Oh, dear heaven above. I can't believe I said all that. I didn't even mean it.

Do you even know who I am? I'd laugh at the ridiculousness if I wasn't currently making unladylike snorting noises as I continue my sobbing. I reach up and wipe my running nose with the back of my hand. Oh, if the gossip sites could see this version of me.

I deserve all the bad press I'm getting right now. But I also sort of don't. Aren't I allowed a moment of weakness? A bit of time to be human, to make a mistake like humans often do? Not in this industry, I'm not. Not when I'm America's Sweetheart, which is what a few gossip magazines have deemed me.

I do try to be a sweetheart, for the most part. One very bad instance aside. I set out to not let this industry jade me, to not get used to the lifestyle, to never stop appreciating the hookups and the handouts. I've tried my darnedest to keep both feet on the ground at all times.

I don't make unnecessary demands. I don't stipulate there be only green M&Ms in my dressing room, no all-white trailer with an on-demand masseuse to pamper me between takes. None of that. I treat my assistant with respect, and I get stuff done myself—I don't load it all on her. She's amazing, though, and I've often wondered out loud what I'd do without Shani. I guess I'll soon be finding out because even she doesn't know my current whereabouts.

I take a deep breath, leaning my head back on the seat. That's right, Presley, enough with the crying. It's not going to help anything anyway.

I need a distraction, something to tide me over until I arrive at the Fort Myers airport, but I've got nothing. I don't have my phone. Before I left LA, I got a new one—a cheap phone without all the bells and whistles so nobody can figure out how to track me, and a new number so no one can call me. This means I don't have anything to keep me occupied, no social media for obvious reasons, no apps for reading or listening to books, not even Candy Crush. I didn't think this through. I should have at least gotten a phone that would allow me to play Candy Crush.

I lean my head back against the chair and sigh, although it comes out as more of a hiccup. I've only got to make it through the summer. That's my goal. Three months of hiding away on an island should be enough time for everyone to forget about my big faux pas or at least move on to something else. That's my hope, or really, my need, because that's when I start a big project—possibly the biggest of my career. So I need everyone to move on, for all the gossip sites to focus on something else by then so I don't get dropped from the movie. And it's a possibility, considering I've already been dropped from another project in the fallout. My agent, who has no idea I'm on a plane right now, guesses there might be more fallout to come. But they can't cancel my contracts if they can't find me, right? This is my plan, as faulty as it is. My entire career hinges on this idea.

Three months. I can do this.

WELCOME TO SUNSET HARBOR

BELACOURT RESORT

GOLF COURSE

NOAH'S HOUSE

JANE'S HOUSE

NATURE PRESERVE

DAX'S DUPLEX

SEASIDE OASIS RETIREMENT HOME

SUNSET REPAIRS

PHOENIX'S OFFICE

CITY OFFICES

SCOOPS AHOY ICE CREAM

SUNRISE CAFE

KEENE B&B

GULF OF MEXICO

TOWN SQUARE

BAKERY

BRIGGS'S APARTMENT

THE BOOK ISLE

CUTS AND CURLS

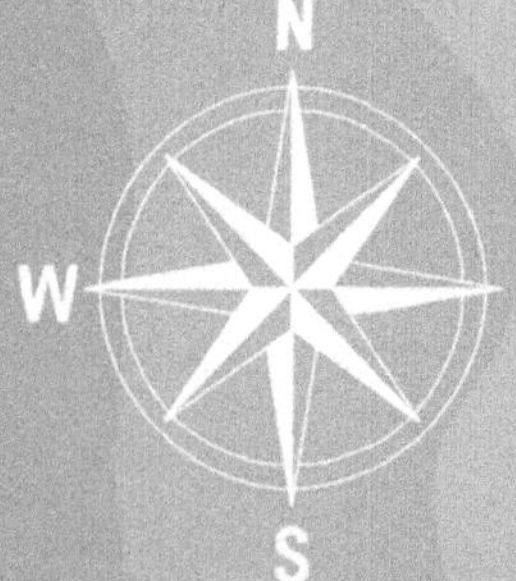

CHAPTER 2

Briggs

THEY SAY NEVER put all your eggs in one basket.

Well, I'm here to tell you that they—whoever they are—are right.

"What can I help you find, Carl?" I ask the only handyman on the island of Sunset Harbor as he peruses the shelves of the bookshop, his brow pulled downward as he concentrates, sweat glistening on his forehead.

It's too early in the morning to be dealing with this. He was knocking on the glass door of the shop before I came downstairs to open.

"I need a book about refrigerator repair, particularly for the Samsung brand," he says, not bothering to look in my direction.

I push my glasses up my nose and will my eyes not to move to the ceiling, like they are straining to do, wondering if it's possible for a man who's been a permanent fixture on the small island where this bookshop has been for many years to think he could find that kind of book here.

"Sorry, Carl, this is mainly a fiction bookshop," I tell him. The Book Isle, my mom's third child, opened its doors nearly thirteen years ago, not long after I turned fifteen.

"Yes, well, doesn't hurt to ask," Carl says. "You ought to consider carrying some nonfiction books."

"I'll be sure to pass that on to my mom," I say.

"It's good business practice," he says with a confident nod.

"I'm sure refrigerator-repair guides will fly off the shelves."

He nods in agreement, clearly missing the sarcasm.

I'll pass it on for sure, but mostly as a joke. Marianne McMannus, an avid reader of fiction, bought the store for the sole purpose of housing the books she loves. Which means this quaint bookshop, with the soft lighting, the framed prints of vintage book covers on the walls, and the plush chairs placed thoughtfully around the space, carries mainly romance books, even though that hardly turns a profit. Of course, there's a smattering of other books, especially the classics. My mom is a big fan—my sister, Scout, and I were both named after characters from her favorite books. I didn't get a literary first name, but I did get a middle one. I rarely tell people what it is because I hate it. Most of my closest friends don't even know. Not that I have many of those these days. If they were right about not putting all your eggs in one basket, then they—again, not sure who they are—

were even more right about not going into business with friends. It's just a bad idea. I know that now.

Carl lets out a large breath, his round belly moving up and down with the effort. "Well, I guess I better figure out how I'm going to fix this dang ice machine for the Vanderduesens."

"You could maybe . . . check YouTube?" I say, giving him a little shrug of my shoulders.

He reaches up and scratches the side of his neck, just under his jaw, his eyes squinting. "Yeah, I guess. Do you think they have something like that on there?"

"I do," I say.

Carl turns his face toward me, his gaze curious. "Say, Briggs, what are you doing back here anyway? I thought you started some big, important company in Miami."

"It was Fort Lauderdale, actually," I say, not sure why I bothered to correct him. I adjust my glasses, a tic I seem to get when I feel suddenly anxious.

He pulls his eyebrows together. "What're you doing back here?"

Oh yes. The million-dollar question. It was the basket that held all my eggs, and when they broke, I had only one option, which was to come back to Sunset Harbor, my figurative tail between my legs. That was the first part of May, and here I am, one month later, still without a clue about what to do next.

I take a deep breath, feeling a sort of ache in the pit of my stomach, a pain that's been showing up every now and then since I came back. A reminder of how lost I've been feeling lately.

"It . . . didn't work out," I tell Carl.

It was a combination of things that caused the inevitable demise of the start-up I'd been working to get off the ground with friends from college. But the main one was money. We just simply ran out of it.

I'm not sure why it rankles to admit this to the island handyman; it's not like I was some small-town star, the boy expected to go places. I've mostly lived under the radar since moving here in the seventh grade when my mom married Keith McMannus, who'd been a Sunset Harbor staple for pretty much his entire life.

But maybe that's why. Because I wasn't someone people talked about growing up, and now I feel like they will be for all the wrong reasons: Briggs Dalton is a failure.

"Well," he says, reaching out and patting my arm. "I'm sure your mom is happy to have you back."

"She is," I say, giving him a nod. That's the one silver lining—my mom was more than happy to get me back here. So was my sister, Scout. They've been pestering me for years, ever since I graduated college. Now I'm back and working at the bookshop, and also living in the apartment above it. Not exactly how I pictured my life going.

Carl takes a small step closer to me, his chin dipping slightly. "Do you know . . . is she, uh, your mom, seeing anyone?" he asks in low tones, even though we're the only ones here.

My eyes widen of their own accord. Carl's . . . interested in my mom? I have no idea if my mom is seeing anyone, because, well, I don't want to know. My guess is probably not. It's only been three years since Keith passed away unexpectedly. "Carl, I—"

I'm cut off—or saved, essentially—by the bell that rings whenever the door to the bookshop is opened. Carl jumps back like we've just been caught in a shady deal.

"Sorry . . . I'm just . . . gonna . . ." I hook a thumb over my shoulder, toward the entrance of the store.

I walk away from Carl without a backwards glance, around the corner from the shelves we were standing by, and to the entrance. I expect to see my mom, who's supposed to be here this morning, or someone else from the island who's hopefully not here to ask me about my mom's current dating status, but instead I find someone else.

I've been away from the island for a while now—nine years, to be exact. I'm sure there have been new people who've moved to the island since then, and the woman standing in front of me, petite build, black running shorts and a white tank, dark hair pulled back into a low ponytail, a baseball cap on her head and dark glasses covering her eyes, is definitely someone I've never seen around here before.

And yet, she looks familiar.

"Can I help you?" I ask, after I realize I've been staring, trying to figure out how I might know the person standing in front of me. I reach up and push my glasses up the bridge of my nose.

"I'm looking for a book," she says, tilting her head up to compensate for the several inches of height difference between us.

"Oh, right. Well, we sell those here," I say, holding out a hand toward the rows of shelves that take up most of the space.

She gives me a closed-mouth smile, and I mentally slap myself for sounding like an idiot.

"Bye, Briggs," Carl says as he walks past. He does a double take at the woman standing in front of me before exiting out the door, the bells ringing as he leaves.

I clear my throat once the door shuts. "Anything in particular I can help you find?"

"Yes. I was hoping to get a copy of Secret Crush by Sunny Palmer," she says. Her voice is lower and raspy sounding. Very sexy, in my just-formed opinion. Again, I'm hit with the feeling that I've met her before. Maybe if she weren't wearing those shades, I'd figure out how I know her. It doesn't seem like she plans on taking them off, though.

"Yah-yes," I say, stammering over my words. "We've got a few copies. My mom ordered them for the book club they have here on the island. It's usually just a bunch of ladies from the retirement center. I can find out when they meet if you want to join?"

What am I even talking about?

"That's okay," she says. "I'm not really a book club kind of person."

"Right. Of course."

I weave my hands together in front of me because they're suddenly feeling like misplaced appendages on my body. I clear my throat unnecessarily. She sniffs.

"Can you . . . maybe show me where the book is?" she finally asks.

"Uh, yes," I say. What is happening to me right now? I've been body snatched by a moron. I've always been awkward, especially around the opposite sex, but this is above and beyond. "It's just . . . um . . . over here."

I turn toward the shelves and she follows me. I know exactly where the current Sunny Palmer books are located because I sold a copy to someone from the book club just the other day.

"Here it is," I say, pulling the last one from the shelves and handing it to her.

She takes it from me, and I notice her fingernails are ragged looking, as if she's scraped off her nail polish. "Thanks," she says.

"Do you . . . need any other books?"

"Actually, yes," she says, her eyebrows peeking over the top of her sunglasses. "Do you have any recommendations?"

"Recommendations?"

Her lips pull slightly upward. "Yes, anything else I need to read?"

"I . . . uh . . ." I may be working in a bookshop, but I don't actually read. Not fiction books, at least. Maybe Carl's right and we should add some nonfiction. Who knows, I might find refrigerator repair manuals compelling.

She grabs a book off the shelf. "Like this one. Is it any good?"

I look down at the cover. "Oh, yeah, that one is . . . great. The Rule Book by Sarah Adams. Everyone is reading it."

She cocks her head to the side, the corner of her mouth moving up slightly. "What's it about?"

"Well, it's a rule book of sorts. There are these rules."

"Sounds fascinating."

"It really is."

She takes it from me and stacks it on top of the Sunny Palmer book. "Any others?"

"Uh, sure," I say as I reach out and grab another book off the shelf. "This one right here is a breakout sensation." I hold it out toward her, the words breakout sensation in bold at the top.

She looks down at it. "The Love Hypothesis?"

"Yes. It's by—" I pause to search the cover. "Ali Hazelwood. It's a New York Times bestseller." I point to the gold sticker with the white lettering stuck to the front of the paperback. Why do they put stickers on paperbacks? I'm pretty sure everyone hates it.

"Sounds interesting. What's it about?"

I look down at the illustrated drawing of a man and a woman kissing on the cover and then awkwardly back at her. "It's definitely a page turner. It's about people who . . . hypothesize about love."

She smiles now, lovely, bright-white teeth on display. "Sounds like a good one."

"Oh, it is," I say.

"You haven't read any of them, have you?"

"No," I say, shaking my head.

She giggles at that and my stomach does a weird dipping thing, a feeling I haven't had in forever. It's almost foreign.

A little voice in my head, one that has been quiet for a long time, nudges me to ask her out, or at the very least ask for her number. It's been a while since I've had that thought. This time is unfounded, because even though she looks familiar, I can't place how I know her. Plus, she might not even be single, or even be interested. Not to mention, I'm in no place to date. Not with the back-to-square-one turn my life has taken.

"Well, I'll take them. All three." She holds out a hand, and I give her the third book, which she stacks on top of the others.

"Excellent choices," I say.

We stand there again, and I rack my brain, still trying to figure out where I could possibly know her from. Was it here on the island? During college? If she'd take off the sunglasses, that might help—they're keeping me from getting a good look. All I'm basing this off is a perfect button nose and full lips in a lovely shade of pink. Why can't I figure this out?

"Can I . . . buy them?" the woman asks, snapping me out of what might have been a short trance. Good hell, was I staring at her lips? I think I was.

"Right," I say, berating myself for acting like a fool. I feel disarmed around her. It's a strange feeling.

She follows me to the front of the store, and once I'm behind the register, she hands me the books. I ring them up while she peruses the odds and ends my mom has for sale on the front counter—small notebooks, a variety of pens, and some gimmicky books of questions.

She hands me cash from a black cross-body bag once I tell her the total. I'd hoped for a credit card so I could see a name to help jog my memory, but no such luck. I guess I could just ask her, but it feels like I've missed the timing on that. I bag up the books and hand them to her.

"Thanks for the help," she says as she takes them.

"You're welcome. You'll have to let me know if you enjoyed the books."

"Rules and hypotheses—how can I not?" She gives me a smile.

"Have we . . . met before?" I finally ask. It's taken me too long to ask, but I've already made a fool of myself—might as well run with it.

She shakes her head. "No," she says definitively.

"Are you sure?"

"I'm sure," she says.

"You just look so familiar."

"I have one of those faces."

"I don't think that's it," I say, shaking my head. "Do you live here? On the island?"

"No, just visiting." She slides a hand through the handles of the bag of books, looking like she's about to make a run for it, her demeanor changing to something more anxious, which makes me even more curious. I may lack a lot of things in life, but reading a room has always been a talent of mine, and this room says, Stop asking stupid questions.

"Thank you for these," she says, with a head bob toward the books.

"Of course," I tell her.

She turns and leaves the store, the bells jingling as she exits.

I stare at the door after she leaves, still trying to work out how I might know her. After a minute, I give up and busy myself with organizing a stack of notebooks on the counter.

It doesn't matter anyway; I'm not trying to see people on this island besides my mom and Scout. I can't get around running into people when they come into the shop, but other than that I've been hiding in the apartment above the store that my mom kindly offered when I told her I was coming back. It's a small, one-bedroom place, and it's got some interesting decor. But I'm grateful for it.

It's not that I'm avoiding particular people—I just don't want to see anyone. I don't want to have to answer questions about why I'm back, what happened, what I plan to do with my life, how I'm going to get back on my feet . . . I don't even know the answers to the last two questions. I'm giving myself the summer to figure it all out. And hopefully I will.

The bells on the door ring as it opens, and I can instantly feel the warm, humid air that's slipped in, fighting for dominance with the air-conditioning. My eyes dart toward the entrance, hoping she—the mysterious, yet familiar, woman—might come through the door, back to tell me who she is and put this unsolved mystery to rest. Instead, my mom enters the bookshop, carrying a bouquet of flowers in one hand and a canvas tote full of who-knows-what in the other.

"Hello, Mom," I say before giving her a faint smile.

"Briggs," she says, sounding out of breath. It's not a greeting, it's the start of a sentence. She has something to tell me, and from the look of her wide eyes, it's very important information. That, or not at all important. You never really know with my mom. It could be anything. A dolphin sighting on her morning beach stroll or seeing someone doing something out of the ordinary on her walk here. Not a lot of exciting things happen on this island.

"Carl was here earlier, and he thinks we should be carrying some refrigerator-repair manuals," I start, purposely cutting off whatever story she was about to tell me, just to be annoying, and also so I wouldn't forget. I told him I would say something, after all. I also want to tell her that he was fishing around about her relationship status, but I decide to keep that to myself.

She lets the bag she's holding drop to her side, a punctuation to the irritated expression on her face: brows drawn low, lips pursed.

"He said it was good business practice." I emphasize the last three words for added effect.

Her eyes move to the ceiling briefly. She shakes her head as she flings the tote she was carrying onto the only empty space on the front counter. The bag teeters before it sags to the side. The contents—which look to be books, go figure—surprisingly stay put. The flowers are next, but she's gentler with those.

"Do you know who I just saw?" she asks, obviously done with talk of Carl and his refrigerator-repair-manual needs.

Marianne McMannus's green eyes—the ones I inherited—stare me down, and her sandy-blonde hair, also the same as mine, looks a little bit frizzy, which means she definitely did her morning beach stroll.

"A dolphin?" I ask, taking an educated guess. It's a common thing around here.

She scrunches her brow, looking at me like I've sprouted another head. "I said who," she says.

I shrug a shoulder. "I don't know, maybe you named the dolphins."

She bobs her head from side to side. "That does sound like something I'd do. But that's not what I'm talking about." She leans in toward me, dipping her chin as she does, like she has the juiciest of gossip. "I think I just saw Presley James."

I cock my head to the side, "The . . . actress?"

"No," she says, scoffing. "The gardener. Yes, of course the actress." She shakes her head like she can't believe the cluelessness of her only son. "I heard a rumor she was here, but I didn't believe it. And you know I'm not one to gossip."

"Oh yeah, absolutely," I deadpan. My mom is actually the opposite of someone who isn't one to gossip. She might even be the town queen of it.

She blows air out of her nose, giving me a disappointed look. "I don't gossip, Briggs," she reiterates. "But I'm telling you, I think it was Presley James."

“What did she look like?”

“She’s a tiny thing. Dark hair under a baseball cap and sunglasses on. I just passed by her on the way here.” She inhales quickly. “Oh my . . . was she here? In our store?” She points out toward the main area of the bookshop, figurative stars in her eyes.

Presley James . . . Presley . . . James.

Oh no.

I slap myself on the forehead with my palm. That’s why she looked so familiar. Not because I’ve met her before, but because I’ve seen her on a movie screen.

Briggs, you idiot.

“She was in the store,” I tell my mom.

Her jaw drops. “She was in the store?” Her voice is so loud someone on the moon could probably hear her. “Scout is going to freak out! Did you at least get a picture, Briggsy?”

I narrow my eyes at her, not because of the nickname that she’s called me probably since birth—I don’t mind that—but because of her ridiculous assumption.

“Yes, because I make a habit of snapping pictures of all our patrons,” I tell her. I drop my chin and purse my lips to accentuate my sarcastic retort.

“We had someone famous in the shop and you didn’t even think to snap a picture?”

"Maybe it's not Presley," I say, hopeful that I'm right. I'm feeling waves of embarrassment work their way down my spine as I think about all the stupid things I said to her when she was here. Presley Freaking James.

"It has to be," she says. "Word is she's staying at the Belacourt Resort."

Note to self: stay away from the Belacourt Resort. Not that I have any reason to be at the posh hotel.

I'll just have to hope I never see her again.

CHAPTER 3

Presley

WHAT AM I DOING?

What am I doing, what am I doing, WHAT. AM. I. DOING?

Presley James, what the heck are you doing right now? You're not supposed to be here; you're supposed to be locked in your room, not off gallivanting around the town. Have you lost your mind?

"You'll ruin your back sitting like that, young lady," an older woman says to me. Well, I think it's an older woman, at least if I'm going on her voice alone. It's raspy with a slight quiver and full of condescension. So, basically exactly how my grandma—a.k.a. Mimi—sounds. Especially the condescending part.

I can't see the woman standing in front of me because I'm currently sitting/slouching on a bench in the downtown square of Summer Harbor Island (oddly fitting since this place is currently my safe harbor) with my bag of newly purchased books beside me and my face buried in my hands.

I pull my hands away to see Birkenstocks and flamingo socks. My eyes travel up to white Bermuda shorts adorned with palm trees and then to a blue cotton T-shirt with the words *I'm too old to care what you think* printed on it. Continuing my gaze upward, I notice oversized hot-pink-rimmed sunglasses and a wide-brimmed visor perched atop the woman's short, dyed-brown, curly hair. I'd guess she's in her late sixties, maybe early seventies. There is zero recognition in her eyes, something I've become accustomed to gauging.

"Yes," I say. "That's . . . excellent advice." I'm not just saying this—it really is wise counsel. If I want to keep working as an actress until I'm Meryl Streep's age, then I'd better work on my posture.

Of course, I don't even know if I still have a job in the industry.

No one warns you when you make it in Hollywood that one day it might all come crashing down on you.

Oh no . . . yep. I'm tearing up again. I'd hoped I had finished with all that on the flight here. Thank goodness for these sunglasses to cover my shame. I'm so sick of crying. There's been way too much of it lately. I feel a lot like the water fountain behind me, except instead of the melodic trickling sound it's making, I tend to make not-so-pleasant noises when I cry—*really* cry, not the acting kind. There's lots of gasping, and hiccupping, and snorting.

I'm not blubbering like that right now, though. Not in front of Brash Betty standing in front of me, her hands on her hips. I'll push these tears back to where they came from if it's the last thing I ever do. And it just might be. This is hard.

I take a deep breath.

"Let's see you sit up taller now," the woman instructs, or rather demands, as a soft breeze ruffles the hair peeking out of the top of her visor.

"Right," I say after a sniffle. I play along because, aside from the quick conversations with the resort staff and the man I just talked to at the bookstore, she's the only other person I've talked to in days. Even if she is judging my posture—or lack thereof, as it were—I miss talking to people. I didn't realize how much I like being around other humans until recently, when all the people I thought were my friends turned their backs on me. One person in particular literally gave me her back. I've never been so snubbed.

I sit up, lifting my chin a bit higher as I force my spine straight, pushing my shoulders back.

"That's more like it," she says. "You young people looking at your phones all the time—you're ruining your posture."

"I wasn't—"

"There's a whole world out there, you know," she cuts me off, continuing her nitpicky lecture, punctuating her words with a bony, arthritic-looking hand directed toward nothing in particular. "And yet you'd rather be on that TokTok and the Twitters."

"Well, Twitter isn't really a thing any—"

"I think you're all a bunch of nitwits and nincompoops," she interjects.

"Right," I say. I'm not sure why I'm agreeing to this. Although, I am considered a bit of a nitwit *and* a nincompoop by millions of people right now. That, and some other more colorful words that have been thrown around, all of which would probably make the hair on the back of ornery Betty's neck stand up straight.

The older woman mutters something about young people and their phones before pivoting in her Birkenstocks and walking in the other direction, past a cute café I'd love to spend time in, but for obvious reasons cannot, and back in the direction I just came from.

I feel like I should call after her to defend myself because I wasn't looking at my phone. I didn't even bring it with me. It's sitting on the bedside table back at the resort. It's basically useless to me, especially with its lack of Candy Crush. And yes, I did consider ordering a new one but thought better of it. I don't need to be tempted to look at social media or the gossip sites and see all the nasty things people are saying about me right now.

One thing is for sure: not *all* publicity is good publicity. I'm living proof of that.

I start to tear up again. No, no, we'll have none of that. I blink rapidly, what's left of my eyelash extensions hitting the frames of my sunglasses as I do. I won't be able to get those fixed for a while. Neither will I be able to fix the nails I picked all the gel off last night. Sadly, it was the most exciting thing I did all day. And oddly satisfying.

I slouch in my seat and then sit up straight again, not to be caught by rude Betty. How sad that I kind of miss her company. I'm so lonely that a curmudgeonly old woman lecturing me is welcome, and maybe even appreciated.

She was right. My posture is horrendous, and also there's a whole world out there, one that I'm missing, not because of my phone, but because pretty much everyone in that world hates me right now. And my answer to it all is to hide at the resort.

I don't know if I can do it. I don't know if I can stay holed up in my room at the Belacourt Resort. I've got a gorgeous suite overlooking the beach, with beautiful, white sand and crystal-blue water off my balcony as far as the eye can see. The resort even has its own private beach. The Belacourt is fully booked, but it's on the small side, so I rarely see other patrons, and I sort of feel like I have the place to myself sometimes. Yet, it all feels like a prison.

I'm in my own personal tropical-island hell. Which sounds ridiculous, I realize. Even more ridiculous, it's only been three days since I got here. Three days since I took a flight from Los

Angeles to Naples and then took the ferry over to the island. I couldn't even make it in a fancy resort overlooking the ocean for more than three days. Actually, today is the third day, so technically I only made it two.

Wow. Just . . . wow.

What am I going to do? I'm supposed to be hiding all summer. No one knows I'm here, apart from Noah. He'll keep my secret because he knows how it is. He's sort of famous himself, and his sisters are massively famous. But now I've got cute-bookstore-boy—or man, really—who'll figure it out soon enough, and I'm fairly confident the lady I ran into on the way out of the shop recognized me. I'm clearly not good at going incognito. How did I already screw this up so badly?

I guess I could have put on a better disguise. A baseball hat and sunglasses were the best I could do, under the circumstances. I didn't bring anything else to hide my identity because I had no plans to leave the resort once I got here, but I've never been able to sit in one place for too long. It's a flaw of mine. I was a fool to think I could do that for an entire summer.

What if this doesn't even work? This hiding thing I'm currently failing at executing. What if it doesn't make a difference? What if humans aren't as fickle as I'm counting on, and they don't move on so easily? Many others in the industry have made a comeback after a mistake. Shouldn't I get a chance, too? I don't need to be America's Sweetheart anymore. That was a lot of pressure anyway. I'd settle for America's Quirky Cousin. Or maybe just the weird next-door neighbor? I could be America's Kimmy Gibbler.

I really could use a friend right now, someone to talk to. Maybe I can track down surly Betty and see if she'll spend time with me. I've got plenty of other flaws for her to nitpick.

I see something in my peripheral vision and look to my right to see a tiny, light-colored lizard perched on the armrest of the bench.

"Hello there," I say, leaning toward the petite reptile. "Would you by chance want to be friends with me?"

Maybe I can catch him and bring him back with me to my room at the resort and he could keep me company. I'll name him George, and he'll be my little sidekick for the summer. He can perch adorably on my shoulder.

"What do you think? Do you want to be my buddy, George?"

The lizard sticks out his forked tongue before he quickly scurries away.

Great. Even lizards hate me.

Well, I guess that's my sign to go back to my resort prison. I've gotten what I came here for. I needed something to pass the time and a book sounded like the perfect thing, and now I have three. Yes, I could have ordered them, but I didn't want to wait. I also know I could have purchased the e-books, but I've always loved the feel of a real book in my hands. The smell of the paper and the soft sound of pages turning are some of my favorite things.

I'm not quite ready to leave this bench in the center of this quaint town yet, with the ocean breeze on my skin and the melodic trickle of the fountain behind me. This could be the last time I get to come to this area of the island once I restart my self-imposed sentence. Just eighty-seven more days to go. My shoulders fall and my posture falters just at the thought. I don't correct myself this time. I just want to wallow in it. Plus, there's no sign of cantankerous Betty around.

I sigh audibly. It's possible I've already ruined everything just by risking this shopping trip. I'll have to hope that cute-bookstore-guy and that woman I passed didn't realize it was me, and if they did, that they don't sell the information to the gossip sites. I'll know soon enough if the paparazzi show up. Then I'll have to find another remote island to hide away on. Or someone's basement. Maybe someone out there will want to harbor a runaway actress until the news blows over, or a different celebrity does something that gets all the wagging tongues and tails to look in their direction and away from me.

I'll never find a lovelier hiding spot than this one, though. It's hot and humid, like you'd expect an island off the Florida coast to be in the summer. But the breeze that softly whips around me makes everything sort of perfect. And there's also the no-cars-allowed-here thing, which is kind of strange, but also refreshing. It's a small island and easy to navigate on foot. I'd love it more if I didn't hate the reason I'm here.

Oh gosh. Will I actually be able to do this?

I just want a happy summer. I've never had one, not in my entire life, not since I was a kid and my parents divorced. And then not long after that, my summers became about filming sitcoms and movies, whatever my mom would sign me up for. I've never had an entire summer to myself to just . . . be. I thought I was going to get one this year, an entirely free summer. But that obviously didn't happen.

"You're slouching again!" I look to my right to see sour Betty across the street, one hand on her hip, the other pointing a finger in my direction. That's my cue to leave, since I don't need more eyes drawn in my direction, more chances to be recognized, not that there are a lot of people out and about on this sleepy island.

I wave at her before pushing the strap of my bag up my shoulder, grabbing my books, and standing up from my bench.

Back I go to prison and another sucky summer.

WELCOME TO

SUNSET HARBOR

BELACOURT RESORT

GOLF COURSE

NOAH'S HOUSE

JANE'S HOUSE

NATURE PRESERVE

DAX'S DUPLEX

SEASIDE OASIS RETIREMENT HOME

SUNSET REPAIRS

PHOENIX'S OFFICE

CITY OFFICES

SUNRISE CAFÉ

SCOOPS AHOY ICE CREAM

KEENE B&B

GULF OF MEXICO

TOWN SQUARE

BAKERY

BRIGGS'S APARTMENT

THE BOOK ISLE

CUTS AND CURLS

TRISTAN & BEAU'S HOUSE

CAPRI'S HOUSE

GEMMA'S HOUSE

HOLLAND'S HOUSE

BEACH BREAK BAR & GRILL

PUBLIC BEACH

N

W

E

S

CHAPTER 4

Briggs

"BRIGGSY," MY MOM SAYS, looking up from her phone where she's been searching images of Presley James for proof. If it is her, the entire island will know by tonight—she'll make sure of that. "Can you run down to the bakery and get me an iced coffee?"

"Sure," I say, having just had the thought that some fresh air would do me good. Somehow Marianne has always been able to read my mind, generally when I don't want her to. She knew right away when things had gone south with the start-up in Fort Lauderdale. I'm not sure how she does it.

"Oh, and let's be daring today . . . How about one of those cookie-croissant thingies," she says, smiling brightly before her eyes move back to her phone, a finger moving up her screen as she scrolls.

"Sounds good," I say.

The bell above the door rings as I exit the establishment that my mother has aptly named The Book Isle and walk down the street toward the bakery, taking my fogged-up glasses off my face and hanging them on the collar of my shirt. Freaking humidity.

I pass the pet store, a tourist shop, the candy store, and the bank before turning the corner toward the bakery. I look to my left and see the top of someone's head bobbing up and down across the square—curly hair under a massive visor. I can't see who she's talking to, as the fountain's blocking whoever it is, but I recognize that hat. It belongs to an older lady, newer to the island, I think. I can't remember her name, but she was in the bookshop last week and was quick to offer a lot of unsolicited advice. *Don't you think that chair would look better over there? You really should get some sort of air freshener in here—it smells like books.* There was more, but I sort of tuned her out, especially after the book-smell comment. I'm pretty sure that's a universally loved scent.

Best of luck to whomever she's talking to. Or perhaps she's talking to herself, offering unwanted opinions.

The small downtown area is pretty serene today, not a lot of people out and about. I forget how quiet it is on the island during the summer months. It's more touristy in the late fall and especially during the winter when people are dying to get out of cold weather. Spring can be pretty busy too, and then around the end of May it all sort of dies.

I'm assuming it's because people think that, like most of Florida, it gets unbearably hot and humid here. But what they don't know is Sunset Harbor gets a lovely sea breeze from both sides, which keeps the island kind of perfect during the summer. Still hot and humid, but nothing like you'd find on the mainland. It's probably a best-kept secret around here, and for the most part we hope to keep it that way. It's nice to take a break from all the tourism we get during the rest of the year.

I open the door to the quaint bakery that is decorated like you'd expect for a shop that sells a variety of pastries and coffee on an island—various shades of blue on the walls and framed pictures of seagulls and watercolor paintings of seashells.

My senses are immediately filled with the smell of baking bread mixed with coffee and other sugary confectioneries. Is there a person in the world that hates this smell? I doubt it.

"Briggs." A bright-eyed woman named Amparo smiles when she sees me. She's standing behind a large metal table, rolling out some dough. She reaches up and swipes her brow with the back of her gloved hand, leaving a small trail of flour. There's also some on her T-shirt and some sprinkled in that nearly black hair of hers, which is pulled up into a bun atop her head.

"Hey there," I say, giving her a gentle smile.

"What can I get for you?" she asks with a slight Mexican accent, walking up to the bakery case which is full of different kinds of breads and pastries.

"Can I get a couple of iced coffees, and one of these croissant-cookie things?" I ask, pointing to the top shelf of the glass-covered case.

She nods, removing her plastic gloves. "Just give me a minute," she says.

I take a seat at one of the small round tables and pull out my phone to see a missed text from Jack. My shoulders slouch of their own accord. Anytime I get a text from Jack—one of the friends I started AssistGen with—I feel something dark in the pit of my stomach. I'm using the term *friend* loosely; I have no idea where I stand with Jack. And based on the argument we had before I left town, I'm thinking it's not a good place.

Jack: Let's get on a call tomorrow

I let out a breath, my cheeks puffing out with my dramatic exhale. I've been mostly avoiding Jack since I got back to Sunset Harbor. The way I see it, there's not much for us to talk about. Not unless he's figured out a way to get some funding. And hopefully he's not trying to get ahold of me to tell me that we owe more money, because that would not bode well for my current circumstances, working only for room and board at my mom's bookshop.

I stare at my phone screen for a bit before clicking out of my messaging app and setting it down on the table. Every time I get a text from Jack, I feel a pang of hatred for my phone. I wish I lived in a time when people weren't so accessible.

"Here you are," Amparo says from behind the counter, two cups of iced coffee and a white paper bag folded over at the top in front of her.

"Thank you," I say as I walk up to her. I pay for everything and then tuck the bag under my arm, and with a drink in each hand, I give her a little head bob and a smile before turning toward the door. Just as I go to use my hip to open it, someone else enters. It's the opinionated lady.

She scrunches her nose.

"Can I help you?" Amparo asks, a smile on her warm, welcoming face.

"Yuck. You should consider some kind of air freshener in here," the older lady says. "It smells like bread."

Amparo lets out an uncomfortable-sounding chuckle, unsure if this woman is being serious or not.

I give her a nod, nonverbally telling her that I see and understand the crazy she's about to experience before opening the door with my hip and walking out into the humid air.

It takes a minute for my eyes to adjust to the bright sunlight, and for a second I wish I had a pair of large-rimmed sunglasses on my face, ones like she-who-might-be-Presley-James was wearing.

Then I wish I hadn't thought of her, as I get firsthand embarrassment over our interaction and my inability to act like a human.

My eyes adjust and I start my walk back to work, feeling the sun on my face and admiring the clear blue sky overhead. I wish I didn't have to spend the day at the bookshop and could play in the water and wriggle my toes into the sand for a while, but unfortunately my bank account would dictate otherwise. How I'll ever dig myself out of the mess I'm in is not something I like to think about, but it creeps into my head often, like a story I can't seem to stop telling myself.

Maybe if Jack would stop texting me and reminding me. Stupid Jack. Stupid phone. Wait . . . my phone.

I curse under my breath when I realize that I've left my phone at the bakery. I spin around to head back to the store and end up running directly into someone.

"Ahhhhhhhh!" the woman screams because not only have I run into her, I've also spilled both cups of iced coffee all down her front.

And to make matters so, so much worse, it's her: Possibly Presley James.

"I'm so sorry," I say, averting my eyes from her shirt because I've just doused her with cold coffee and the shirt is completely soaked and it's a bit . . . um . . . see-through. So much so that that I can see a perfect outline of her bra. Or, I could. If I were looking. Which I'm not.

"It's so cold," she says, holding a cross-body bag and also the plastic one full of books I sold her not that long ago in one hand, and attempting to pull the wet shirt away from her skin with the other. It makes a sort of squelching sound as she does.

"I'm just . . . so sorry," I say, at a loss for what I can do for her. I have no napkins, or anything, on my person. I don't even have a croissant-cookie thing to offer as penance because I dropped it on the ground in the shuffle.

She lets out a sort of frustrated-sounding breath. She's still got the sunglasses on, but I imagine there's a lot of irritated eye rolling and probably some brow pinching going on right now. Or maybe I'm projecting Scout onto her.

"I have a shirt, back at my place. You can borrow it, or you can just have it," I tell her.

Her lips pull downward.

"Sorry." I shake my head. "I'm not a weirdo. And my place, it's not far. The bookshop you were just in, the one just over there. I live above it, and I can get you a shirt. A clean one. Well, I think I have a clean one." What the hell am I even saying? What is it about this woman that gives me verbal diarrhea?

"Um," she says, sounding flustered. She's still holding the shirt away from her stomach, her lips pinched. I notice it's dripping down her legs now. Perhaps I should offer her an entire new outfit. Not that I have shorts that will fit her. As it stands, she will be swimming in any of my T-shirts.

"Okay . . . yeah, that would be great," she says.

"Really?" I say, with a sort of golden-retriever energy I didn't know I possessed. I honestly didn't think she'd agree.

"I'd appreciate it," she says. "I'm staying at the resort, and I walked here because that was my only option."

"You could have ridden a bike," I offer.

"Well, I didn't, so . . ." She stops talking and looks down at her soaked shirt.

"Right. Follow me," I say. I abandon my phone at the bakery because I can get it later and I don't want her to continue suffering with not one, but two cups of cold coffee I managed to drench her in. With an awkward little hand gesture in the direction of the bookshop, which is just around the corner of the square, we head that way together.

We don't say much as we walk, and as we approach the door to the shop, I realize something.

"Hold on," I say. "Actually, let's go around back instead of through the bookshop."

"Why?" she asks.

"There could be people in the shop, and I—" I stop talking and gesture toward her shirt.

"Oh, yeah, thank you . . . for . . . thinking of that."

I don't want to tell her that the real reason she shouldn't go in the shop is because my mother is in there, and wet, coffee-soaked shirt or not, she might fangirl and ask to take a picture or something. I don't know what my mom is capable of in this scenario. I'm sure we've had celebrities visit the island—we've even had some that used to live here—but none of this caliber.

I mean, if she is, in fact, Presley James. I'm still holding out hope that she's not. Although the fact that she won't remove those sunglasses leads me to believe it could be her. It just seems like a famous-person thing to do, not taking them off. Trying to hide from prying eyes. Not that I have a ton of experience with fame.

I lead her past the bookshop, around the post office, and to the back side of the row of buildings where the shop is situated. The back door is unlocked, and I open it as she follows me in and up the set of narrow, creaky stairs to the entrance of my current place of residence.

I open the painted blue door, but I freeze at the threshold. I didn't really think this through, did I? She's going to have so many questions.

I turn around quickly, shutting the door behind me, my hand still on the knob.

"Is there a problem?" she asks, her brown eyes searching my face.

Yes, I can finally see her eyes because she's pushed her sunglasses up on her head. And now I can admit she is 100 percent Presley James. Presley James, who I made a fool of myself in front of at the bookshop, dumped two cups of iced coffee on, and am now about to show the apartment I'm currently living in.

This is just . . . great.

When Keith died, my mom decided that she would eventually sell the house after Scout moves out and live out her days above the bookshop. She's been working on it ever since, making it into the bedroom she never had as a child.

I think I'd choose death right now. This might sound dramatic and definitely like something Scout would say, but I believe I'd rather die than have Presley James see this apartment.

"You know what, I'll just bring you a shirt," I say with a head bob toward the door. I feel good about this. It's a solid plan. *Good job, Briggs. Way to think on your toes.* Relief rushes through my body.

"Oh," she says. "Um, sure. But . . . I was kind of hoping to use the bathroom so I could maybe wipe off some of the stickiness." She gives me a sort of sheepish-looking grin.

I give her one back because it's my fault she's in this predicament right now. We're so close on this tiny landing that I can feel her body heat, and it's giving me enough nervous energy to power this entire island. There's no air-conditioning in the stairway, and it's starting to feel stuffy.

"Yeah, of course," I say, the relief sucking out of me in an instant, as if it were done by one of those high-powered vacuums you find at a car wash. "I should . . . uh . . . warn you about the apartment."

"Okay," she says skeptically.

"There's nothing wrong with it, except it may be a little messy—I wasn't expecting company and all that. But—" I stop and run a hand through my hair and remember my glasses are still hanging from my collar. "It's my mom's, as is the bookshop downstairs. All of this—living here and working here—is temporary for me."

"No worries," she says.

"It's just that it's, um . . . well, you know what? I'll let you see for yourself."

I open the door and walk in, Presley just behind me. She takes in a breath when she sees it.

"Oh . . . wow," she says.

"Yeah," I respond, looking around the space as she does, taking it all in like I'm seeing it through her eyes. There's a small entry space and then directly in front is the galley-style kitchen. Off to the left is a nice-size living room, where there's a pair of my boxers I pray she doesn't notice haphazardly just hanging from the arm of the gray couch.

"It's so . . . pink," she says.

“Well, I mean, the walls are pink, but the, uh, cabinets are purple, so that’s something,” I say, a hand directed toward the kitchen like I’m her tour guide. “It’s princess themed.”

She nods. “I gathered that, with the castle on the wall over there, and the pink frilly curtains on the windows.”

I reach up and scratch my jaw, feeling quite awkward in this moment. But I’m just rolling with it at this point.

“The, uh, bathroom is fairy inspired, as in Tinker Bell,” I tell her.

“Perfect,” she says, her lips pulled up into a smile.

She seems to be taking this well, so I continue. “And the bedroom—which I’m just telling you for information, not because I’m planning on showing you,” I say, holding out my hands, palms facing toward her to show my innocence, “has a four-poster bed with draped pink ruffles.”

She sucks her lips into her mouth, I’m assuming because she’s trying not to laugh.

“You can laugh,” I tell her. “I get it. This is my mom’s childhood dream come to life, and . . . I get to live in it.”

Her inclination to laugh falls away. “Oh,” she says. “I kind of love that.”

I bobble my head side to side. “I mean, it’s great for my mom, but for me it’s . . . a little strange.”

"I'm having a hard time picturing you sleeping in a frilly pink bed, to be honest," she says, and I try not to read into the fact that she's even picturing me at all.

"You know, it's a very comfortable bed, actually."

She lets out a lilting laugh. Melodious and light. I kind of like it . . . a lot.

"So, about that T-shirt," she says.

I nod my head in little rapid movements. "Yes, sorry. I'll go grab that for you. I'll . . . be right back."

I quickly walk through the living area while grabbing my boxers off the arm of the couch, hoping I was stealthy enough she didn't notice. I really should keep this apartment clean for guests. In my defense, I haven't had anyone up here since I moved back, save my mom and Scout.

I walk into the bedroom, which has a window with a view of the ocean, but right now it's dark in here, since I never opened the light-blocking curtains this morning—they're floral pink and match the drapery hanging from the bed, of course. I quickly go to my laundry basket and rifle through it, praying I find something usable. I throw each piece of clothing out in a sort of panicked rage and do a full-body sag of relief when, at the bottom, I find a clean white athletic tee. I grab it and exit the room, finding Presley waiting at the door when I open it.

"Here," I say, holding out the shirt.

"Thanks." She grabs it and gives me a soft smile.

I point at the closed door just behind her. "The bathroom is right there."

"Great," she says, turning to her left to grab the handle. "I'm excited to see the fairies."

"I hope you enjoy them," I say and give her my best pained look because that was a weird thing to say. "There are some clean washcloths under the sink."

I briefly wonder if I should go in first, just to double-check that everything is okay in there. I may leave clothes around the place, but my mom taught me to always keep a clean bathroom, and I just cleaned it yesterday, thank goodness.

I hear the water turn on, and I stand there by the closed bathroom door for a bit before realizing I'm being unintentionally creepy right now. Like, what if she opens the door and finds me loitering here like some lost puppy? I should make myself scarce, and probably have a chat with myself about being cool.

If that's even possible.

CHAPTER 5

Presley

"PRESLEY JAMES, WHAT are you doing?"

I say this to myself after I've splashed cool water on my face, because even though it feels like sticky iced coffee is on all parts of my body, I don't think it made its way to my cheeks. Still, I'm in need of a good slap in the face right now, and this was the best I could do.

Not only am I *not* back at the resort prison, I'm in a stranger's apartment. One that's decorated in a princess motif, which is neither here nor there, but being here was not part of the plan.

But, okay. Wow. This bathroom is so much cleaner than I was expecting. I honestly didn't know what to think when I was invited here. I suppose I wasn't thinking at all.

Too bad Tinker Bell is just a painting on this wall and not real, or maybe she could offer me some pixie dust to magically transport me back to the Belacourt Resort.

Of course, being doused with a cold, caffeinated beverage was also not part of my plan when I set out to go back to my room, but I certainly didn't need to come to the apartment of a guy I barely know. What has gotten into me? Am I losing my mind from the time I've spent alone? Two and a half days in solitude should not an unhinged person make. Yet here we are.

Unhinged might be a tad over the mark, but that's how I'm feeling. I don't do things like this. Unless you count the time I tried to break into Zac Efron's trailer. I was a dumb teenager back then. Fun fact: I could have just knocked on the door since we were filming the same movie. Which is what he nicely told me as he helped pull my stuck body out of the tiny window. So embarrassing. At least we can laugh about it now. Still, that was the only time I'd done something that crazy.

Oh, right . . . I've been crazier. I guess my big faux pas that brought me to this island might be more proof. Maybe I am unhinged. Maybe it's always been a thing I've done and I'm just now learning this about myself.

I look in the mirror. Am I a nutjob? I don't look like one. Right now, I look like a kid in her dad's shirt with how this one hangs on me. I've tied it in a knot at the front, my cross-body bag sort of helping it stay in place, but it's not working that well. At least it's clean and not soaking wet.

I wring out the coffee-drenched tank I was wearing in the sink, and then, grabbing it, I make my way out of the fairy-decorated bathroom and into the princess-themed living room to find cute-bookstore-boy sitting on the out-of-place plain gray couch—shouldn't it be some kind of regal purple with a high back and gold detailing?

"Everything okay?" cute-bookstore-boy asks as he jumps out of his seat. Then he moves his hands around awkwardly before he tucks them in the back pockets of the jeans he's wearing, as if he doesn't know what to do with them. He's wearing his glasses again, and although he's handsome without them, the rectangular frames take him to a whole other level.

"Yes, thank you," I say. I hold out my wet tank top. "Do you have a bag I could put this in?"

"Sure," he says, walking over to the small kitchen. I stifle a giggle as he walks over there with his hands still in his back pockets. It just looks ridiculous. He's kind of adorable.

He disappears behind the lower cabinets, and I hear him rifling around them until he pops back up, a grocery sack in hand.

He walks over to me and offers me the bag. "Here you go," he says.

"Thanks," I say, and as I take it from him, our hands brush and a pleasantly comfortable feeling settles in my belly. I quickly stick the soaked shirt in the bag.

"I'm glad the shirt worked," he says, pushing his glasses up the bridge of his nose.

"Oh, yes. Thank you." I look down at the oversized T-shirt and then back up at him. "This is a strange time to be asking you this, but . . . what's your name?"

His eyebrows shoot up. "Yeah, no. It's not strange. I mean, I guess it is strange since you're in my apartment—or, my mom's apartment." He reaches up and runs a hand through his hair before letting out a breath. "I'm Briggs. Briggs Dalton."

I hold out a hand, and he takes it in his, practically engulfing mine. My grandma Mimi, my dad's mom, says *big hands, big idiot*. She really is such a snarky woman. Briggs doesn't seem like an idiot, though, and he has nice, big hands that are oddly soft. When he shakes mine, it's with a sturdy sort of confidence—something he hasn't been demonstrating so far. He's mostly seemed awkward, but adorably so.

"It's nice to meet you, Briggs. I'm Presley."

His eyebrows go even higher. I'd thought I'd seen recognition in his face earlier—is there a chance I read that wrong?

"James," I add. "I'm Presley James."

"Yes," he says, his face falling into a sort of resigned look.

He removes his hand from mine, and then we stand there in silence for a few seconds. It feels awkward now. More awkward than it's been. Briggs reaches up and adjusts the arm of his glasses, moving them up slightly before settling them down again at the top of his nose.

"It's nice to meet you," he says, finally, and then adds, "officially."

I give him a small smile. "Yes, nice to meet you as well. Officially."

"Just to clarify, you're not the actress Presley James, are you?"

I nod. "I am, actually." Why do I feel like I need to apologize for that? It might be because his shoulders are now doing a sort of drooping thing.

"Is that . . . okay?" I'm not sure why I asked, because take me or leave me, I am Presley James.

"Yeah, of course, sorry," he says. "I guess I was kind of hoping it wasn't you."

This makes me huff out an unexpected laugh. "I'm sorry to disappoint you."

He shakes his head. "No, sorry, that's not what I mean. I've just acted like a complete idiot since you came into the bookshop, and then I spilled coffee on you, and well . . ."

I shrug my shoulder. "All in a regular day for me."

He chuckles. "Oh, I'm sure. Anyway, I'm sorry about all that." He bats a hand back and forth between us, as if to sweep away all the actions he's deemed embarrassing.

"It's totally fine," I say. And it really is. See, world? I'm not the diva the gossip sites are making me out to be.

"So, what brings you to the island?" Briggs asks.

"I'm . . . um, taking a little break from life. From everything, really," I tell him and then hold my breath, waiting for the fallout—for him to remember. To put it all together. I'm sure, so far, he's only just been working out whether it was really me, but now he'll remember: Presley James did a bad thing and is now hiding from everyone on a tiny island.

"A break?"

"Yeah. Yes . . ." I stop myself because he's not giving me an understanding nod, or an acknowledging gaze, or even a disappointed how-could-you glare. Instead, he's wearing more of a questioning expression—his lips parted, his eyes searching my face.

I can't help the brow furrow I make in response. Is it possible he doesn't know? That he hasn't heard about my shame? There are plenty of people not into pop culture or the goings-on of Hollywood, I realize, but someone his age would have at least seen something on social media? A headline on the news? One of the eleventy billion subreddits about me?

"I'm sort of hiding right now," I finally tell him. That should clue him in.

"Hiding from what?"

Okay, so he doesn't know. How absolutely refreshing. I feel lighter, suddenly.

"Just . . . life," I tell him. I have no intention of cluing him in to my big blunder.

"Well, you picked a great place to hide," Briggs says.

I nod. "I'm not doing the best job of it, though," I say, holding up the bag containing my wet shirt.

"Sorry about that," he says, looking chagrined.

"It's not all your fault—I was trying to get myself back to the resort before anyone else saw me. I just needed to escape for a minute. I was restless."

He gives me an understanding nod. "How long have you been in town?"

"Three days."

He chuckles. "Three days?"

"I'm not good at staying put."

He gives me a closed-mouth smile. "I get that."

I lick my lips before asking him the next question, feeling slightly nervous about it. I don't know why; I guess it's the anticipation of his answer. I don't expect him to say no, but I don't know if I'll believe him when he says yes.

"Could you . . . would you mind not saying anything to anyone? About me being here?"

"Of course," he says without even the slightest hesitation, and I smile because I believe him. In a business where you're basically taught by experience to trust no one, and after finding out recently who my true friends are (the answer is: I don't have any), it's an odd feeling to trust this guy so quickly. But I do.

There's something in those green eyes of his that just looks trustworthy.

"Thank you," I say, feeling relieved.

He fiddles with one of the arms on his glasses, his forehead creasing. "Actually, I think people might already know," he says.

"Really?" A feeling of dread fills my stomach.

"My mom said she saw you outside the bookshop."

"That was your mom?" I ask, remembering the flustered-looking woman who did a double take when I passed her on the sidewalk.

Crap. I knew she'd recognized me.

"She said she'd heard a rumor you were here and staying at the Belacourt Resort." He reaches up and rubs the back of his neck. "Word does spread fast around here."

"Great," I say. "Well, serves me right for going to a small island." I guess I can't beat myself up for leaving my room today if people were already talking. I wonder who's spreading the news? Noah? That doesn't sound like something he'd do.

"I might be able to help," Briggs offers.

"How so?"

He lifts a shoulder and lets it drop. "A lot of people come through the bookstore. I can shoot down any rumors I might hear there and when I'm out and about."

"You'd do that?"

He smiles. "Of course."

"Would it work?"

"Possibly. Like I said, word travels fast. If I tell people it's not you, that will spread as well."

"Briggs, that would be so amazing." A little tiny voice in the back of my head wonders if Briggs would be so willing to help out if he knew why I'm hiding. Probably not.

"Well, thank you so much for the shirt," I tell him.

"No problem."

"I'll figure out a way to get it back to you."

He shakes his head. "Keep it. I don't need it back."

"You sure?"

"Absolutely. Think of it as payment for dumping iced coffee all over you."

I bob my head from side to side. "I think that covers a bit of it."

The corner of his mouth ticks up. "If you think of another way for me to even the score, let me know."

"I'll keep that in mind," I say, giving him a grin.

I turn and walk toward the front door of the apartment, Briggs following behind me. He opens the door for me, and I walk out onto the threshold. I turn around before going down the stairs.

"Thanks again."

"No problem. Maybe I'll see you around?" He looks at me, his eyes behind his glasses bright and focused.

How I wish I could tell him that yes, I'll be back at the bookstore, back for more conversation with this charming man who has no idea how adorable he is. I think that's the best part about Briggs Dalton. At least, from what I can gather about him.

"Maybe," I say, knowing it probably won't happen. I've got to stay in my resort prison now. No more real world for me. Even if it does come with pretty green eyes and a handsome face.

I give him a little wave and he gives me one back, then I head down the stairs, hearing the click of the door shutting just as I reach the bottom.

A sort of sadness lands in my gut. I'm not sure why. Probably because Briggs was a real person who actually talked to me. He expected nothing of me, didn't want me to act a certain way or give off a certain vibe. I could just be myself. It's been a long time since I've had a genuine conversation where no one wants something from me.

I walk out into the humid air, resigned to go back to the resort and keep myself secluded—now more than ever, with word getting around the island. If there are no more sightings of me, the rumor will go unfed, and maybe it will die.

At least I've got some books to keep me company now.

The books! Crap. I think I left them in the bathroom. I look around me like they might magically appear, before turning back toward Briggs's apartment, going inside and up the stairs.

I knock on the blue door of his apartment, feeling little butterflies dance around in my stomach, wondering how I can be so elated that my visit with Briggs isn't quite over yet. Is it him? Or is it just the fact that I need human interaction so badly?

"Just a second," I hear him say through the door.

"Oh, hello," he says as he opens it and sees me standing there. He's smiling like he's happy to see me, which makes my stomach do a little dipping thing. It has to be the human interaction thing, right? I'm just starving for it, that's all.

"I forgot my books," I tell him. "I think they're in the bathroom."

"Sure, of course. Do you . . . want me to grab them?" His eyebrows peek out above his glasses.

"I can do it," I say, walking inside the apartment.

"Hopefully they're still there and Tinker Bell hasn't sprinkled them with pixie dust and sent them off to Neverland," he says. Then he closes his eyes and shakes his head. "I can't believe I just said that."

I smile because he's all kinds of adorable right now as he's running a hand through his hair, and suddenly I know the excitement and the butterflies in my belly are because of him and not just because I've missed being around people. It's all just Briggs. A man I barely even know. Strange.

"I better go see if they're still there, then." I play along, heading toward the bathroom.

It dawns on me, as I grab the bag of books off the yellow-and-white checkered tile floor and walk back into the princess living room, that this interaction with Briggs reminds me of something.

"Have you seen the movie *Notting Hill*?" I ask Briggs.

He shakes his head. "I haven't."

"It's one of my favorites. I've seen it like probably ten times or maybe even more," I tell him. "Julia Roberts and Hugh Grant. He owns a bookstore, and she's an actress."

"Oh," he says, giving me a small smile. "Sounds familiar."

"In the movie, he even invites her back to his place after spilling orange juice on her shirt."

"That's . . . really strange," he says, that space between his brows pinched.

I smile as I think of the rest of that scene—Hugh Grant standing there, looking surprised, the slight raise of his brows indicating he didn't think he'd ever see Julia Roberts's character again, and then there she was.

Kind of like how Briggs is looking at me now.

"She even leaves his place and then has to come back because she forgot her shopping bags."

"Wow," he says. "Was his apartment princess and fairy themed, by chance?"

I shake my head. "Sadly, no."

"That's a shame," he says. "That could have taken the film to a whole other level."

"Definitely a missed opportunity."

"So, what happens after she comes back for her stuff? In the movie?"

The corner of my mouth lifts up of its own accord. "She kisses him, actually."

"Oh," Briggs says, his eyes going a little wider behind his glasses.

"It's kind of a weird kiss, to be honest," I tell him. "Very out of the blue, and a little stilted."

"And this is your favorite movie?"

"I mean, there are better kisses after that first one. But yeah, it's funny and lighthearted," I say. "You should watch it."

"I apparently just lived it," he says.

We both have silly grins on our faces now. "Okay, well, I'm really leaving this time," I say, holding the bag of books up as evidence.

I walk to the door, Briggs behind me, just like the first time I tried to leave. He opens the door, and I step out.

Maybe I'm caught up in the moment with *Notting Hill* in my head, or maybe it's the thought of going back to the resort to live out my self-imposed solitary confinement sentence, or maybe I really am unhinged, because there's no good explanation for what I do next.

I turn back toward Briggs, lift up on my toes, wrap the arm that's not holding my books and wet shirt around his neck, and I kiss him squarely on the mouth.

I only mean for it to be a quick peck, but as soon as my lips touch his, my eyes flutter closed, and I'm entranced.

His lips are soft and pillowy, and not what I expected. I can't stop myself from leaning in, adding more pressure to the kiss.

For a second, he's a statue, caught off guard by my forwardness, but then his body melts into mine, his arms snaking around my back and practically lifting me. The smashing of our lips morphs into movement then, soft and slow, both of us giving and taking.

I can feel his hands solid on my back, fingers splayed as he holds me, and our lips move together. One hand moves up and presses against the base of my skull, angling me back just so, giving him more access.

Oh man. I totally get why Julia Roberts's character kissed the nerdy-cute bookstore owner in *Notting Hill*. This kiss is everything. Not awkward and stilted like the movie, though—hotter and more intense. Not in a chaotic I-want-to-rip-your-clothes-off sort of way, but like a slow sort of dance.

The distant, muted sound of bells jingling on a door makes Briggs pull out of the kiss. I can feel and hear his startled intake of breath. Or maybe that was me.

Presley James, what have you done?

He slowly sets me back down so my heels touch the floor beneath them, and removing his arms, he takes a tiny step back.

"Sorry," I say, breathlessly, feeling a bit shell shocked. Did we really just do that? Did *I* just do that?

"Sorry," I say again. "I think I got caught up in the moment, or the sea air or something." I reach up and touch my lips that now feel sort of empty. Maybe *lonely* is a better word.

Briggs reaches up and runs a hand through his hair. "Yeah, yeah. Me too," he says. "It's definitely the sea air . . . or the moment. Or something."

"Or the movie," I add.

"Right. What was it called again?"

"Notting Hill."

He nods. "I'll make sure to watch it."

"You definitely should."

I want to apologize again, but I don't. Instead, I take a big, kiss-recovering breath.

"I'd better go," I say. I search his face, not sure what I'm looking for. If he invited me back inside his apartment, I'd probably take him up on it.

He doesn't, though. Which is good. That's what I'm telling myself. It's good. Great. Excellent.

I turn and walk down the stairs. Before I exit, I look back up and see him standing there. He gives me a little wave, and I return it before I leave for real this time.

WELCOME TO
SUNSET HARBOR

BELACOURT RESORT
GOLF COURSE
NOAH'S HOUSE
JANE'S HOUSE
NATURE PRESERVE
DAX'S DUPLEX
SEASIDE OASIS RETIREMENT HOME
SUNSET REPAIRS
PHOENIX'S OFFICE
CITY OFFICES
SCOOPS AHOY ICE CREAM
SUNRISE CAFE
KEENE B&B
TOWN SQUARE
BAKERY
GULF OF MEXICO
BRIGGS'S APARTMENT
THE BOOK ISLE
CUTS AND CURLS
TRISTAN & BEAU'S HOUSE
CAPRI'S HOUSE
GEMMA'S HOUSE
HOLLAND'S HOUSE
BEACH BREAK BAR & GRILL
PUBLIC BEACH

N
W E
S

CHAPTER 6

Briggs

THE BELL OVER the door rings, and someone else enters the fray. The bookshop is busier than it's ever been, with people looking through the shelves and all the cozy chairs around the space filled. A quiet moves across the room as they all look at the entrance to see who's come in, and then go back to talking when it's not who they were hoping for.

It's the older woman with the big visor who was in earlier this week with her unsolicited advice. She's wearing super high-waisted, dark-gray pants and a T-shirt haphazardly tucked into them.

Her face scrunches when the door shuts behind her, blocking the humidity from the air-conditioned room. "I see you didn't get an air freshener like I suggested."

It didn't seem like a suggestion.

From behind the counter, I school my features and don't allow my face to give this woman the disdainful look it's wanting—more like dying—to send her way. Instead, I plaster on a closed-mouth grin. I've been giving a lot of fake expressions today.

Her eyes scan the room. "Why's it so busy in here?"

Why indeed.

It's a long story, but the short version goes: I didn't make it back to the bookshop fast enough, after Presley left the apartment, to stop Marianne McMannus, who *never* gossips, from spreading the word that she saw the actress.

I'm sure it was a chain of texts and probably phone calls (she wouldn't fess up), but in my head I picture her with a bullhorn in her hands, standing in front of the fountain in the middle of the town square.

I did my best, telling her I ran into the woman she thought was Presley James while I was getting us coffee, and I verified it wasn't her.

So, basically, I gaslighted my own mother.

It doesn't matter because whether she believed me or not, she wasn't about to retract that juicy piece of gossip, so the damage is done.

Because the Belacourt Resort doesn't like it when people loiter there, hoping for a celebrity sighting, everyone has come to the only other place Presley James has allegedly been spotted: The Book Isle.

Well, not everyone on the island, but plenty of people from around here have stopped by, or are just sitting here, waiting.

It's dumb logic, really. If she's already been to the bookshop, then she'd probably try another place the next time, like the bakery, or the Sunrise Café, and not loiter around here.

True to my word to Presley, I've tried to tell everyone in here that it's not really her, but no one believes me. I have no clout since I haven't lived here permanently in nine years, whereas my mom has been here for sixteen years and owns a business in the town center. So her word trumps mine. And also, hers is the better story. Everyone wants to believe one of the most popular actresses in the world is visiting their island.

"Can I help you?" I say to the scowling older woman, ignoring her question about why it's so busy. I push my glasses up my nose.

"No," she says, her voice flat, then turns and heads back outside. The bell jingles, drawing everyone's attention in that direction, only for them to realize it was just someone leaving. The disappointment is palpable.

A few seconds later, someone else enters the shop, and everyone goes quiet again until they realize it's not Presley James and then go back to whatever they were doing. And the cycle continues. Why won't anyone believe me?

I've told so many people that it's not really her, I'm starting to wonder myself. It all feels sort of like a fever dream . . . spilling coffee on her, going back to my apartment, the kiss I can't stop thinking about. I still can't believe she did that. I also can't believe I kissed her back. I kissed Presley James.

Because I told her I would, I watched *Notting Hill* last night. It's funny how similar the beginning is to Thursday's encounter. I think that's where it ends for my story with Presley, though—at the kiss that I can't get out of my head. I doubt I'll have another run-in with her. At least I won't have to pretend I'm from *Horse & Hound* magazine if our story were to keep going. I don't have the acting chops.

Our story? Good hell. I sound like an infatuated fool. And I'm not. It was just one day. One very strange day. I'll tuck it away, a memory to think about later. Maybe it'll be a story I tell someday—that time I kissed Presley James, or really, she kissed me. Maybe I'll forget about it . . . yeah, that's not going to happen probably ever.

I did get curious about why she's here, hiding on the island. I'm not really one to stay up on pop culture. Not when my Google searches tend to be more about tech trends and market analysis. Or at least they used to be. Now my searches are more along the lines of what I should do next. I still don't know. I've gotten two more texts from Jack that I've ignored. I'm not ready to talk to him yet. I should apologize at the very least. But I'm also nervous I'll find out we owe more money and just this morning I got a balance alert from my bank because I'd gone below the minimal threshold I set, which is concerning.

Anyway, I searched Presley's name, and it brought up a bunch of recent articles . . . It was easy to put two and two together about what happened. I was even able to find the leaked video on YouTube.

I can see why people are upset, but also, it's hard for me to reconcile the Presley I saw and heard on that leaked recording, yelling and red faced, with the Presley I met here on the island. They seem like two different people.

All I know is there are two sides to every story and I'm sure Presley has a good reason for why she went off like she did.

It doesn't matter anyway. I doubt I'll see her again, especially if everyone around here keeps acting like they are. How long before word spreads from here? I've never been around the paparazzi, but if they are anything like in the movies, the people on this island wouldn't like it if they showed up.

"This is the worst Saturday of my life," Scout says as she sidles up to me behind the counter. She's wearing a bathing suit under cutoff shorts and a white button-up shirt she's left open. She had plans with friends that our mom quickly put the kibosh on, telling her she had to work today instead.

Scout wasn't happy and isn't good at hiding her feelings. Especially when she thinks it's unfair. And making her work on a Saturday when she had plans to go to the beach with friends is "totally not fair."

It's not fair, really. She can't help her mother's big mouth and the fact that there truly is an A-lister on this island. Even though I will go to my grave saying otherwise.

Scout tucks some of her naturally-highlighted blonde hair behind her ear and lets out a long-suffering sigh. "Mom is the worst."

Our mom isn't here to defend herself; she had to take the ferry over to the mainland to run some errands. And so, as Scout's older brother by fourteen years, I probably should correct her, but I, too, think my mom is the worst right now. Sure, the bookshop is busy and making quite a bit of money because apparently the islanders waiting on a Presley James sighting aren't just sitting around—they're shopping. But they wouldn't be here if it weren't for my mom's gossiping ways. The money does help, though. It's not like this shop turns over a huge profit.

"You can go," I tell a sulking Scout. I take my glasses off and clean them with the hem of my shirt.

Her eyes go wide. "Really?"

"I've got it handled."

It's been busy, but nothing I can't take care of.

"What will you tell mom?"

"That you left me here to work by myself without even asking," I say.

She whacks me lightly on the arm. “Briggs,” she whines.

“Fine. I’ll tell mom I told you that you could go,” I say. Teasing Scout is so fun. She falls for everything. Or at least she used to. I once had her totally convinced the animals on the safari ride in Animal Kingdom were animatronic. It was a couple of years before she figured out the truth. She still gets mad when I bring it up.

“You’re the best,” she says, wrapping her arms around me for a quick hug.

“Where are you going anyway?” I ask her when she’s pulled away.

“We’re going to crash Belacourt Beach.”

“Why?”

“To see Presley James, duh.” She says the last word like I’m an idiot.

I reach up and rub my forehead with my fingers. “I told you it’s not her.”

“And I don’t believe you,” she says. “Maybe if you didn’t lie to me about robot animals and that Bigfoot sighting in the nature preserve, I would.”

I forgot about that. That was another good one.

“Besides, I don’t care if I see her; I’m hoping to catch a view of Declan Stone.”

“Declan Stone,” I repeat, my face scrunched. “Why would you be looking for him?”

"Because he's hot," Scout says, and I cringe at her word usage. I don't like knowing that my fourteen-year-old sister likes boys. If I had my way, I'd keep her away from them until she's thirty. I know how boys think, and frankly, it's almost always inappropriate.

"But why do you think he's on the island?"

Scout gives me an are-you-stupid glare. "Because he and Presley James are a thing."

I rear my head back, tucking my chin in. "What?"

I didn't see anything about that in my Google search. Not even one mention.

"They've been together for a few years," Scout says. "Everybody knows about it."

"They're together?"

"Yeah," she says, picking something out of her nails like she didn't just drop this bomb on me. "They met on the set of that alien movie *A Star-Crossed Love*." She lets her shoulders drop, her face taking on a dreamy look. "Declan Stone was the hottest alien I've ever seen."

I remember that movie. He played an alien that crash-landed on Earth and met a quirky hairstylist played by Presley. I didn't think Declan was all that great in the movie. He's definitely better suited to play Alex Steele in the Shadowstrike Chronicles.

But . . . he and Presley are together? Something sour swirls around in my stomach. Suddenly the kiss from two days ago that

I've been replaying in my head feels like a deception. A scam. Something A-list stars do to pass the time when they're bored. Presley's viral video instantly feels more believable. My perspective in the rearview mirror changes in a blip. The bright, happy frame my brain had put around her and Thursday's events now looks rusted and broken.

I feel like Hugh Grant's character when he finds out Julia Roberts's character has a boyfriend. Awkward and naive. I'm William Thacker.

"I'm leaving now," Scout declares, not even noticing the fact that I've gone silent and most likely have a confused look on my face.

"Have . . . fun," I say, absentmindedly.

"Thanks for being the best brother ever," she says before basically skipping out of the shop.

The bells chime as she leaves, and everyone looks toward the door before going back to whatever they were doing.

When the last person exits the bookshop, the dimming summer sun casting shadows across the town square, I lock the door, flip the sign to *closed*, and slump against the glass.

This wasn't the worst Saturday of my life, but it might have been the most tedious. I wasn't in the best mood either since

Scout dropped the Declan Stone bomb on me. And then I was annoyed I allowed it to affect my mood. I'd known I wouldn't be seeing Presley James again, so what did it matter that she kisses men who aren't her boyfriend for fun? Nothing was going to happen between us anyway.

And Declan is her boyfriend, at least according to the internet and the many, many pictures and sightings of the two of them together—laughing at dinner, holding hands as they walk into a movie premiere, sitting together on a beach. I'm not sure how I missed it in my initial search about her. Maybe I didn't want to see it at a subconscious level.

Even despite knowing all that, despite feeling like a total idiot for giving any of my mental bandwidth to Thursday's events, I kept up the ruse that she is not really on the island. I don't know why I did. But a promise is a promise.

Not that it worked. People filtered in and out of the bookshop all day, eyes peeled and bright as they searched the store and kept an eye on the door anytime the bells chimed, no matter what I said. The patrons did taper off toward closing time, but that's probably because they all have homes to go to and dinners to eat.

The bookshop is closed tomorrow since it's Sunday, thank goodness. I don't know if I could have endured another day like this. Keeping up the lie on my end and dealing with dumb questions about books we don't have in the shop (I'm talking to you, Carl, and your refrigerator-repair manuals that we still don't carry). I'm looking forward to cleaning up and going back to my princess-decorated apartment, where I can sleep this day away and try not to think about a certain star.

A tap on the glass door behind me makes me jump, and I turn around quickly to see who it might be.

It's someone in a dark-colored sweatshirt, the hood pulled up over their head, the strings drawn so tight over dark sunglasses, I can't tell who they are.

Am I . . . Am I being robbed? On Sunset Harbor? Has that ever happened here? I don't think it has, even during peak tourist season. We don't have any cars to make a getaway, and our one part-time police officer, Beau Palmer, drives a golf cart, so it's hard to run away from him. Plus, you have to take a ferry to get on and off the island. Robbing someone here would require a lot of effort with not a lot of ways to get away fast.

"Briggs," the person says, and even though it's muffled, I can definitely hear the high tones of a woman's voice.

I look closer, my face so near the glass that my breath fogs up a small spot on the door. "Presley?"

She holds a finger up to her mouth—or at least I'm guessing that's where her mouth is since the drawstrings of the hoodie are pulled so tight, she looks like a minion. What a terrible disguise. Isn't learning to hide from fans and the paparazzi part of Famous Actor 101?

I look around me, making sure I didn't accidentally miss someone still in the shop, and quickly unlock the door. I open it, and she slips inside. I grab her lightly by the arm and guide her over between the shelves of books, just in case someone walking by might see us through the windows.

I let go, and she removes her hood. Her hair springs out with static cling, while some of it stays plastered to her face.

"Hey," she says, her tone bright, a smile on her face.

"Hey," I say, confused. "What are you doing here?"

She lets out a breath. "I'm bored."

"You're . . . bored?"

"I know," she says, running her fingers through her hair, calming the static and fluffing the rest up. "I'm so bad at this."

My hands are being weird appendages again, and I fold them in front of me. "I'm not sure this is the best place to escape to," I say. "I spent the entire day telling people you aren't really here."

Her head falls to the side. "Did you?" She reaches up and grabs some of my T-shirt in her fist, pulling herself closer to me. It's flirtatious and I don't appreciate it.

"You're the best," she says.

I shake my head. "No one believed me, and word has spread. We've had people in and out all day hoping you might come back."

"Crap," she mutters, letting go of my shirt. Then she lets out an exhale that's a whole upper body effort, shoulders and head drooping. "Thanks for trying."

"No problem," I say. "But you probably shouldn't be seen around the island if you don't want to feed that rumor."

She nods. "You're right. But . . . I just needed to get out of there, you know? I needed some air. I was stuck in my room yesterday because of a wedding at the resort, and then I couldn't even sit on my veranda today because there were a bunch of teenagers that kept sneaking onto the private beach. They were persistent. Every time I called the front desk, I'd see them asking them to leave, but they'd find a way to sneak back in."

I guess I'll be needing to have a conversation with Scout about breaking and entering in the near future. Like tomorrow.

"I borrowed a bicycle from the resort and came straight here." She looks down at the floor, and swallows. "I needed to get out, and also, I wanted to say sorry . . . uh . . . about the whole kissing thing the other night. It was like *Notting Hill*, you know? And I got caught up, and . . . I'm . . . just . . . sorry." She looks up at me, her expression soft, her eyes searching.

I give her a single nod. Is she sorry because she was cheating on Declan Stone? Or sorry that it was me she kissed? I don't want to know the answer because either one sucks.

"No worries," I say, even though I do have some concerns. But why bother bringing it up? What will it even change?

"What are you doing now?" she asks, with a very obvious upbeat change to her tone.

I look around the store. "Closing up here, and then I was going to go home."

"To the princess apartment?"

"That's where I live." I give her a nod.

"Well, I'm already here. Do you . . . want some company?"

I tap the side of my glasses with a finger. "I don't think that's a good idea," I say.

"Oh," she says, her eyebrows moving quickly up her face. "Right. Of course. Sorry." She grabs hold of the drawstrings on her hoodie and pulls on them.

"It's been a long day."

"Is that all that's wrong?" she asks, her brows lowered.

"I mean, yeah," I say.

She lets out a long, sad-sounding sigh. "You saw the video, didn't you?"

I pinch my brows together. "I did, but that's—"

"And now you hate me."

"What? No, that's . . . I don't hate you." I shake my head back and forth. She looks so sad right now. So small.

"My gosh, it was a stupid moment caught on film," she says, holding her hands up toward the ceiling, a pleading look on her face. "I've never lost it like that. I've always kept my cool. But no one seems to care. Everyone is just waiting for you to mess up. That's all they care about."

"Presley," I say. "I don't care about that video."

"Yes, you do," she says. "You must."

I rub the back of my neck with my hand. "It's not that. I just think that it's probably not a good idea for us to hang out when you have a boyfriend."

"A . . . boyfriend?" She looks at me like I have two heads.

"Yeah, Declan Stone?"

"What?" She shakes her head. "Declan's not my boyfriend."

"Really?" The word comes out more accusatory than I intended.

She looks to the side, then back at me. "Wait, you thought I had a boyfriend? That's why you're annoyed? This isn't about that stupid video?"

"Well, don't you have a boyfriend?"

"Wait . . . I kissed you, and you thought . . . Oh my gosh, Briggs. I'm so sorry." She lifts her hands and presses them against her cheeks.

"So, are you saying he's not your boyfriend? But the internet . . ."

"Haven't you heard not to believe everything on the internet?" She removes her hands from her face and lets them hang at her sides.

"There are pictures. A lot of them," I say.

She bobbles her head back and forth. "Declan and I are . . . I don't know what we are. We were sort of dating in the past, but that's been over for a couple of years at least."

"So then why does it seem like you're together? At least online."

"We have the same publicist and we get buzz every time we're seen together, so she tends to put us . . . together. That's it. It's just a facade, really."

"But . . . you're not dating."

She shakes her head in slow movements. "No, we are not."

I rub my temples with my fingers. "I'm an idiot," I finally say.

She shakes her head. "You're not. How would you know? I could have warned you, but I wasn't really thinking about Declan when I saw you last."

The corner of her lips pulls up in a very adorable way. I can't help the return smile that spreads across my face.

"Okay, so now that you know I'm not cheating on Declan Stone, and I did come all the way here, risking getting seen . . . Will you hang out with me tonight?"

CHAPTER 7

Presley

"FAVORITE BOOK?" I ask Briggs as we sit together on the couch in his regally decorated apartment, the movie we were watching abandoned before it even really got started. Now it's just background noise.

It was *Notting Hill*. I wanted him to watch it, but apparently Briggs already had. He admitted to it just before Julia Roberts comes back for her bags in the movie. I don't know why he didn't tell me when I suggested watching it. It's kind of cute that he watched it on his own.

Briggs looks up at the ceiling as he thinks. He's reclined on the couch, his back sinking into the lower cushion, legs stretched out before him, his fingers intertwined and resting on his stomach. He looks like the epitome of relaxation, with not a care in the world, and I aspire to be him. He's also two cushions' worth of couch away from me.

Not that I'm keeping track of that.

Except, I totally am. Presley James, what is wrong with you? I can't help that it feels like he's a mile away. I'm not sure if he still doesn't believe me about Declan, or if he's just trying to be a gentleman. But he could sit a little closer.

I have hateful feelings toward my publicist right now. The are-they-aren't-they thing with Declan is so old. We are most certainly *not*. No way. And definitely not now after everything . . .

Nope. Not going there.

I didn't come here tonight with the expectation of more kissing, even though the one outside his door keeps replaying in my head and I wouldn't mind engaging in more of it because I am only human, after all. But I did apologize for it, and I meant it. It was really presumptuous of me. Honestly, I'm doing all kinds of idiotic things lately. What if he has a girlfriend? Somehow, I doubt it. Not with how he reacted about the Declan thing. And not with how he kissed me back.

It doesn't matter, because it's for the best that we stay on our separate ends of the couch—me on my end and he on his. I'm here for the summer to hopefully fix my life, not complicate it more. I don't think Briggs wants to get caught up with a disgraced actress anyway. Even if the video didn't seem to bother him. Which is . . . odd. And also lovely.

We can just be friends. Friends who never see each other again since I must go back to my resort prison and stay put this time for real. I can't leave again.

I don't know what compelled me to leave this time. I'd made it nearly two days by myself. It might have been the lack of fresh air since I couldn't go out on the veranda, or the fact that even though I'm loving the Sunny Palmer book, I just can't focus. But just as the sun started setting, I couldn't take it anymore. I borrowed a bike from the hotel and flew over here, a woman on a mission.

Sitting here with Briggs, I feel like I should have regrets, or at least be mentally punishing myself right now for once again not being able to stay put, and yet . . . I can't even bring myself to feel regretful.

But I am staying put. After tonight. I swear it. No more leaving the resort for me.

"I haven't read a fiction book in a while," Briggs answers my question, his eyes on the TV, even though he hasn't been watching. "But I'd say it's probably Harry Potter."

"Good answer," I say, giving him an appreciative nod. "I love those books too. And the movies."

"Don't tell me about the actors in real life," he interjects quickly, looking toward me. "I don't want to know if they're horrible."

"They're not," I say through a laugh. "Am I . . . tainting Hollywood for you?"

He gives me a side-eyed glare through his rectangle-shaped glasses. "Maybe a little."

"I'm ruining the magic with all my name-dropping, aren't I?"

"You do drop a lot of names," he says, tilting his head to the side.

I let my jaw fall open, placing a hand on my chest. "I'm not a name-dropper—you told me you wanted to know."

"I've changed my mind."

I grab a throw pillow out from behind me, a red velvet one that looks like it might be used to present a glass slipper, and toss it at his head.

"Um, my mom would have you kicked off this island for that kind of roughhousing," he says before setting the pillow gently beside him and giving it a little pat like I've hurt its feelings.

"Apologies to your mom," I say. "I promise to never attempt to damage anything of hers again."

"Thanks. But if you do, maybe next time you could go for the curtains," he says, pointing to the ruffled, pink billowy things on the window across the room. "I actually like this pillow." He pets the velvet material again.

I chuckle. "I'll do my best."

Being around Briggs is delightful and also kind of calming. Like a healing balm to my heart. So unlike anything I've experienced in a while.

For so long I haven't known if people are spending time with me because of the fame thing or if they actually want to be my friend. It's something that's always in the back of my mind, hanging over me like a dark cloud. And after the video went viral, I found out the truth: It wasn't my friendship they wanted. So, that was fun.

With Briggs, it feels different. Genuine. Real. I've hardly spent time with the guy, but I recognize it because I haven't had much real in my life in . . . well, I actually don't know when the last time was. Eighth grade? Wow. That's sad. And maybe a little pathetic.

He could be faking it. Maybe he's only interested in the fame part of my life and is just using me for my social status too. Somehow, I don't think that's true. Not as I watch him practically snuggle a red velvet tufted pillow.

"So, how did you get into acting?" he asks.

See? Right here. This is what I'm talking about. Most people would have read my Wikipedia page and then regurgitated it back to me thinking it would give them some sort of clout with me. But not Briggs.

"In middle school, actually," I tell him, reciting the story I've told probably hundreds of times. But it feels fresh and new, telling him.

"We did a play—*Anne of Green Gables*. I played Anne, and my teacher, Mr. Davis, called a talent scout friend of his to come watch it, specifically to see me. I got signed to an agency pretty quickly after that and was filming my first movie that summer."

"So you were thirteen? Fourteen?"

"I'd just turned fourteen. My mom moved us to LA, and that was the start of it."

Then my mom made my career her entire personality, but no need to bring that up. Or think about it.

"Is that unusual? To be discovered like that?" he asks.

I shrug. "I guess."

"Are you being modest right now?" The corner of his mouth pulls up into a smirk.

"Maybe," I say. "It's not uncommon to be discovered like that."

"But it isn't all that common, is it?"

I don't answer him. I just give him a little shrug in response. He obviously knows. Because yes, it's not how things are usually done. It's the dream, to not have to struggle or keep going from audition to audition, experiencing rejection after rejection, while dealing with overdraft fees from your bank because your only source of income is waiting tables at The Cheesecake Factory.

It's not that this career has been handed to me on a silver platter. It was at first. It felt so easy, and I was too young to truly comprehend it—to really appreciate it. But I've worked hard to get where I am now. I've taken classes and studied with world-renowned coaches. I take my job seriously.

Funny how easily all that hard work can be ruined in an instant. Or not funny, actually.

"So, what's next for you? I mean after this summer of hiding . . . or not hiding," he says, giving me another smirk.

"After tonight you'll never see me again."

He twists his lips to the side, doubt in his expression. "Should we bet money on that?"

"I need that pillow back so I can throw it at you again," I say, holding out a hand.

"No way," he says, hugging the pillow close to him, petting the top of it like it's a beloved pet.

The man is adorable.

I sigh. "Fine. After the summer—the one where I'll be hiding in my room, thank you very much," I eye him dubiously. "I start filming a new movie . . . That's the plan right now, at least."

"Could it change?"

"Things change all the time in Hollywood. But this time there's a small chance they might release me from my contract."

This makes me sad to consider. I worked hard to land this role. A lot of the movies I've done in the past have been pretty much handed to me, some even written with me in mind. But this one . . . It's an epic fantasy, an adaptation of a beloved book, with a lead that on the character breakdown looked nothing like me—Callis, a futuristic warrior who's tall with long blonde hair. But I waltzed into the audition with platform boots on my short legs and a wig over my dark-brown hair and . . . I nailed it. It was a proud moment in my career.

And then, not long after, I had a very not-so-proud moment. Bleh.

Because of that not-so-proud moment, the script for the movie is sitting in my suitcase untouched, even though I should be running lines. But what if I do and it turns out to be a waste of time?

"What happens if they release you from the contract?" he asks, his eyebrows peeking out over the top of his frames.

"I don't know," I tell him truthfully, feelings of unease swimming around in my stomach. I've already been released from at least one role in the fallout. "I guess I'll quit working and live out my days on this island."

"That serious?"

"Probably not," I say. "At some point the gossip will move on and I'll start getting work again. People forget."

Probably. Hopefully. Please, oh please, oh please.

"Of all the places in the world, why would you pick Sunset Harbor?" he asks.

"That's a great question. I'm friends with Noah Belacourt—do you know the Belacourts?"

He nods once. "Of course," he says, and I feel stupid, because who doesn't know the Belacourts? They're almost more famous than I am. I expect Briggs to point that out, but instead he says, "If they've been on the island a long time, then I know them. And the Belacourts have been around for a while."

I want to let out a sigh. He's just so refreshing.

My mind goes back to Thursday and Bratty Betty. If she's been on the island awhile, maybe he knows her? Is she a permanent fixture on the island, going around telling everyone to sit up straight and stop looking at their phones?

"How do you know Noah?" he asks.

"I met him at a party a while back, and he told me I should visit the island and stay at his family's resort. So, when everything went to crap recently, I took him up on it," I say. "I figured it's a remote island, not easy to access, so it's kind of perfect. Well, except that people talk on tiny islands. I didn't know that when I decided to come here."

"And except for running into men who spill iced coffee on you."

"Yes, that too," I say, giving him a teasing smile. The truth is, I'm really glad Briggs spilled iced coffee on me. I'm also happy I came here tonight, even though I should be in my room at the resort.

Ugh. The thought of going back to my place makes me feel sort of sick to my stomach.

"Anyway, I'm hoping if I stay put and word doesn't spread too much, then maybe I can go back to life as usual," I say, my hands in prayer pose. "It'll just be another crappy summer for me."

"Another one?" he asks, frowning.

"I never had a good one growing up, and adulthood hasn't been much better, so what's one more dumb summer for me?" I know I sound like I'm joking right now, but somewhere deep inside, my inner child is stomping her foot.

"You've . . . never had a good summer," Briggs repeats, his tone dry, clearly not believing me.

I let out a dramatic exhale. "Summer is the worst."

"No, summer's the best," he says.

"You live in permanent summer," I say, throwing my arms up.

"Well, yes, that's true." He reaches up and scratches the side of his face, his fingers moving slowly over his clean-shaven jaw. "But this island has always been more fun in the summer, since tourist season is over and things feel more relaxed. And maybe there's some nostalgia there from when I was younger . . . that feeling of not having to go to school was so freeing."

"Ah, but see, I never had that. My parents divorced when I was young, so when school was over in Nashville, where I grew up, I was packed up and shipped to my dad's place in North Carolina. He was always busy working during the summer, and it was so incredibly boring. I was at his house all day, with no friends, and a babysitter who most days would sleep on the couch while I played all by myself. And then when I started acting, it filled every summer after that."

It's hard to believe that at twenty-nine, I've never had just a regular old summer—time to spend with my friends, playing in the sprinklers, swimming at the community pool, all the things I used to dream about doing when I was younger.

It's always touchy for me to complain about my life, since from afar it looks ideal to most. The picture painted about acting and fame and the lifestyle that comes with them isn't the full view. Sure, it's extravagant parties and red carpets and all the things you see online, but there's also a lot of loneliness, a ton of comparison—not just from others, but from yourself—and constantly feeling judged.

"And this summer was supposed to be different?" Briggs asks, his head resting on the back of the couch and lolling toward me.

"This summer I purposefully left open for once, and I was going to travel."

"That sounds like a good summer plan."

"Not the entire summer, but for some of it. And then I thought I'd do other summery things like, I don't know, have a barbecue, or play beach volleyball, or make a bonfire on the beach." With what friends, I have no idea. Of course, I still had friends—or at least I thought I did—before the stupid video.

The corner of his mouth lifts. "Things you've never done, I gather."

I shake my head. "I've been on short beach vacations, but when you're in the spotlight and paparazzi are always around . . . you feel like you're constantly putting on a show, or worried about an accidental wardrobe malfunction that will haunt you for life." To be honest, I haven't been on a lot of vacations. I've just been working, working, working the past fifteen years of my life. No wonder I don't know how to take a break.

He gives me an understanding dip of his chin. "That makes sense."

"And because of how I grew up, I missed out on all the things that are quintessential summer childhood things. I've never run through the sprinklers, or jumped on a trampoline, or made a sandcastle, or gone camping. I've never even roasted marshmallows or slept under the stars."

"That's not every childhood," he says.

"Was it yours?"

"Well . . . yes, I guess it was."

"And you probably took it for granted."

He doesn't respond, and he doesn't need to. I feel stupid for complaining. But it doesn't seem like Briggs is judging me right now. He looks more contemplative.

"And now I get to spend the summer cooped up in a hotel."

"You're not in a hotel right now," Briggs says. He's giving me a teasing grin. It's in the upward curve of his lips and the look of mischief in his eyes.

"Okay, I'm supposed to be in a hotel room. And after this, I'm going to stay there."

He gives me a questioning stare. "I don't know. You've been here for, what, less than a week? And you've already left the resort twice."

I cover my face with my hands. "I know. I don't know how I'm going to do it."

Briggs is quiet for a minute, and I pull my hands away from my face to see him looking at me.

"It can't be that bad at the resort," he says.

"It's not; the resort is beautiful. It's not that, anyway. I'm just not good at staying put. I don't know how to do it."

Briggs looks off to the side, going quiet as if he's thinking about something.

"We could do some of those things," he says.

I pull my chin inward. "What . . . things?"

"The summer stuff. While you're here."

"I'm supposed to be hiding in my room, remember?" He was literally just teasing me about it.

He reaches up and adjusts his glasses. "Yeah, but you just said you don't know how you're going to do it. So . . . don't. I'm here for the summer and feeling pretty directionless right now, so we could, I don't know, do stuff . . . together?"

I can't help it when my eyes tear up a little. I blink the moisture away and hope he doesn't notice. I'm an actress, after all. But I'm completely touched by the fact that he wants to spend time with me, especially after seeing the video of me losing my crap. Why did everyone else turn their backs, but not him?

I know right away that I can't spend the summer gallivanting around with Briggs. Even if I really, really want to. But just the fact that he's offered means so much to me.

"That is seriously the sweetest offer, and I'd love to take you up on it, but it's for the best if I stay at the resort," I tell him.

I want to say yes. I want to scream it, actually. A whole summer doing summer things with a guy who is so unexpectedly not what I'm used to. But, I can't. I can't risk it. This is my career. If word gets out and the paparazzi catch me roaming around an island having what would probably be the best summer ever—because, let's face it, any kind of summer activity would be better than what I've been doing my entire life—the headlines would be scathing.

Presley James Living Her Best Life, Despite Video

Presley James Doesn't Care What We Think of Her

Did She Think We Forgot Already? Presley James is at it Again

"We could be discreet," Briggs says.

"We could," I say. "But with everyone already talking and the teens sneaking onto the private beach, the damage might already be done. I think right now I probably need to lie low."

It's for the best, even if I hate it with a passion.

He nods. "Well, the offer stands if you ever change your mind."

Even as I want to say *never mind, let's have the best summer ever*, I know I can't change my mind.

This is how it has to be.

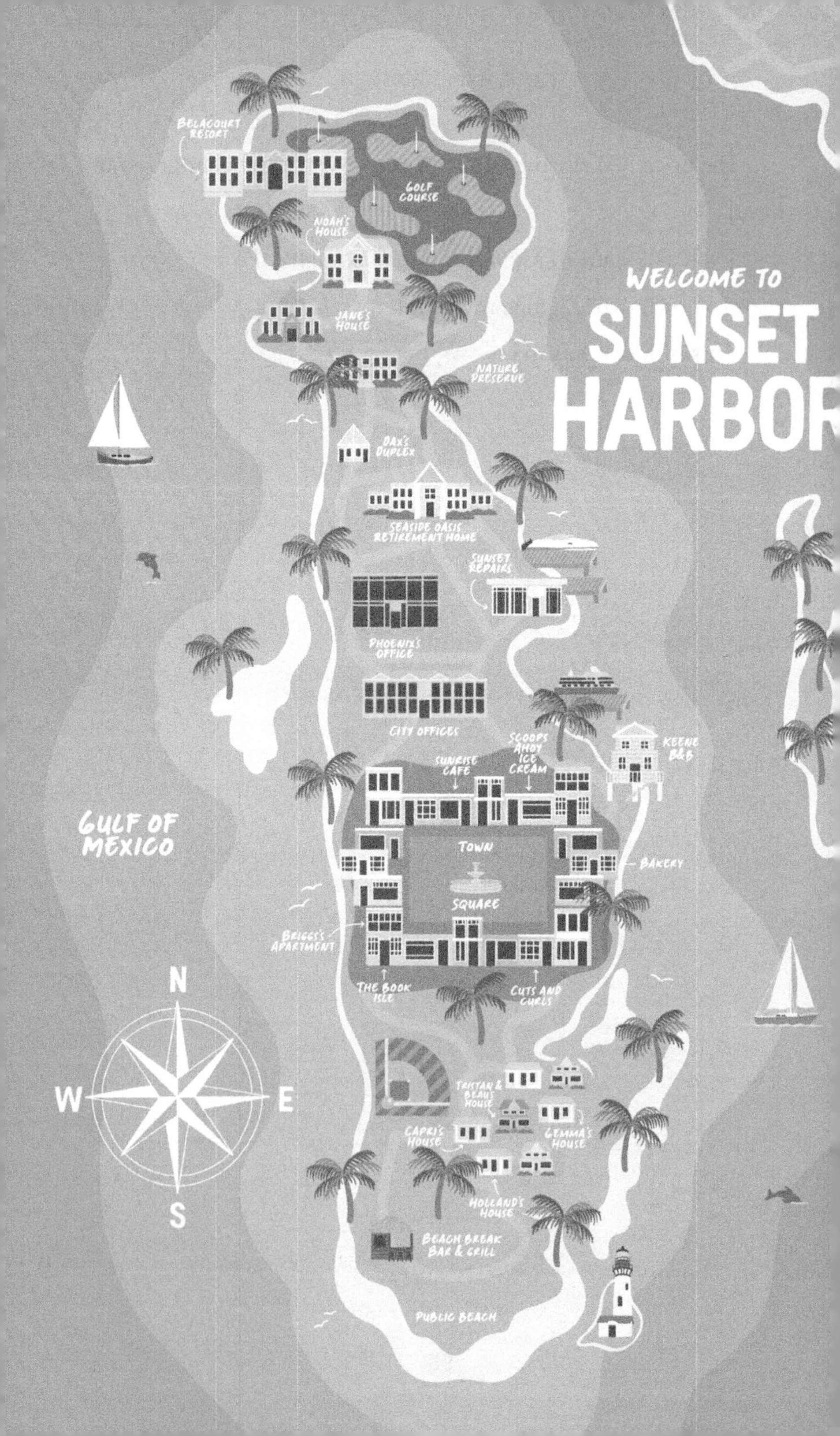

WELCOME TO

SUNSET HARBOR

BELACOURT RESORT

GOLF COURSE

NOAH'S HOUSE

JANE'S HOUSE

NATURE PRESERVE

DAX'S DUPLEX

SEASIDE OASIS RETIREMENT HOME

SUNSET REPAIRS

PHOENIX'S OFFICE

CITY OFFICES

SCOOPS AHOY ICE CREAM

SUNRISE CAFE

KEENE B&B

GULF OF MEXICO

TOWN SQUARE

BAKERY

BRIGGS'S APARTMENT

THE BOOK ISLE

CUTS AND CURLS

TRISTAN & BEAU'S HOUSE

CAPRI'S HOUSE

GEMMA'S HOUSE

HOLLAND'S HOUSE

BEACH BREAK BAR & GRILL

PUBLIC BEACH

N

W

E

S

CHAPTER 8

Briggs

Jack: Let me know when we can talk, B.

I set the phone down on the counter at the bookshop with more force than I mean to use. He's called me twice since the last text and I haven't responded. He should catch on by now. But apparently not. Jack has always been a little thick. I should call him, but I'm not ready to talk just yet. The wounds from how everything went down are still too fresh. But honestly, what is there to actually talk about? Maybe he wants to apologize, and I probably need to as well, but is it really necessary? Can't we just let it die like our failed business?

Some of the things I said to him were pretty awful though, and he didn't deserve it. I mean, he said things too, but that doesn't excuse my actions. I definitely need to apologize. I'm also still worried he'll have bad news and my struggling finances can't really take that hit right now.

A few stragglers at the bookshop slowly make their way out as I get ready to close up, leaving one person still hanging around, apparently until the last minute. The day hasn't felt as long as I thought it would. It was still busier than it normally would be in the summer, but not as bad as it was Saturday. Hopefully the whole gossip mill has moved on, or maybe because no one saw Presley, they realized it was fruitless. Little did they know she did show up and spent the evening with me.

I did have a strange run-in with a woman named Jane—someone I went to middle and high school with. I thought she was fishing around for information about Presley James, but it turns out she wanted to ask me out. Which was . . . very random. I couldn't say yes; I'm not in a place to date right now. Even though I sort of offered that to Presley. But it's not really dating. Just she and I doing summery things . . . alone.

Okay, well, that does sound a bit like dating.

I felt sort of dumb for even offering it. Who do I think I am, anyway? I'm just some penniless island dweller at the moment, living in an apartment that's been decorated by the inner child of a fifty-two-year-old woman. If my college professors could see me now. Especially after all the *you're going places, kid* accolades they gave me at graduation.

Yes. I'm really going places right now. So many places.

I hope what Presley is doing works for her. I hope the rumors about her staying here on the island will die down and she can move on with her life. I told her that as I walked her back to the resort late Saturday night. There was no spontaneous kiss when I left her at the entrance to the Belacourt Resort. It's not like I wanted one anyway. Okay, that's a total lie. I almost went for it when she went up on her tiptoes and kissed me on the cheek before walking away.

The rumors will settle here, and the islanders will move on to something else, like they always do, and Presley will become a blip in my life. A blip I'm not going to tell anyone about because no one would believe me anyway. I still don't fully believe it myself.

"Closing up?" Carl asks, looking up from a book he's been reading for the past two hours. I just turned off half the lights in the store, the universal sign for *please leave this establishment*.

"Yep," I reply. "Off to have dinner with my mom and Scout."

"Oh?" His bushy eyebrows shoot up.

I think he might be fishing for an invite, and heaven knows there will be plenty of food because Marianne McMannus doesn't know how to cook for only three people. But since I never told my mom about him digging for info on her dating status, I'm not sure inviting him would be the best idea. Plus, let's be honest here: Carl is annoying.

"Yep," I answer him. "And I'm running late, so I'll see you around, Carl."

I go to the door and hold it open for him.

"I'll be in later this week," he says, giving me a single nod as he walks out the door.

"Sounds good," I tell him. He's after the refrigerator-repair manuals I did finally order for him. Apparently, YouTube was too confusing. There was too much information.

I lock the door behind him, turning the sign over to *closed*, and then start closing up the shop, doing a checklist of things I have memorized: shutting the shades on the windows, putting any misplaced books back where they belong, and organizing all the things on the checkout counter. My mom comes in and deep cleans the place on Sundays, so there's not much to do cleaning-wise, but I pick a few things up off the floor and move a few chairs back into place.

I'm just about to turn off the lights when I hear it. A knock on the door of the shop. Unexpectedly, my heart does a little speeding-up thing.

I shake my head as I walk to the door, seeing someone in a pair of shorts and that same black hoodie and sunglasses, the hood covering her head and pulled tightly, just like Saturday night.

I quickly unlock the door and open it, letting Presley James inside.

"Hey," she says, removing her hood and then messing with her hair so it's no longer flat to her head.

"What are you doing here?" I can't help the smile that's evident in my tone.

She smiles back. "It's my thing," she says, in that lower raspy voice of hers. "I stay inside for two days and then I can't take it anymore and I come here to bother you."

"Were the teenagers bugging you again?"

I talked to Scout yesterday when I took her to get ice cream at the shop on the other side of the square from the bookstore. She acted like she had no idea what I was talking about, and I couldn't tell her that it was Presley who told me she saw a bunch of teens sneaking in, or she'd have been back with her friends attempting it again today. I just reiterated the lie I've been telling that Presley James isn't here and not to waste her time or get in trouble for doing something dumb like that.

"No teenagers today," Presley says, shaking her head.

"Bored?"

"Always."

"So . . . what are you doing?"

She sighs. "Being stupid, I guess."

"You really can't take more than two days by yourself," I say.

She shakes her head. "I know. That seems to be my limit."

I lift my shoulder briefly, wondering if I should say what my mouth wants to say right now. I decide to just go for it.

"You know, you could just come here at night, and we could hang out, sometimes . . . when you're bored, that is. If you want to, or you know . . . whatever."

Right. Really smooth, Briggs. I mess with my glasses, pushing the bottom of the frames up with the back of my finger.

"Actually," she says. "I was thinking that . . . I mean if you're still up for it, that maybe . . . we could do your summer plan?"

I rear my head back, confused. "But what about—"

"I know," she says, holding up a hand. "I know what I said, and it's probably a very bad idea, but I can't do it. I can't stay in that room. I feel like I'd rather risk it than lose my mind at the resort. And I am . . . losing my mind. We can be careful, right?"

"Of course," I tell her, having already worked out some ideas, even though at the time it felt fruitless. I give her a grin that she returns. "Let's do all the summer stuff."

"Really?" she asks, her eyes doing a sort of twinkling thing.

Did she really think I'd turn her down?

I grab my phone out of my back pocket and pull up my notes app. I was bored myself yesterday, what with not working at the bookshop and also not having a five-foot-nothing famous actress keeping me company.

"What's that?" Her eyes go from my phone to me.

"I made a list of things to do."

"You . . . made a list?"

I give her my best sheepish smile. "I figured it could end up being useful."

"You assumed I wouldn't be able to stay at the resort, didn't you?"

"No," I say, pushing my glasses up my nose with a finger. "Of course not. I made it just in case."

Her mouth pulls up into a full smile, and it's pretty dazzling.

"What's on it?" She tries to peek at my phone, but I hold it away from her.

"It's a surprise," I say. It's not a surprise, but it feels sort of vulnerable to let her look at the list I made. What if she hates it? What if it's stupid?

"I love surprises," she says.

"Good," I tell her. "Because that's why . . . I mean that's what it's going to be. A surprise." Great. I'm fumbling over my words again.

"So, what should we do tonight? Can we knock something off the list?" She points to the phone in my hand.

I scan my screen to see what we could do this evening before remembering that I already have plans. "Oh crap," I say, shaking my head and briefly looking up at the ceiling. "I have dinner with my sister and my mom. But I can cancel it."

"No," she says as I start to pull up my mom's number. "Do you think . . . would they . . . would they care if I came with you?"

I stare at her, unsure I heard her right. She fumbles with the drawstrings on her hoodie, and I put the phone in my back pocket, which begins to vibrate as soon as I do, but I ignore it.

I open my mouth to say something, but she talks first. "If it's too much to ask, don't worry. I'm . . . sorry. We can meet up tomorrow, or the next day, or whatever?"

The way she's fumbling through her words and her nervous energy makes me smile. She's Presley James, famous actress extraordinaire. And I'm . . . well, I'm nobody. And yet, with the way she's acting right now, you'd think she was trying to ask for a meeting with King Charles.

"Sorry, was that dumb to ask?" she says, now taking the ends of the drawstrings and nervously tapping them together.

"No, my mom would love to have you," I say. "That's not the problem."

"Really? Then what's the problem?" She looks around the room for a possible answer, and then back at me when it seems like she's landed on one. "Oh, did you . . . were you planning on bringing someone with you? Like a date or something?"

I shake my head, quickly. "No, no date. It's just me and my family. The problem is"—I reach up and adjust my glasses—"my mom happens to be the person who most likely spread the news that you might be here, and my sister was probably part of the teenage group that kept sneaking into the resort."

Not probably—they literally did those things. But I don't want to tell Presley that.

Her face falls, just the slightest bit, but I see it, and I hate that it's my own family that's been some of the cause of her seclusion.

"That does pose a problem," she says.

I don't respond; I just nod.

A noise from the back of the shop has us both turning our heads in that direction.

"Briggs! Mom made me come here and tell you to come to dinner. You ignored my call," I hear my sister say as she walks into the main area of the shop with her phone in her hand, having most likely used the back entrance.

She stops dead in her tracks, only a few feet away from us, when she sees me standing there with Presley James.

"Holy crap," Scout says, her eyes wide. "It's true!" She covers her mouth with her hand.

"Scout," I say as I take the few steps toward her. "She's not who you think she is."

"Briggs," Presley says. "It's okay." She moves to stand next to me.

"You're Presley James?" Scout finally says, her words muffled behind her hand.

She nods. "Yes, and you must be . . ." Presley looks at me for some help.

"Sorry," I say, shaking my head, trying to get my bearings. "Presley, this is my sister, Scout."

"You really are Presley James?" Scout asks, her eyes still wide. "You're in Sunset Harbor?"

"It's really me," she says, holding her hands out, like she's presenting herself.

"Oh my gosh, Briggs." Scout turns toward me. "You liar."

"Sorry, Scout, I've been trying to keep Presley's secret. She doesn't want people to know she's here."

"Oh, right, because of that video," Scout says, like it's no big deal, like it didn't completely upend Presley's life. "Was that AI? Because I've been telling people I think it was."

"Uh," Presley starts, but you can tell she's not sure where to go with that.

"Scout," I say, attempting to save Presley. "You can't tell people she's here, okay?"

Scout nods her head in quick little movements. "Sure, yeah. Okay."

"It's really important that you don't tell your friends or anyone else."

"Briggs," Scout huffs, putting her hands on her hips. "I heard you the first time. Stop being an annoying weirdo."

This makes Presley snort out a laugh. She takes a step toward Scout, reaching out and taking one of my sister's hands in hers.

"I think your brother is just trying to protect me, but it would mean the world to me if you kept the secret . . . at least until the end of the summer."

"You're here for the whole summer?" Scout asks, her eyes wide.

"That's when I have to go back to work," Presley says.

"Can I tell people after you leave?"

This makes Presley smile. "Absolutely."

"Done," Scout says. "But . . . could I get like an autograph as proof? I mean, for after you leave. And probably a picture too, so people believe me."

"Scout," I chastise.

"I can definitely make that happen," Presley says.

Scout claps and does a little dance in place. "Everyone is going to freak out."

"Okay, but they can freak out after she leaves," I remind her.

"Briggs," she says, with a roll of her eyes. "You're so annoying."

"Yeah, you . . . said that already." According to Scout, the word is starting to become synonymous with my name.

Scout's phone beeps, and mine vibrates in my back pocket. It doesn't take amazing deduction skills to know it's our mom.

"We need to go home for dinner," Scout says, looking at her phone and then at me.

"Yeah, okay," I say, nodding my head at her and then at Presley.

"Oh! Presley should come with us," Scout says, practically jumping in place now.

"I'm not sure," I say at the exact same time that Presley says, "Okay."

"Really?" Scout asks, her focus on Presley like she didn't even hear my response. "You'll come to dinner?"

"Scout, you know how Mom is with secrets," I admonish.

She waves my words away with her hand. "I can handle Mom."

I look to Presley. "I'm not sure this is a good idea." A sick feeling swims around in my stomach, thinking about my mom and her inability to keep gossip to herself. I don't even think she does it maliciously—she just likes to talk and know things.

"Briggs," Scout says, putting her hands on her hips. "If we tell Mom that Presley needs to keep it a secret, she will."

"Are you sure?"

"She's kept lots of secrets from you about me."

I lower my brow. "What secrets?"

"Never mind," she singsongs. "You don't need to know. But she's also never told me about what went down in Fort Lauderdale and why you're really back home."

My face feels instantly heated. I haven't told Presley why I'm here, and I kind of wanted to keep it that way. There's a reason I kept directing our conversation back to her on Saturday night.

"Trust me," Scout says. "Mom won't say a thing."

"This is the best pulled pork sandwich I've ever had," Presley declares.

My mom is practically bursting at the seams. Half because Presley James is sitting at her dinner table, and the other half, I'm pretty sure, is because she can't tell anyone about it.

I'm still skeptical, but Scout seems to be right about our mom. Once we explained the situation, that Presley needed to hide this summer, Marianne McMannus swore herself to secrecy, promising she'd never say a thing and even offering to tell people Presley isn't here to try and throw them off the scent. She'll probably succeed where I clearly failed because people in this town believe her, hence the crowd in the bookshop on Saturday.

She readily and heartily agreed to not tell a soul, and when Presley offered the same deal that she gave Scout—that my mom could tell everyone once summer is over—that pretty much sealed it.

"I'm so glad you like it," my mom says.

Presley's eyes widened when we arrived at my mom's place and, after we got through the hoopla of Presley James really being Presley James, she saw that my mom had made us barbecue for dinner.

"My first summer barbecue," she'd whispered to me after we sat down at the round table in the dining room of the two-story house we moved into when my mom married Keith. That was sixteen years ago, and a little more than a year later, Scout was born.

I didn't tell Presley that, like her, I split time in the summer with my dad, who lives on the mainland in Naples. Mostly because it was a different experience for me. I had a slew of friends there and did a lot of summer things. It seemed like rubbing it in her face that we had similar upbringings, and yet mine wasn't at all like hers.

"What was it like working with Austin Butler?" Scout asks around a mouthful of food, which our mom has reprimanded her for more than once already tonight. Scout gets like this when she's excited, like nothing can get in her way when she's got something on her mind. There have been many conversations with the bathroom door between us, her screaming a story at me while I'm trying to take a shower.

"You may not want to ask her about actors," I say before Presley can answer Scout's question.

"Briggs," Presley says, pushing my arm lightly.

"I'm just saying, you might not want to know the truth about people."

Presley rolls her eyes. "Austin Butler is probably one of the coolest people I've worked with."

"Yes! I knew it," Scout says, clapping her hands excitedly. "Was he a good kisser?"

"Scout Genevieve McMannus," my mom says, an appalled look on her face.

"What?" Scout scrunches her button nose at our mom. "It's a good question. He's got really nice lips. Like, they're so pillowy. He looks like he'd be good at it." She puckers her lips and mimics kissing the air.

"Scout!" both my mom and I say at the same time.

Presley looks like she's trying not to laugh, and having a hard time holding it in.

"Ignore her," I tell Presley.

When Scout moves from air kisses to kissing her hand and making exaggerated smooching noises, Presley can no longer hold back and bursts into giggles. She leans in toward me, her head landing on my shoulder as she laughs. It feels like something you'd do with someone you've known for a long time. Even though I only officially met Presley four days ago, it doesn't feel strange at all.

I look over at my mom, who should be putting a stop to Scout's antics, and instead find her holding a half-eaten pulled pork sandwich in her hands, frozen as she watches Presley and me. I can actually see the calculations going on behind those green eyes. She's picturing romance and weddings and grandbabies, and I will need to put a stop to it as soon as possible because there's nothing romantic between Presley and me.

Sure, she kissed me, and I liked it . . . a lot. But that's all that's happened, and Presley apologized for it because it was a mistake. One that won't happen again. My life is kind of a mess right now. I don't have a job, nor any prospects, and my bank account is nearly empty—the last thing I need is to become romantically entangled with someone, especially Presley, who has her own stuff going on. Even if that weren't the case and we were both in healthy places in life, that doesn't mean anything would happen between us. We're from two different worlds. She's a famous actress, and I'm just a regular, small-town boy.

Even beyond all that, Presley would have to like me in that way, and I just don't see it happening.

"Okay, if you won't tell me about Austin Butler, then what about Zac Efron?" Scout says, her eyebrows wagging.

"He's a great guy," Presley offers.

"But is he a good—"

"No," I say, shaking my head and cutting her off. "No more kissing questions."

"Fine," Scout replies to me, although her eyes are looking up toward the ceiling. "You're so boring."

Boring is a step up from annoying, I'd say.

"Well, Presley," my mom says, her voice indicating that we are changing the subject. "What do you think of the island?"

I look to Presley, who's smiling kindly. "It's great, very beautiful," she says. Oh, she's got the acting thing down. I know she doesn't think it's great and feels more like she's trapped here.

My mom dips her chin once. "It is, isn't it? It's been home for sixteen years now."

"What brought you here?" Presley asks.

"My husband, Keith," my mom says, a sorrow-filled smile spreading across her lips. "I'd given up on love and all that after I divorced Briggs's dad. But then I met Keith, and he swept me off my feet. He's from the island, and so he convinced me to move here."

Presley must not notice the solemn look on my mom's face, because she looks to me and then back at my mom. "Did he . . . have to work tonight?"

"Daddy passed away three years ago," Scout says.

Both my mom and I look at Scout, who, up until this moment, hadn't been able to say that to anyone without breaking into tears. But she looks fine right now, her lips pulled into a straight line, her eyes bright and dry, her expression calm and composed.

My mom clears her throat, unable to hold back her own feelings as her eyes shine under the pendant light hanging above the dining room table. "It was a heart attack," she finally says.

Presley looks to me with big eyes, nonverbally asking me why I hadn't told her this. It wasn't that I was purposefully keeping it from her—it was just never part of the conversation. We didn't talk all that much about me on Saturday night except for superficial things. Favorite books, favorite movies, that kind of thing. There was no diving into the nitty-gritty of my past because we just never went there. And also, I didn't want to.

"I'm so sorry," Presley says, her voice almost a whisper.

"Oh, it is what it is," my mom says, dismissing the sentiment with a shake of her head. She's trying to keep it in, but her words come out wobbly. I've never been married, but I'm assuming you don't ever get over the loss of a spouse, especially one you loved very much.

And my mom did love Keith, even if he and I didn't always see eye to eye. My relationship with him wasn't bad—it just wasn't all that good, either. Still, I miss him, especially for my mom and for Scout, who was only eleven when he died.

My mom takes a big breath. "Okay, let's talk about something lighter, shall we?" Her head bobs up and down as she looks around the table.

"Well, I love the bookshop," Presley says, and that's the perfect topic change, as my mom's sad eyes instantly turn to heart ones.

"Thank you. I've loved running it. It doesn't make much money, but we're staying afloat for now. It did help when there was a rumor Presley James had been in the store."

"And we can spread the rumor again after she leaves," Scout says.

"Perfect," says Presley.

"Oh!" Scout says, her loud voice reverberating off the walls. "Maybe we can do a photoshoot of you in the bookshop that we can hang all around the room! Like different poses of you with the books and stuff." Her eyes are wide, full of ideas.

I give Presley my best apologizing expression. It's shrugging shoulders and downturned lips, a silent plea to forgive my nutty family.

Presley just smiles at Scout. "I'm sure we can do something like that."

"So, Presley," my mom says. "Has Briggsy here given you a tour of the island?"

"I haven't," I tell her. "Not yet."

I feel Presley's gaze on mine. "Briggsy?" she asks. I can tell by just her tone, not even having to look at her, that she will be using that later.

"I'll take you on a tour," Scout excitedly offers.

"So you can parade her around the town and introduce her to your friends?" I ask.

Scout smiles. "I said I'd keep her secret, but you know if we accidentally run into people . . ."

"No," I say, emphatically. "I'll figure out a way to show her around the island so we have less chance of running into people." How I'll do that is a mystery at the moment.

"But you have to work at the bookshop, so it should be me," Scout says, giving me a smug grin.

"I'll work at the shop so Briggs can show you the island," my mom pipes in. I think she might be back to imagining weddings and babies.

The fact that she's offering bodes well, though. I'd told Presley I'd give her a fun summer but hadn't really thought out the logistics of how I was going to actually do that, since I'm supposed to be working at the shop so I can stay in the apartment for free and give my mom a break. I didn't think the details through because I didn't expect it to really happen.

"That way, I can make sure I spread the rumor that you're not really here to people in the bookshop," my mom says.

"I really appreciate it," Presley says.

"It's my pleasure," says my mom, and I can tell by the twinkle in her eyes she's going to enjoy spreading the lie more than she would have telling the truth.

Maybe this will work out after all.

CHAPTER 9

Presley

"BRIGGS!" I SCREAM after he does some sort of double-bouncing thing that shoots me up so high off the trampoline, I can see above the houses and to the ocean in the not-so-far distance.

I can also feel my dinner flopping around in my stomach. Is there a rule for how long after eating you should wait before jumping on a trampoline? Like with swimming?

We finished dinner with his family, ending with some delicious peach cobbler and ice cream, and then Briggs told me he wanted to show me something in the backyard. I actually squealed when I saw the trampoline sitting in the corner of the well-manicured lawn.

I immediately ran over to it, and with a little help from Briggs, I climbed up and started jumping.

It was everything I thought it would be as a kid. I never got to jump on one because it was always in my contracts to stay off trampolines and away from basically anything that might cause me to break a limb or dislocate a shoulder. No skiing, on snow or water, rock climbing, or extreme sports of any kind. Nothing that could delay production of a film or show. I surely have the same clause in my latest contract, but I don't really care. No one is here to hold me to it.

"Have you had enough?" he asks, looking up at me and smiling as the next bounce throws me much less high.

"I think I might need a little break," I say as I flop on my back and bounce lightly there until I come to a complete stop. The air is thick with humidity, but the ocean breeze makes it tolerable.

Briggs comes over to me, his steps on the flexible mat forcing my body to roll toward the center of the trampoline before he flops down on his back next to me, the bottom of his light-gray T-shirt moving up before he yanks it back down.

I look up at the night sky, bright and beautiful and full of stars without all the city lights to dim it. How long has it been since I've seen a sky like this?

"So, how did your first time on a trampoline feel?" he asks, his arm brushing up against mine.

"Well, except for the possibility of my dinner coming back up, it was amazing."

"Sorry if I bounced you a little too much."

"I think I just ate too much. Your mom's macaroni salad was amazing."

"That was your favorite part?"

"Pasta is my favorite thing in the world, and I never get to eat it because I'm always on a diet for my next role," I say, my tone sounding slightly dramatic on purpose. I am an actor, after all.

He nudges me. "Don't you have a role coming up?"

"Yes, I do, and don't remind me." I probably need to up my cardio game while I'm here to start getting myself ready since I don't have a trainer or anyone forcing me to do it now. Of course, I might not even have the role anymore. Negotiations could be happening right now to take me off the movie and I would have no idea. It's so weird to not be in contact with anyone—not my manager, or my mom, or my assistant. And I've stayed off social media, so I don't even know what's going on there. I'm kind of proud of myself for that, for not breaking down and finding a computer at the hotel to use. Every once in a while, I get the notion to see what people are saying, to have a little peek. But then I remember that a tailspin is not what I need right now.

"What's the role? Or are you not allowed to say?" Briggs asks.

"I'm not supposed to say much, but you're already keeping my secrets, so why not one more?"

He chuckles, and it's rich and warm, and my stomach does a little spinning thing that has nothing to do with the food in my belly.

"It's a movie adaptation for the book *Cosmic Fury*," I say. "Have you read it?"

"I haven't," he says.

"Well, it's kind of a big deal. It's a beloved book in the fantasy world."

"That explains it," he says. "I only read rom-coms."

I snort out a laugh. "Ones about rule books and love hypotheses?"

"Exactly," he says.

"Well, in this adaptation, I'm playing a character named Callis who heads up a team of warriors tasked with defending the galaxy against an ancient evil." I can't help the voice change that happens when I mention *ancient evil*. I do it every time I give the elevator pitch for this movie.

"That sounds interesting," he says, turning his head toward me. I realize I've been staring at the side of his face like a weirdo since the chuckle that did strange things to my insides, and I quickly look away.

"I think it will be good for my career," I say to the twinkling sky above us.

"Why's that?" Briggs asks. "Isn't it pretty similar to other roles you've taken? Like the Zenith Trilogy?"

Ah, the Zenith Trilogy. That was a fun one, and where I first worked with Declan Stone. It wasn't until the third movie came out that we started fake dating, which turned real for a bit before it turned fake again. And then it just got weird, like so weird. Too weird to even think about right now.

It's all a big publicity game. That's the part of this work that I hate the most--putting on a show outside of movie making. If I could get rid of any part of the job, it would be that. Oh, and probably not being able to go to Target anytime I want to without the paparazzi following me everywhere.

"Yes, but this one is the most epic," I tell Briggs. "It's epic-er than the other ones I've done."

"Epic-er?"

"The most, most epic," I say, feeling silly but also comfortable enough to be this way around Briggs. It's refreshing—*he's* refreshing.

He turns his body toward me, now on his side, his arm tucked under his head, and I do the same, turning toward him.

"If you could have any role, what would it be?" he asks.

I let out a breath. "I don't know. I like doing all the sci-fi and fantasy movies, but I think I'd like to try my hand at a rom-com sometime."

"A remake of *Notting Hill*?"

"Heck no," I say, giving him my best appalled look. "That movie is perfection and should never be remade."

"Agreed," he says. "I've only really seen it the one time, but it should never be redone."

"Never, ever."

"Why do they keep remaking movies? Have we run out of new ideas?"

"Guaranteed audiences," I say. "Humans love nostalgia."

We stare at each other for a bit, the sound of the ocean tides and buzzing and chirping insects in the background.

"I'm sorry about your stepdad," I tell him after a little while.

I know it isn't my fault that I didn't know he'd passed away. I've learned to be good at reading people—you kind of have to be in the business I'm in. I've gotten very good at catching the small details, the nuances. A solemn glance, a sad smile. But nothing registered with me at dinner tonight. And Briggs hasn't been very forthcoming about himself, I've noticed.

"Thanks" is all he says.

"Were you close?" I prod, deciding I'm going to get him to talk right now on this trampoline under the stars.

He rolls over to his back, weaving his fingers together and laying them atop his chest. He's quiet for a few seconds, and I wonder if maybe I won't be able to get him to open up. But then he takes a resigned-sounding breath, a clear sign he's going to talk.

"We weren't all that close, no," he begins. "He was my mom's husband for more than half my life. But it was mostly strained, and I blame myself for that. It was hard for me to treat him like a father-type person when I already have a dad. At the end of the day, Keith was a good guy. It was incredibly sad when he passed away. Especially watching my mom and Scout and their grief."

I continue lying on my side, once again studying his profile as he talks. His glasses are off because glasses and trampolines make a bad combo (he's apparently broken a pair or two on this very trampoline). I like the glasses on him—they only add to his attractiveness. I know I called him cute-bookshop-boy previously, but he's more than cute. With that perfect-shaped masculine nose, and that well-defined jawline, as well as his thick head of dark-blond hair . . . *cute* is not the right word. Cute is for bunnies and puppies and little trinkets you can put in your pocket. Briggs isn't any of those things. He's handsome. Attractive. Dashing.

"What about your dad? Where is he?" I ask, still looking at his profile like a creeper. I don't even care. It's a pretty place to look.

"He lives in Naples," he says.

"Italy?"

He chuckles. "No, Naples, Florida. It's a beach town about an hour and a half from here."

"Oh, got it. So, what's your relationship with him like?"

"We're good. I saw him in April. He remarried not that long ago, and his new wife, Kate, is pretty nice."

"Do you feel like you need to be around your mom because of what happened to your stepdad?"

He lets out his breath heavily through his mouth. "I did feel like that when it first happened, but I was also in the middle of getting a start-up off the ground and couldn't be here as much as I wanted to be. It was a tough time for all of us."

"I bet," I say. "Your mom and your sister seem to be doing okay, though?"

He turns his head toward me. "Yeah, I think so."

"You're not really an open book, are you?" I say, reaching over and poking him on the arm.

"Sorry," he says, with a lilt. "It takes a lot for me to open up."

"You don't say," I tease.

He rolls over onto his side, facing me again. "What else do you want to know?"

I place an index finger on my chin as I contemplate. "Ever been married?"

"Oh, no. Not even close."

I laugh. "Me either. Um . . . let's see . . . last girlfriend."

"Wow. You're really grilling me now."

"This is my subtle way of asking if you're dating anyone."

"The last boyfriend for you was Declan Stone, I'm guessing?"

"If you want to call it that," I say. "And stop trying to bring it back to me. I'm asking the questions now."

"No girlfriend," he says. "And the last one was probably three years ago. I've mostly been focused on work."

"And that is not running a bookshop?"

He makes a sort of uncomfortable-sounding laugh. "No, the bookshop was me coming back home after a business I started in Fort Lauderdale failed."

"Oh yeah, that's rough."

"You ever own a business?" It's so dark out here in this backyard, I can barely make out the ribbing eyebrow lift Briggs gives me.

"Nope, but I once played a cyborg who owned a trinket shop, and we were having a hard time getting supplies because of an intergalactic war that was going on. So, I'm basically an expert."

He laughs, and I can barely see the white of his teeth. "It's . . . a little different than that."

"What kind of business?"

"Software," he says. I think that's all he's going to tell me but then he takes a breath and continues. "AssistGen was the name. At its core it was a virtual assistant app we designed to anticipate the needs of the end user. It could do a bunch of things, like schedule appointments and manage tasks and even offer personalized recommendations based on preferences."

"Oh wow, I didn't take you for a nerd."

He chortles. "A nerd who lost his company. So not a very good one."

"I wonder how many times Steve Jobs had to start over."

"Yeah, he didn't, really."

"Shoot, I was going for something inspiring," I say.

"Thanks for trying. There are plenty of them out there to inspire me. But right now, inspiration isn't enough, and I'm not sure what I want to do next."

"I'm sure whatever you decide to do, it'll be great," I say.

He lets out another heavy breath. "I'm not so sure right now. Maybe you should ask me next year."

"I will," I tell him, and I mean it.

Slowly, we've been inching toward each other as we've been talking. Not on purpose, but I'm guessing because of the trampoline mat and probably something to do with physics, which I have zero understanding of, but it must be science that's happening here. It's science that's drawing us toward each other. At least that's what I'm telling myself. I don't want to think it's possible that we've been doing it on our own, like a magnetic sort of attraction that can't be avoided.

Briggs is so close right now that if I leaned in, just a little, I could kiss him. If I wanted. Do I want to? I kind of do. But I also don't because I already did that once and it was a total foolish jerk-girl move. It was a really great kiss, though . . .

Presley James, stop it right now.

There will be no kissing. I'm grateful to Briggs for wanting to help me get through this summer, and I need to keep things on the friendly side. It's for the best. Plus, and this is a big plus, except for kissing me back the other night, he's shown no signs of wanting anything other than friendship. This is a good thing. I'll keep repeating that until I believe it. This. Is. A. Good. Thing.

Briggs and I can be friends, and that's exactly what I need for the summer.

I turn away from him, lying on my back, looking at the twinkling stars above us. That was a good decision to put some distance between us. I'm proud of myself.

I, Presley James, solemnly swear to keep my lips and hands to myself this summer.

It's how it must be.

"You don't need to do this, you know," I tell him as we walk back to the resort, the humid air and the lovely sea breeze surrounding us. We took a pathway along the coastline, and honestly, it's kind of a perfect night.

Just like Saturday night, I escaped via bicycle, which Briggs, glasses restored to his handsome face, is currently walking back, his big hands on the handlebars as he guides it.

"I don't mind," he says. "Since I can't drive you back, this is the next best thing."

"Do you even have a car?"

He chuckles. It's low and deep. "I do—it's on the mainland. Parked in a lot near the port where the ferry stops. We go there often, since there aren't a lot of options for food and clothes on the island."

"It feels so secluded here, like another world," I tell him, keeping my eyes on the darkened path we're on.

"It's definitely unique."

"It's also really dark out here," I say, a little tiny chill creeping up my spine. There are hardly any lamps along this path. Anything could jump out at any moment.

He bumps me with his elbow, and I look over to catch a smile on his face, even in the limited lighting. "You scared, Presley James?"

"No, Briggsy," I say, my tone mocking.

"Ah, you remembered," he says.

"I filed it under things to keep forever," I say, tapping the side of my head.

"Well, you don't have to worry about the dark, because we're not really known for crime around here. Or gator attacks."

"But . . . there are gators?" I ask, moving slightly closer to Briggs. Not because I think he can save me, but because he is much more muscly than I am and would probably be a better meal.

He chuckles again, and I swear the sound is like a warm blanket. I also love how easy it is for Briggs to laugh. I feel like most of the men I've spent time with don't get my humor, or they just don't really laugh. I think Declan Stone was born without a humor gene. The man is so full of himself.

Briggs and I are silent now, our feet padding along the walkway, with the sounds of the bicycle wheels and the waves breaking against the shore as our background soundtrack.

"Thanks for tonight," I finally say. "I had a summer barbecue and jumped on a trampoline. Look at me."

"You're a summer gal already," he says.

"I do feel like a summer gal," I say, lifting my chin.

"How have you never jumped on a trampoline?"

"Neither of my parents had one, and then there were contracts forbidding it so I didn't get hurt."

"I'd never thought of that."

"I haven't done a lot of things because of contracts," I say.

"So I'm guessing you don't do your own stunts?"

I snort out a laugh. "No way. I mean, I'd love to fall off something onto one of those big, huge, stunt airbags they use. But alas, they've never let me do it."

"Hmm," Briggs says. "That does sound like fun."

"Got one of those around here?"

"Sadly, no. It's a very small island."

I chortle. "So, what's next on the list and when can we do it?"

"I have to work for a little bit tomorrow, but I have an idea for the afternoon. Should we say around two?"

I reach up, putting an index finger to my chin. "I better consult my schedule first. I'm very busy, you know."

"Yeah, right, of course. How silly of me to assume you had nothing to do when you keep telling me you have nothing to do."

It's my turn to laugh. Bantering with Briggs might be my new favorite thing.

"What are we doing tomorrow?" I ask.

"It's a surprise, remember?"

"I don't know why I told you I love surprises the other day. I actually don't . . . love them."

"You shouldn't have told me that. It only makes me want to do it more," he says. "Just be sure to wear a bathing suit."

"Something on the beach, then? Wherever will we go to find one around here?"

We both look over as a large wave crashes against the shore, the moon hanging just above it.

Briggs looks to me. "That's a good question. We'll just have to make do."

I feel so light right now, walking toward the resort with Briggs. Lighter than I have in a long time. Like I could float away right now, not feeling that heavy weight I've been carrying around for so long, even before that stupid video.

And I think it might all be because of the man walking next to me.

CHAPTER 10

Briggs

I MIGHT HAVE to set up some ground rules with Presley.

The first one being that she can't wear that red bikini ever again.

That's it. It's just the one rule. Now to figure out how to tell her that without sounding like a creep.

"I literally have no idea what I'm doing," she says as she packs sand into a turret-shaped bucket. I grabbed a bunch of supplies from my mom's house before meeting up with Presley. My mom was more than happy to find them for me, as well as work at the bookshop this afternoon so I could be here. And she agreed to it all with stars in her eyes, which I quickly shot down, but I don't think she's buying it.

She's already started her Presley James is Not at Sunset Harbor campaign, and it must be going well since the bookshop was pretty much dead for most of the day. Which is sort of a double-edged sword, since when it was busy, the shop was making good money. It's not like the shop is in trouble or anything—it's just not making a decent profit. My mom never expected it to when she bought it all those years ago, but I don't want her to end up losing money on it, money she needs for retirement.

Scout is also part of the campaign, confirming that she started texting her friends last night after dinner claiming the same thing. They may have run with the rumor when it started, but they just might be the best allies for Presley in the end.

Now, Presley and I are both on our knees in the sand under a large beach umbrella, even though we're lathered up with sunblock, attempting to make a sandcastle. We pushed the fancy beach chairs to the side to give us enough space.

That was my plan for today, the first thing on the list I made. I could have taken her on a boat ride, or done something more extravagant, more like something she's used to, but for some reason when she said the other day that she's never made a sandcastle, it stuck in my head.

I could picture us on the beach working together to build it, and of course, in my mind, I'd be masterful at it, showing her how to do it with the utmost confidence as I formed towers and turrets with ease. Unfortunately, it's been a while since I've made one, and I'm kind of at a loss for where to begin. And also, that red bikini is distracting me.

We're on the private beach that's only for guests of the Belacourt Resort. It's on the north corner of the island, palm trees blowing in the light wind, the water a beautiful blue under the afternoon sun.

It's hot and sticky from the humidity, but the great part about being on the beach is you can run into the water and cool off, even if the water is only slightly cooler than bathwater right now.

"Maybe we should google it," I say, grabbing my phone out of a beach bag my mom insisted I take. I instinctively look for my glasses and then remember I've got contacts in. I wish I liked them more, but I usually have to suffer through wearing them. But I don't mind suffering today, here with Presley.

She places her hands on her hips, looking over at me, those large-frame sunglasses covering so much of her face. "Briggs Dalton, you've lived by the ocean your entire life and you don't know how to build a proper sandcastle?"

"No, I mean, I'm looking it up for you. So you have some instructions."

"You have no idea what you're doing, do you?" she asks.

"I'm rusty, okay? It's been a while. And apparently building a sandcastle is not like riding a bike."

She smiles, and I'm grateful those glasses aren't big enough to cover that part of her face because she has a great smile. Big and warm and inviting. It's easy to see why she's become an A-list star. There's just something about her . . . like someone you can picture hanging out with and forgetting they make movies for a living. Or maybe that's only how it feels for me.

I quickly type *how to build a sandcastle* in the search bar, and in just a few seconds I have a list.

I sit back on my heels. "We need water," I say, shaking my head, because how did I forget that? The water helps to stabilize the sand, making it easier to form.

Have I really forgotten, or is being around Presley in that red bikini short-circuiting my brain? I'm going to bet it's the latter. Honestly, I'd rather it be that than the chance I'm already going senile.

"Well, crap," she says, letting her shoulders fall dramatically. "Where are we going to find water around here?"

"That's a really good question," I say, looking out into the vast ocean that stretches as far as the eye can see.

She's smiling again, and I'm smiling back, and we're looking at each other. I think this is what the kids call *a moment*. I feel like I've had a lot of those with Presley since she first came into the bookshop last week. I haven't had a moment with someone in so long, I think I'd forgotten how it feels. How my stomach does a little dropping thing like I'm on a roller coaster. How my pulse quickens and my palms feel sweaty. Although that could also be attributed to the heat index.

Last night I felt it on the trampoline, when we were facing each other, inching closer together as we were talking. I wanted to kiss her. I wanted to lean in and feel her lips against mine. I almost did before she turned away. I was going to throw caution to the wind and just do it, right there under the stars.

It was the right thing to happen, Presley turning away like she did. Having a summer fling, because that's exactly what this would be, isn't a smart move. Maybe if we were teenagers and could afford foolish things. But we're both adults, with fully developed brains. And my fully developed brain is a bit lost and wandering right now, not to mention broke, and I should probably figure that out. I don't fit into her world, and she absolutely doesn't fit into mine, even if right now on this beach it feels idyllic.

"Okay," Presley says, snapping us out of the spell. "Let's go get some water." She takes off her sunglasses before grabbing a pail.

We walk quickly over the hot sand until we hit the water, wading in up to our ankles. We move a little deeper, and then I bend over, filling the bucket with water, and Presley follows suit. I turn to walk back toward the umbrella, and just as I do, water lands on my head and drips down the side of my body.

I turn to see a laughing Presley bent over at the waist, her hand covering her mouth.

"That was so worth it," she says through her laughter, pointing a finger at me.

"You do know I have a bucket of water myself, right?"

She rights herself and tries to quickly move away from me, but I've got much longer legs and reach her in no time, dumping the entire contents of my pail on top of her head.

"You're dead," she says through giggles, looking a bit like a drowned rat. Only, still adorable.

She fills her bucket again, but I'm too fast, filling mine and dumping it on her once more.

She makes a sort of laughing-shrieking noise before abandoning the bucket on the sand and running toward me, water splashing as she moves, looking like she's ready to pounce. I toss my bucket toward the shore and ready myself for whatever she has planned. What I don't expect is for her, in some sort of ninja move, to use my knee as a hoist as she flings herself onto my back, her arms going around my neck and legs wrapping around my waist.

"What the hell?" I say. "How did you do that?" I put my hands under her knees for balance, but I don't think she needs it. Her grip on me is so tight, it's kind of making it hard to take a good breath.

"You forget I was in *Lady of the Blade* and had to learn how to jump on the back of a Viking who was trying to invade our farmland."

"I saw that one," I say. It was years ago, though, and I barely remember it. I do, however, remember her in that torn-up gown, dirt on her face and sword in her hand as she fought for her land.

"But I did have a mounting block that they edited out in postproduction. I'm kind of surprised I was able to do it today," she says, her breath on my ear as she talks, wreaking havoc on my already straining resolve.

"Well done," I say. "But now what do you have planned?"

"I have no idea," she says on a laugh. "In the movie I choked the Viking."

"I'd appreciate it if you didn't do that," I say, locking my arms around her legs and holding her tight as I go farther out into the water.

"Briggs, what are you doing?" she asks as I move us deeper and deeper, holding on so she can't get away.

"Exacting my revenge," I say before dunking us both under.

I bring us both back up, still holding on to her, and hear her sputtering and coughing. I feel a little bad for doing that, but then she twists and breaks free from my grasp, slipping off my back and going under the water. I barely have time to react before she launches herself back up and onto me. I'm laughing as I lose my balance and fall back under the water, managing to grab her arm and take her down with me.

When we come back up, we're both laughing and swiping water from our eyes.

"Are we calling a truce?" I ask, out of breath but feeling so much lighter than I have in a while. Playing with Presley in the water like this feels like a soothing relief for all my worries. A temporary one, but much needed.

"No way," she says, doggy-paddling in place to keep afloat. I've got both feet on the ocean floor, my head easily above water.

She looks like she's preparing to launch herself at me again, but then her eyes go wide, and she jumps at me, but it's more like straight into me, her arms wrapping around my neck.

"What's wrong?" I ask, looking her in the eyes.

"I felt something touch my leg," she says, her body basically suction-cupped to mine.

My arms go around her, feeling instantly protective.

She lets out a little scream. "I felt it again," she says.

I look down in the clear water, seeing something dark toward the bottom. I kick my foot around at whatever it is before realizing what I'm touching.

"It's seaweed," I say, a laugh bubbling up in my throat.

"What?" she asks, searching my face. "No, it wasn't. It was a fish."

"I'm pretty sure it was just seaweed, but even so I'm a bit shocked that the Lady of the Blade, who can jump on a Viking's back, would be scared of a little fish."

"It could have been a barracuda," she says, still plastering her body against mine. I won't lie and say I'm not enjoying holding her like this.

"I'm pretty sure it wasn't."

"Are there barracuda in this ocean?"

"Absolutely," I say, and she makes a little squeaking noise, her arms going tighter around me to the point that it does feel something akin to being choked.

"In all the time I've lived here, I've never seen one in the water," I say, wiggling my neck a little and she loosens her grip, but only slightly. I'm mostly being truthful about never seeing a barracuda. I have seen one once, when I went deep sea fishing with Keith years ago and he caught one. But I didn't know it was a barracuda until we brought it above water. It might have been the ugliest fish I've ever seen with its pointed head and huge, elongated mouth filled with sharp, jagged teeth. I hope I never see one again, to be honest.

"Really?" Presley asks, her eyes still wide. I can see tiny droplets of water on her long, dark lashes.

"Really," I say.

She releases her grip a little, her body relaxing. Then, as if it finally dawns on her that she was practically adhered to me just seconds ago, she lets go completely, and I feel sort of disappointed.

"Should we make that sandcastle, then?" she asks, as if the last few minutes never happened.

"Sure," I say.

We make quick work of getting back to the shore, grabbing our buckets and filling them with water before making our way back to our towels and things under the large beach umbrella.

We spend the next hour working on the sandcastle—very seriously, I might add. It's obvious Presley likes to do things right, making me redo a couple of the spots when they weren't up to her standards.

By the end we've done a decent job of making our castle. There's even a walkway to the entrance and a moat around the circumference.

"My first sandcastle," Presley says, while I'm taking pictures of it with my phone since the camera on hers is terrible.

"On the summer rating scale, where does this one land?" I ask her once I've completed my role as photographer. Feeling hungry, I grab a small bag of chips I'd thrown in the beach bag before coming here.

"I'd say it's an eight," she says.

"That high, huh?" I say as I open the bag. I offer it to her, and she reaches inside, pulling out a chip. "What about the trampoline?"

"Also an eight," she says, before popping the chip in her mouth.

"What gets a ten from Presley James?"

"I have no idea," she says, talking around the food in her mouth. "We've still got a lot more summer activities to experience."

"Now I have a goal," I tell her, giving her a smile.

"What's that?"

"To do something that earns a ten."

She grins. "I have to warn you: I'm a tough audience."

"Challenge accepted," I say.

"I think the castle is a two at best," a woman says, and we both look up to see that same opinionated older lady, that big visor on her head. She's got a T-shirt on that says *Hot Grandma*. I hadn't seen her in a few days and thought maybe she'd gone back to the hole she'd crawled out of.

"Thanks?" Presley says, looking up at her.

"I need a drink," the woman declares.

"Okay, I can . . . grab someone for you?" I say, wondering for a second if she thinks I work here.

I'm also wondering if she's even supposed to be on this beach. Should we tell her it's private? I still have no idea who this woman is, and I keep forgetting to ask my mom about her.

"I'll do it myself," she says, her tone sounding frustrated. Then she points at Presley. "Sit up straight—you're killing your posture."

I watch as Presley does, in fact, sit taller. The woman gives her a nod before walking away, muttering to herself about people these days and something about a daiquiri.

"Who is that woman?" Presley asks, when she's walked out of listening distance.

I lift my shoulders. "I have no idea. I think she moved to the island after I left home."

"She's so . . . weird."

"And has a very strange aversion to smells," I add.

"Hmm?" Presley asks, confused.

"It's nothing," I say, waving the words away with my hand.

We spend the rest of the afternoon sitting under the umbrella on lounge chairs, talking about mostly superficial things, similar to the other night when we were at my apartment. I now know Presley James hates mushrooms and tried going vegan for all of one day. And she knows that I wrestled in high school and was rejected publicly by a girl named Brittany when I tried to kiss her at the homecoming dance, subsequently causing my aversion to public displays of affection.

"I never got to go to a school dance," she says, now wearing an oversized white swimsuit coverup over her red bikini. She takes a bite of a club sandwich, which we each ordered from the resort. They delivered them to us on fancy trays and on real dishes. Food service on the beach is something I've never done before and will probably never do again. Especially since my bank account wouldn't allow it at the moment. I argued to, at minimum, pay for mine, but Presley insisted it all be put on her tab.

"How did you do school?" I ask her, and then take a bite of my food. It tastes amazing, like all food seems to on the beach. It's a strange phenomenon.

"Tutors, mostly. And some online classes," she says.

"I can't say you missed out," I tell her honestly. High school for me was a rough time. I struggled with making close friends and resisted listening to Keith when he tried to be a father to me. I was kind of a jerk to both him and my mom, which, luckily, I was able to apologize for before Keith died. Still, it doesn't make up for how I acted. I wasn't terrible, but I wasn't all that considerate or understanding either.

"Did you like college better?"

"Much," I say. "I think I like being on my own."

"Which is why you're not happy being back here, working for your mom?"

I bob my head from side to side as I think about answering that. "I'm not unhappy about being back. I'm just not happy about how things turned out with my company."

"I'm sure," she says.

Once the sun is close to setting, employees from the resort bring out tiki torches and place them around the private beach. The umbrella we've been sitting under all afternoon has been taken down by one of the beach attendants, and we're now lying flat on our lounge chairs, looking up at a purple sky as a few stars start to appear.

"Thanks for spending the afternoon with me," Presley says, and reaching over, she grabs ahold of my hand and gives it a little squeeze. I expect her to pull away, but she keeps it there, and I wrap my fingers around hers. Her hand feels dainty in mine, and soft. It's a friendly handhold. That's all it is. Just friendly.

"It was my pleasure," I tell her. And it really was. Today has been a good day. I haven't felt this free in . . . well, I don't even know how long. Probably not since college?

"So, what's the plan for tomorrow?"

"I have to work all day," I tell her, feeling disappointment weigh on my shoulders.

"Oh," she says, turning her head toward me so we're lying on our chairs, still holding hands and now face-to-face. "Sorry, I didn't mean to assume."

"No." I shake my head in tiny movements. "My mom and Scout had a shopping trip planned for tomorrow on the mainland that I don't want them to miss."

"Yeah, of course. They should definitely do that. We've got all summer, anyway," she says, giving me a soft smile. "Maybe Thursday?"

"Or ... you could maybe come over tomorrow, after I close up the shop?" I ask, feeling instantly nervous, for no reason really. Maybe it's because, in my head, I'd just assumed we'd hang out tomorrow night, and now I feel sort of ridiculous for thinking that.

"Okay," she says, her lips pulling into a wide grin, putting my nerves at ease.

Her head lolls back to the sky, and mine does likewise, and we lie like that, holding hands, looking at the stars until the sun sets fully.

WELCOME TO SUNSET HARBOR

Belacourt Resort
Golf Course
Noah's House
Jane's House
Nature Preserve
Dax's Duplex
Seaside Oasis Retirement Home
Sunset Repairs
Phoenix's Office
City Offices
Sunrise Cafe
Scoops Ahoy Ice Cream
Keene B&B
Gulf of Mexico
Town Square
Bakery
Briggs's Apartment
The Book Isle
Cuts and Curls

Beach Break Bar & Grill
Public Beach

CHAPTER 11

Presley

"YOU'RE SERIOUSLY NOT going to tell me your middle name?" I ask, leaning across the bookshop counter toward Briggs, who's printing out some kind of sales report from the register after closing.

"No," he says, adamantly. "I hate it."

We've been going back and forth like this for a few minutes, not long after I showed up outside the bookstore, knocking on the glass door with my hoodie pulled up over my head. We were talking about our first names and how we got them (mine is after Elvis, of course, and his is an old family surname), but we've now moved on to middle names. Briggs is refusing to tell me his, which is both infuriating and exhilarating because I feel like I have to know. Like it's now become the most important thing in my life.

"Did you know Presley James isn't my real name?" I ask him, crossing my arms in front of me, bunching up the front of the pink tank I'm wearing.

He furrows his brow behind his glasses. "It's not?"

I shake my head. "I'll tell you mine if you tell me yours."

"Couldn't I just google yours?"

"That's not fair," I say, giving him my best pout.

"How about you guess mine," he says, the corner of his lips pulled up into a smirk.

"Okay . . . How about Rufus?" I say, conjuring up the worst name I can think of.

He shakes his head.

"Bartholomew," I guess again.

"Nope," he says.

"Driggs?"

He gives me a confused look. "You think my name is Briggs Driggs?"

I snort out a laugh. "Well, I don't know. But wouldn't you hate it if it were?"

"I definitely would."

"Is it worse than that?"

He nods. "You know, come to think of it, I'd rather be Briggs Driggs. Maybe I can have it changed."

"Give me a hint," I say, unfolding my arms and placing my hands on the counter between us. I feel like I might spontaneously combust if I don't know it right away. Patience has always been a struggle of mine.

"It's literary," Briggs says, grinning slightly.

I think for a minute. Literary? Truthfully, I'd need the help of Google with this one, because it's been a while since I've read any classics. And I'm assuming it's probably a classic name.

"Atticus," I say, wondering if maybe Briggs's mom loved *To Kill a Mockingbird* and likes a theme, since his sister's name is Scout. He does live in a very themed princess and fairy apartment, after all.

"Try again," he says, picking up his phone and typing something into it. The short sleeves of the black button-up shirt he's wearing pull taut around his muscles, and it almost makes me forget my train of thought. But I stay the course.

Anyway, I'm sort of glad it's not Atticus because I like that name and I think I might have been disappointed if he hated it. Why, I'm not exactly sure.

I snap a finger. "Oh, is it Heathcliff?"

"Nope," he says, looking up from his phone.

"Frodo?"

He laughs at that one.

I huff out a breath. "You're really not going to tell me?"

He shakes his head slowly. "Nope."

It has now become my life's mission, my sole purpose, to figure this out.

"Well, I'm not telling you mine until you tell me yours."

"Presley Renee Shermerhorn," he says, looking me directly in the eyes.

"Curse you, Wikipedia," I say, trying not to smile so he doesn't get the satisfaction, but the extra smug look on his face is making it hard not to.

He reaches up and rubs his jaw. "Not gonna lie, I can see why you went with a stage name."

I let my jaw drop, mock appalled. "I like my name, thank you very much."

"Yeah, but Shermerhorn is a mouthful."

I let out a breath. "That's exactly what my agent said."

"Where did you get James from?"

"It's my grandpa's name, and I've always loved him, even though he's gotten crotchety in his old age," I tell him, and then make a scoffing noise. "Why did I tell you that? I could have used it as leverage."

"That was foolish of you," he says.

I give him my best *what am I going to do with you?* look. "I'll figure out your middle name, you know," I tell him.

"I have no doubt," he says. "So, are you ready to get out of here?"

"Sure. What . . . exactly are we doing?"

"It's a surprise, of course," he says, a little twinkle in his eyes. I should have never told him that I hate surprises. But I don't mind them so much when Briggs is behind them. And so far, they've been exactly what I needed.

"Okay, Briggsy, let's get out of here."

"You have a little bit of . . . um . . . chocolate on your face," Briggs says, pointing to my mouth.

"Where?" I say, knowing full well there's a big glob right by the corner of the left side of my lips. But I'm in a silly mood tonight as we sit by a gas firepit in his mom's backyard, roasting marshmallows and making s'mores.

"It's right here," he says, pointing to the spot on his own mouth.

"Here?" I purposefully point to the other side.

"How can you not feel that? It's practically half of a candy bar."

I laugh before swiping the melted chocolate from my face with a napkin.

"So how is your first marshmallow roasting experience?" he asks before taking a bite of a graham cracker, marshmallow, and chocolate sandwich. The firelight reflects off his glasses and casts an orange hue onto his face.

"I like it," I tell him. "Thanks for being a good teacher."

Apparently, there's an art to roasting a marshmallow, at least according to Briggs. You have to hold it just right, just above the flames, so that you get a nice golden color to it. The first time, I'd just gone for it, sticking the fluffy thing right into the fire and blackening the outside. It had a very bitter aftertaste—because of course I ate it. I wasn't about to waste a marshmallow.

"Is this your first time having s'mores?"

"Of course not," I say, my tone mocking. But then I think about it. "Actually, I . . . don't know."

He shakes his head. "How have you missed out on one of life's greatest treasures?"

I hold my half-eaten s'more toward him. "I mean, this is good, but I don't think it's *that* good. I give this an eight point two out of ten."

He feigns shock. "That's sort of blasphemy, you know."

"My apologies to the s'mores gods," I say before cupping my hands with my mouth, angling my head toward the sky, and yelling, "I'm sorry if I offended anyone."

Briggs laughs, and it makes me feel a little wobbly on the inside.

I pull my legs up, my feet now sharing the seat with my butt, my arms wrapping around my knees. It's a stance that makes sense when I'm cold, to use my own body heat, but right now I'm not cold. Not with the warm, summer night weather and the low heat emanating from the gas fire. It's more of a steadying pose because I'm feeling things for Briggs. Bigger things than I should be feeling. Bigger things than I want to be feeling. No, that's not true. I don't mind the feelings. It's just not the best idea. I will inevitably get my heart broken—or worse, I'll break his. Because I think my feelings are reciprocated. It's in the way he held my hand on Tuesday.

Or right now, as I look over to find him staring at me.

I try some levity. "What are you looking at?"

"You," he says, no apology in his voice. "You're just . . . surprising."

"How's that?"

He looks away, his eyes on the fire now. "It's that you're not like I'd expect."

"Seen too many movies with bratty, entitled actors?"

He nods, looking back toward me. "And real stories on social media."

"I wouldn't put too much stock into those. Fame is a weird thing. Most everybody wants a piece of it, and if they can hitch themselves up on your downfall, they'll do it."

There are so many TikToks now of people who've said I was rude to them at restaurants and stores, and it's all a bunch of lies.

He crosses a leg over the other. "That's the thing, though. The video—"

"Oh gosh," I say dramatically, looking up toward the sky, cutting him off. The truth is, I've hardly thought about that stupid video over the past few days. And it's not because I've been avoiding it—it simply hasn't entered my mind.

"Hear me out," he says. "That video of you is more like what people expect of stars, what we're, I guess, taught to expect. But spending time with you, that's not you at all."

I shake my head. "That video was me, Briggs. One hundred percent. I wish I could say it was AI or a body double or something. But it was me having a moment, a real, human moment where I just . . . lost it. I haven't done that in fifteen years, since I started working."

Since I've been working nonstop. Which is why I'm now currently on an island, sitting with a man I've just recently met, eating roasted marshmallow-and-chocolate sandwiches and feeling contented for the first time in a long time. Maybe instead of working so hard, instead of taking every role that came my way to keep my career on an upward trend, I could have taken more time to do things like this. To just be.

"You'd never lost your temper until that moment?" Briggs asks, his brows peeking out from behind his glasses.

"No," I say through a chuckle. "Of course not. But I'd gotten really good at holding it in, and then letting it out when I'm alone. I have a very nice soundproof closet at my place in LA that gets the brunt of it. And when I'm on set, which is a lot of the time, the bathroom in my trailer is usually a good place.

Although I have to be more cautious there. People are always around, always listening."

"I'm . . . not sure if that's terrible or maybe sort of healthy," he says.

"It's not, because you saw what happened. Millions of people have seen it. I just couldn't take it anymore."

"So, what happened?" he asks. But then quickly adds, "I mean, if you want to talk about it. We don't have to."

I rest my chin on the tops of my knees, watching the embers of the fire dancing in the sea breeze. I think talking about it might ruin this lovely night, and I definitely don't want to ruin it. But also, I kind of do want to tell Briggs. Mostly because he's not expecting anything, and I don't think he'd judge me. Actually, I'm pretty sure of that. He's seen the video, after all, and he was madder about the possibility that I was cheating on freaking Declan Stone than about my viral actions.

I haven't fully said out loud what went down that day on set. I didn't want to feel the shame of it, mostly. Maybe if I did, though, it would set it free. I could release all the feelings and emotions from that day that have been sitting deep inside me somewhere.

I sigh. "To give you the full picture, I'll have to go back to the beginning of my career."

"Okay," he says, turning just slightly in his chair, demonstrating that I have his full attention.

Actually, that's kind of a unique thing about Briggs. He listens—like genuinely listens. In my world, people are always half listening to you, their minds always on other things, or looking at their phones, trying to multitask. Ill-mannered Betty with her big-brimmed hat was right about no one looking up anymore. It's a sad fact.

"So, I have a very . . . interesting relationship with my mom," I start. "When I first got signed, she was very supportive of everything. She made sure every contract we signed was good, worked with my agent because I was too young to do it myself, and she hired any staff I needed. She had my back, for the most part. And then, I'm not sure when it shifted, or if it had always been that way and I just finally noticed, but my acting career had become basically her entire personality."

It was more than that, really. Didi Shermerhorn sort of became obsessed with it all. My career was her career. My highs were her highs, and my lows . . . well, those were all mine. She was, and I guess still is, the quintessential stage mom.

"Anyway," I continue. "I've been working pretty much nonstop since I was fourteen, hence why I may have never had a s'more—the jury's still out on that—with only a few breaks here and there. Don't get me wrong, that sounds like I hate it, but I really do enjoy my career. I love acting; it's hard at times for sure, but it's also a lot of fun."

"Is that what you wanted to be when you were younger? An actress?"

I shake my head. "No, I wanted to be a heart surgeon, actually."

"Really?" Briggs asks, a soft smile on his face.

"Right up until I did my first play in middle school, which was basically how I got started. But"—I hold up an index finger—"I did get to play a heart surgeon in a movie once. It was on a pirate spaceship, and I was a green alien doctor."

"*Galactic Heist*?"

"That's the one," I say. "Getting into that makeup was not fun. It took three hours. But still, I loved it. I love acting. I don't care about the other stuff—the fame or the money, although that is nice."

"I'm glad you added that caveat," he says.

"But it's not why I do it."

He nods, a quick dip of his chin showing me he understands, that he gets it. "So, back to your mom."

"Right," I say, giving him a single nod. "So, I've basically been working for fifteen years straight with hardly a break, not getting to go to regular school, and most of my time off was spent with my dad, because that's all I'd have time for."

"Are you close to him?"

I lift a shoulder and let it drop. "I guess. I mean, I love him—he's my dad. But he's kind of played a side character in my life rather than a main one."

"That's pretty sad," Briggs says.

"Yeah, but we're good," I say. And we are. I love my dad, and he loves me. He may not have been a prominent figure in my life for the past while, but he's always been there, in the background. Calling me occasionally, sending me supportive messages.

After everything went down on my last set, I sent him a text telling him I was going offline, and he wrote back right away telling me that if I needed him for anything to please reach out. I almost considered hiding out with him at his house, but my mom would have bullied it out of him. She can be a tyrant, my mother.

"So, anyway, I had filmed three movies since last June, ones where I had big roles. Lots of hours on set, all three were very physically taxing, and I even shot a couple of smaller parts for other movies."

"Five movies in a year?" Briggs asks, and he doesn't sound impressed exactly—more like it's hard to believe.

"Yeah," I say, bobbing my head up and down. It's hard even for me to wrap my brain around it. "I needed a long break. I've needed one for a while. I landed that big role that I may or may not still have, and I was finishing up my last movie and there were no press tours coming up. Suddenly I had an entire summer with nothing going on. So, I planned to go to Europe for a month or maybe two and do absolutely nothing that had to do with acting or any of the stuff surrounding it. I wanted to travel and see things with no one to tell me what I was obligated to do, and I had lots of plans, a whole itinerary full. I'm sure I would have had run-ins with fans and possibly paparazzi, because that's part of the job, but I was going to try to stay away from it if I could. I was going to be on a hiatus of sorts. A little summer hiatus."

"Hey, but you did sort of get one," Briggs says, his arms outstretched, palms up.

I smile. "I did, but . . . it wasn't exactly how I planned it."

"It's not so bad, right?"

I reach over and give his hand a squeeze. "It's not so bad at all, actually."

It's really not. I'm on a small island, hanging out with a handsome man, and there are no paparazzi, or anything like it, around me. No movie sets or publicists telling me where I need to be. And there's no Mom, trying to run my career. If I didn't have the whole viral video hanging over my head, it might actually be idyllic. Exactly what I needed.

"Where were you going to go?" he asks, turning his palm over and intertwining our fingers, which sends a little tingle down my spine.

"Italy," I say. "I've been to Venice before, to shoot a movie. I did a few touristy things during my downtime, but it was barely scratching the surface."

"I'm assuming your plans were thwarted."

"Right, yes. So, I was planning my trip, and none of my friends could go with me." *My so-called friends,* I want to add, but I don't. "And I thought, maybe I should ask my mom to join me for part of it. With all the work I'd been doing, and her basically managing my career, I was feeling sort of disconnected from her. Like our mother-daughter relationship was more like client-manager."

"I get that," Briggs says. "My mom is a tough boss."

This makes me cackle. Like, the laugh that comes out of me sounds more witchlike than human. "She seems like she'd be hard to work for," I say, sarcasm evident in my tone.

He shakes his head slowly back and forth. "You have no idea."

"Anyway, so I invited her to go with me. And she was excited, I think. I started telling her about my plans, and she basically told me we could do whatever I wanted."

Looking back now, I should have seen the next part coming. It seems foolish I hadn't expected it.

"But about a week before the film I was shooting was set to end, she asked for an itinerary, claiming she just wanted to know what I had planned. Little did I know, she'd leaked it to some people so we could get some paparazzi shots while I was on my much-needed vacation. She was going to use it for publicity because 'the world is always watching,'" I say, doing a poor imitation of my mom. "It's something she'd often say to me. Especially when I'd try to go incognito to even the freaking grocery store. She didn't like that."

"I'm assuming you confronted her?" Briggs asks, giving my hand a little comforting squeeze.

"I did," I say, rubbing my thumb over the back of his hand. "It was the last day of shooting, and my assistant handed me an invitation she'd received, inviting me to stay at a hotel in Florence, which surprised me because no one besides my mom knew my plans. So, I called the hotel and they said they had confirmed I was coming to their city and offered me a suite at their hotel. I confronted my mom right after, and she wasn't even remorseful about it. 'It's all part of the job' is what she said."

"Wow," Briggs says. "So then you, what . . . lost it on set, and it was recorded?"

"Yes," I say. "Except, before that happened, it got worse."

He pushes his glasses up his nose. "How so?"

I laugh, and it's an ironic-sounding one because I haven't fully wrapped my brain around it and I've never said it out loud. "I was mad, of course, but right as I was about to do my last shot of the film, she pulled me aside and asked—actually, she told me that Declan Stone would be joining us on the trip."

"Why?" Briggs asked.

"For publicity, of course. More buzz, or whatever. At least that's what I thought. It turns out my mother and my fake boyfriend who's *my* age are dating."

"What?"

"That's right. My mom wanted Declan to come along so it would look like he and I were together for pictures, creating a buzz, when really it was going to be a secret romantic vacation for the two of them."

"That's . . . that's ridiculous." Briggs chortles then. The kind of laugh that just bubbles right out of you.

"I'm glad you find it funny," I say, kind of feeling the same way. Saying it all out loud, it's even more absurd than I realized.

He lifts his glasses with his free hand, since I'm still holding on to his other one, and swipes at his eyes with his fingers. "It sounds like a soap opera," he says.

"It does, right? But it's not. It's my life." I'm giggling as I say this, even though it's not all that funny. But it kind of is at the same time.

"I'm sorry," Briggs says.

I take in a deep breath. "It's . . . whatever. It's frustrating. I just wish I had handled it differently, yelling at the crew and calling them all unprofessional, singling out that poor gaffer who'd done nothing wrong. I especially wish I hadn't swiped all that food off the craft services table."

"That did seem a little over the top," Briggs says, making a pinching gesture with his thumb and index finger.

"Oh gosh," I say, leaning my head back on my chair. "It's so embarrassing."

Even though telling all this to Briggs has been mostly lighthearted and I haven't once felt judged by him, I turn my head away, my eyes tearing up as pictures of the fallout go through my mind. The people I thought were my friends, the online uproar, the lies everyone made up about me, fans canceling me.

"Presley?" Briggs asks, concern in his voice after he hears me sniffle. I thought I'd done it quietly, but apparently not.

"I'm fine," I say, the words sort of choking out of me. The tears are coming faster now.

"Come here," he says, tugging on my hand.

"What?" I ask on a sob, confused by what he's getting at.

"Just come here," he repeats.

I put my feet on the ground, moving to stand, and he pulls me toward him so I'm now in front of him. Then he tenderly guides me onto his lap, where I instinctively turn on my side toward him like we've done this before, curling up while he wraps his arms around me and rests his chin atop my head.

I let out a breath, like I'd been holding it, as I lean into him. This. This is what I've needed. Someone to hold me, not tell me it's okay or that things will turn out fine. But just be with me.

I've always told myself I don't like to be consoled, but maybe that was just something I made up in my head because I've never known what true comfort from another person feels like. This is it, right now, in Briggs's arms. And when I feel him kiss the top of my head, another tear escapes down my cheek. This is what feeling cherished must be like. I realize if none of the story I just told him had happened, if I were in Italy right now, visiting the Vatican or drinking wine at a vineyard, then I'd never get to have this . . . this time with Briggs. I'd never even have known he existed. And right now, snuggled up in his lap, I'm feeling happy to know there's a Briggs in this world and I get to be here with him.

CHAPTER 12

Briggs

"SO, HOW ARE things going with Presley?" my mom asks me, her voice full of insinuation with a dash of hopefulness. It's full of romance and weddings and grandbabies.

We're both behind the counter of the bookshop. I worked the morning and early afternoon, and she came in to work the remainder of the day so I can take Presley out on a boat for a day at sea. Our next summer activity.

I've borrowed a boat from Dax, a guy I knew from school who now owns Keith's boat repair shop. Keith left it to him in his will. There was some chatter around the island after Keith passed and didn't leave the shop to me, but the truth is, I never wanted it. I have no idea how to fix a boat, and it's never been something that interested me. It was right that it went to Dax. That's who should be running it.

Meanwhile, I have no idea what I should be doing with my life. It's weird to be so directionless and nearly penniless right now. I have no idea what to do next, but I need to do something.

Maybe I should call Jack to see what he wants to talk about. Maybe he's got something up his sleeve, or maybe my nightmares will come true and I'll learn he's only been trying to reach me because we owe more money. Since I currently have no money, that would not be good news. Maybe he wants to continue the fight we had before I left. Maybe I should never call Jack again and run away and hide on an island like Presley. Of course, I'm currently on an island, one I also sort of ran away to, so I guess that's pretty much what I did. Huh. How am I just now realizing this?

"Things are fine with Presley, Mom," I say, trying to indicate with my voice that nothing is happening, so she'll stop with the freaking stars in her eyes and the naming of the grandchildren.

"I think you're in love with her," Scout says, walking up to the counter, obviously eavesdropping and not dusting the shelves like she's supposed to be doing right now. Instead, she's stuck the end of the feather duster into the bun on top of her head, and it's looking like some sort of Regency-era headdress. And the only reason I know anything about that is because my mom forced me to watch period pieces with her when I was young. I don't even know the number of times I've watched *Pride and Prejudice*. I think the 2005 adaptation is the superior version, but I would never admit that to my mom. She's a Colin Firth fan forever.

"I'm not in love with her," I say to Scout, taking a quick glance around the shop to make sure Presley hasn't somehow snuck her way inside and is listening to this conversation right now.

I am very much in *like* with Presley, but I'm not about to tell my mom or sister this. It's not a good thing anyway. There's attraction between us for sure. I know we both feel it. I wanted to kiss her last night, which is kind of a theme with me. I've wanted to kiss her every time I've been around her. It's not a good idea. She and I are not a good idea. She's not going to stay on this island, and I . . . well, I don't know what I'm going to do.

And yes, I can hear my mother's hopeful, romantic voice in my head saying that's perfect—I don't know what step I'm taking in life next, so I can go anywhere. But I'm not the type of man who can just do that. I need some sort of direction; I need to feel useful. And I've got neither of those things going for me right now.

The bell above the door rings as someone enters the shop. Her ears must be ringing…

"Hello," says Presley, waving at us as she comes inside, a baseball cap on her head and big sunglasses on her face. She's looking beautiful in a blue T-shirt and cutoff jean shorts.

She bites her lip as she looks around the store and then quickly removes the sunglasses when she realizes it's just us. She's still being careful, even though word has spread around the island that she's not here, thanks to my mom and sister. I haven't heard her name mentioned in days, which is crazy that they have such an influence around here. I hope they use this power for good and not evil. In the past, I fear it's been wielded mostly for evil.

My mom and I both tell her hello, and Scout does some sort of Regency-type curtsy, the feathers still in her hair.

"Welcome, Miss Presley," she says in a terrible British accent.

"Why, thank you," Presley says, falling right into character and curtsying back.

"Okay, well, thanks for that, Scout," I grab her by the shoulders and guide her toward the shelves she's supposed to be dusting.

"She was malnourished as a child," I say to Presley when Scout walks toward the shelves, the feather duster in her hair bouncing with each step.

"She was not," my mom says, sounding insulted.

"I'm sorry about my weird family," I say to Presley.

"I don't think they're weird at all," Presley says. "You have a great family."

"Thank you, Presley," says my mom, and you can probably see the beaming that's happening right now from space.

With a head bob toward the books, Presley and I walk away from my mom and over to some shelves that aren't near Scout either. I caught a quick glimpse of her and she's still not dusting but now currently doing some sort of ballroom dance with a ghost. And yes, the feather duster is still in her hair.

"What are you doing here?" I ask Presley. "I'm supposed to come get you in an hour."

"I need another book to read," she says.

I furrow my brow. "You read the other three already?"

"Yep," she says, putting her hands behind her back and looking up at me with a closed-mouth smile.

The math isn't mathing, considering we've been spending a lot of time together and I've never once seen her reading, and also, she told me while we were building the sandcastle that she hadn't read much since we'd begun the summer adventures. So she had just magically read all three since then?

"What did you think of *The Love Hypothesis*?" I ask, testing her.

"Loved it," she says, giving me very convincing eyes.

"What was it about?"

She purses her lips. "People who hypothesize about love."

My lip twitches of its own accord.

"And *The Rule Book* is about . . .?"

"Rules," she says, emphatically. "And . . . a book."

"You haven't read them, have you?" I ask, reversing our roles from the day we first met, just over a week ago.

"No," she says. "But I did finish the Sunny Palmer book."

"And what did you think?" I'm not sure why I'm asking because it's not like I've read it.

"Loved it; I want to play the main character, Cali, in the adaptation."

"Is that happening?"

"I have no idea," she says.

"Okay, so what actually brings you here? Not that I mind you coming here. You can come to the bookshop whenever you want." I'm rambling. Great. I'd come so far with her and I'm reverting back to nervous me. I reach up and mess with my glasses.

She nibbles on her bottom lip. "I need a favor."

"Of course," I tell her.

She places a hand on her hip and pops it out. "Briggs Fitzwilliam Dalton, you don't even know what I'm going to ask. I could be asking for your assistance in burying a body."

"Fitzwilliam?" I ask her.

"I'm just going to start throwing names out there until I figure it out."

"Well, you were wrong with that one."

"Damn," she says, her lips pushing out in an adorable pout. Yep, and I want to kiss her again. Get yourself together, man. It would be one thing if I'd never felt her lips on mine—I could delude myself into thinking she might be a terrible kisser, or that her lips are rough. But I know how they feel. Soft and giving.

Crap. I'm staring now. I'm staring at her lips.

"So, what's this favor?" I ask, forcing my eyes up toward hers.

She lets out a breath. "I need you to look online and see if they've said anything about the movie I'm supposed to be doing. If they've . . . replaced me."

"Oh, okay, sure," I say, taking my phone out of my pocket and pulling up the internet. "You know, they do have Wi-Fi at the Belacourt Resort."

She gives me a scowl. "I know that. I'm staying offline right now. Maybe forever."

The internet must be hard for people like Presley. It can be hard for anyone, really. Someone could post something they thought was benign and wake up the next morning canceled. Everyone has an opinion these days, and they have a way to share it with the world now.

"Okay, so what am I looking up exactly?" I say, fingers at the ready to type in the search bar.

"Just Presley James and *Cosmic Fury*," she says. "They were supposed to announce casting today." She nibbles on the side of her thumb, nervous energy oozing from her.

"No problem." I quickly type in the words, and a headline pops up almost immediately: Cosmic Fury *Now in Preproduction, but Will Presley James Still Play the Lead?*

"What does it say?" she asks, looking from me to the phone.

"Hold on," I say, quickly skimming the article.

"It's bad, isn't it?"

"It's not bad," I say, my eyes quickly catching on to key words. It's not ideal either. I feel a little whooshing sensation in my stomach.

"Tell me," she says.

"So, you still have the role."

She lets out a breath.

"But apparently, there's still a lot of backlash."

According to the article, because of the outcry to cancel her after the viral video, the producers have gone quiet about the role, but as far as the author of the piece can tell, she's still cast as the lead.

Presley closes her eyes, placing her hands on her face. I put my phone in my pocket and wait for her to talk because there's nothing I can say to her right now that might help the situation. First of all, I don't understand the ins and outs of how things in her industry work. Secondly, for all I know about Presley, there's so much I still don't know. She might be one of those people who needs to process things inwardly before she wants to talk about them.

Presley moves her hands away from her face and takes a big breath, as if she's trying to clear out whatever she's feeling right now.

"Okay, that's not horrible," she says, and I nod. "If the producers aren't saying anything right now and I still have the role, chances are they are also waiting to see if this dies down."

"That makes sense," I say. It's so awkward not to offer some sort of platitude right now. It's my instinct to try to fix things or offer solutions. It's what I do for a living . . . or what I did. Searching for bugs in a system and creating ways to fix them. It's hard for me to just stand here and let her process without offering her something.

But I do have one thing. I take a step closer to her, putting a hand on her shoulder, and when she leans in, I gather her into my arms and hold her. Her head falls onto my chest and her arms wrap around my waist. I rest my face on the top of her head and rub comforting circles on her back.

She feels warm, her body melding with mine, and she smells like vanilla and coconut.

"Thank you," she says, so quietly I almost miss it.

"You okay?" I ask after a minute of holding her. Honestly, if she wanted to stay like this for the rest of the day, I'd be okay with it. I don't have a lot to offer her, but I can give her this.

I feel her nodding under my head. And then she pulls back and looks at me, a sad sort of resigned smile on her face.

"Whatever you had planned today, can we . . . maybe do it another time?"

"Of course," I tell her. I can't help the disappointed feeling that lands on my shoulders. It feels selfish to feel this way. Stupid viral video. Of course, if it weren't for that, I wouldn't get to hold this woman like I am right now.

"I think I just need to lie on the beach or something."

"Read a book?"

She smiles then. "Yes. There are lots of hypotheses and rules to learn about."

"Exactly," I say, returning the grin. But then I let it drop. "I'll . . . be here whenever you want to do something."

She pulls her head back, tucking in her chin. "No, I was . . . I hoped . . ." She stops and takes a deep breath. "Would you come with me? Would you sit on the beach with me?"

I search her face. "Yeah, absolutely."

"Okay, perfect." She pulls out of the hug, grabbing on to the hem of my T-shirt like she's not ready to let go. "You're kind of my emotional support human."

I chuckle. "Glad to be of service."

CHAPTER 13

Presley

NAPPING ON THE beach might be my new favorite thing.

And yes, this is the first time I've done it. Ever. You learn to not fall asleep at the beach when there are cameras around, waiting to catch a picture of you with double chins, mouth sagged open, and drool coming out the side of your mouth.

Not that I look like that right now. I'm actually awake, or rather just woke up, and am currently lying under an umbrella on a padded lounger, Briggs on the one next to me. He's on his side, turned toward me, glasses off, no drool coming out of his mouth. He's just soundly sleeping, his light-brown eyelashes looking like feathery fringes resting against his skin.

I'm loving this little bubble I feel like I'm in with Briggs. My life feels so normal right now. Well, as normal as it can be, staying at a posh resort with people who are here to cater to my every whim, and with an entire world out there that sort of hates me right now.

But there are no paparazzi, no agent or publicist telling me what to do. My mom's not here, trying to micromanage. I'm just lying on a beach, hot and a little sticky, clad in a yellow bikini, next to a man that I really, really like.

I'm not sure I've ever in my life liked someone as much as I do Briggs. I'd say it's more than like. It's a crush. I have a crush on Briggs Ulysses Dalton.

That's not his actual middle name—I tried it on him earlier.

I've had crushes on guys before, and I've dated of course—my dating pool mostly consisting of men I've been on set with. Because how else would someone who hasn't even taken a real vacation in fourteen years meet someone? Online? No thank you. Not in my profession.

And relationships? Yeah, no. Unless you count whatever that was with Declan Stone, which I don't really. I think he was in proximity and I was lonely, and we were already faking it, so why not try for real? And now he's dating my mom. So, that's a fun thing I kind of hate.

Mostly I've just had showmances . . . which are short, on-set flings that fizzle out when filming is over. It might carry over to a press tour, but it's never serious, and my agent likes them because she uses them to her advantage in some way or another. Planned sightings leaked to the paparazzi. Quotes from "reliable sources" about our chemistry or whatever.

Why do I play this game? I've never liked it. When I get back after this break, if and when people forget about my mistake, I want to do things differently. I want to be more real, but also keep some things private.

I wouldn't mind keeping the man asleep in the lounge chair next to me. Could I? When the summer is over and I have to go back to my real life, will Briggs be part of it? Or is this just another showmance? Or maybe an islandmance? A summermance?

Not that there's any *mance* happening, although I feel like things could move in that direction. There's definitely been more touching. And that hug in the bookstore earlier today was everything. Exactly what I needed.

Yes. I've only known Briggs—whose middle name is a mystery—Dalton for a little over a week, and I'd like to keep him.

I shouldn't be thinking like this. It feels too soon to be crushing this hard. All I know is, I should be more worried about the news circulating around, the possibility that I might lose the role of Callis, and right now all I can think about is the man lying next to me, the slow rise and fall of his chest.

He stirs and slowly opens his eyes, blinking away the sleep, to find me staring at him like a weirdo.

"Hey," I say.

"Hey," he says back, his voice sounding groggy, reaching a hand up and rubbing his eyes. "How long have you been awake and staring at me?"

"I have not been staring," I say. "And I woke up only a few minutes before you." This is sort of a lie. I have been staring. I've also been thinking about foolish things, wondering about preposterous possibilities.

Presley James, you silly, silly woman.

"I didn't mean to fall asleep," Briggs says through a yawn.

"I didn't either, but it was exactly what I needed," I tell him.

He sighs. "Me too."

Briggs has a smattering of hair on his chest, and I like that it's a real chest. It's a great one. Not one chiseled out of stone, acquired from many hours a day working out, or covered in spray tan.

Yeah. I'm still staring.

I very purposefully look away, toward the ocean, where small waves are breaking against the sand.

"What plans did I ruin today?" I ask him.

"Hmm?" he asks, not following.

I look back at him. "I mean, instead of coming here, what summer activity did you have planned?"

"Oh," he says. "I was going to take you boating."

"You were?"

"Yes," he says. "Tubing, actually."

"Like where a boat drags you on a tube thingy?"

"That's not the technical terminology, but yes," he says, giving me a smirk.

"I've never done that," I tell him. Mostly because my film contracts specifically say no water sports. Including the one I recently signed for *Cosmic Fury*.

"I figured," Briggs says.

Maybe it's for the best we didn't do that. I've already violated my contract with the trampoline. I probably shouldn't do it again. Except . . . except what if I don't end up getting the part and I miss out on this? I could do it again, sure. And if I don't end up getting the part, I may be taking an even longer hiatus than planned and have a lot more opportunities to do things I haven't done. But when will I get the chance to go with Briggs? My summermance.

I sit up then, resolution on my face. "Do you think we can still go?"

He smiles. "I'm sure we can, if you want to."

"I do," I say, feeling suddenly exhilarated, and to be honest, kind of rebellious.

"Okay," he says. "Let me make a call."

Two hours later, I'm wrapped in a towel, sitting in the front of a speedboat on a padded bench, a can of Diet Coke in my hand, and Briggs is sitting across from me in the captain's chair. He killed the engine after my second round of tubing, and now we're just drifting, rocking slowly with the current, the only sound in the background the rhythmic gentle lapping of water against the side of the boat.

"This is nice," I say, leaning my head back, feeling the sun on my face, the soft ocean breeze moving across my body.

"It is," he agrees. "I haven't been out on the water like this in a long time."

"I feel bad that I'm the only one who got to go tubing," I say. I'd offered to drive while he took a turn but then remembered I've never actually driven a boat, except the one time I played a Bond girl and was involved in a very intense boat-chase scene. But all the driving I did was on a green screen, and we both agreed that doesn't really count.

"It's fine," he says. "I can do this anytime."

"Do you . . . do this anytime?"

"Actually, no," he says with a chuckle. The kind that makes my insides feel mushy.

"Briggs Albus Dalton, have you been working so hard you've forgotten to take time to have fun?"

"That's not my middle name," he says, pinching his brows together in a very adorable way. "Also, *Harry Potter* came out after I was born."

"Whatever," I say, doing a sulking thing with my shoulders. I looked up a bunch of literary names last night and committed them to memory. I will figure it out if it's the last thing I do.

He smiles. "And anyway, you're one to talk about working so hard."

"Yeah, but it's different because I didn't know any better. I hadn't done any of this before. You have, and you still don't make time for it."

"You're right," he says. "Thank goodness you're here to make me do fun things."

"What would you do without me?"

I watch as the smile disappears, his gaze moving toward the water. "I'd be working in a bookstore and probably spending the rest of my time in an apartment decorated for a ten-year-old."

I snicker. "It's not a bad life."

He shakes his head, looking back at me. "No, it could definitely be worse."

"Yes, you could have cameras and stalkers and people following you around all the time," I say. My gosh, it's going to suck to go back to that. I haven't even been away from it long enough for my new life to feel like a normal routine, and yet I'm already so used to not having to deal with all the unwanted attention.

"Yeah, that doesn't sound fun," Briggs says.

We sit in silence for a bit, my gaze dropping down to the blue-and-white-striped beach towel wrapped around me.

"Oh wow," I hear Briggs say, and I look up.

"What?" I ask.

"Shhhh," Briggs says, slowly making his way over to my side of the boat.

"Look," he says, kneeling on the bench next to me, pointing out in the water.

I turn and look in the direction he's pointing. I stare out for a moment, wondering if I missed whatever he was pointing at until I see three fins appear above the water.

"Sharks?" I say in a loud whisper, a little tremble of panic racing down my spine.

"No," he says, laughter in his voice. "Dolphins."

"Shut up." I let my towel fall and get on my knees, facing outside the boat, so I can have a better look.

We stay there in silence, and I wonder if that's all I'll see of them, just three grayish-blue-colored fins. But then they bob up again, this time two of them surfacing a little more above the water. I spot an eye, and misty air sprays out of one's blowhole before they submerge below the ocean's surface.

"Oh my gosh," I say quietly, even though I kind of want to squeal right now. I've seen dolphins in captivity, but I've never seen them in the wild.

They surface again, and one flips its tail up before going back under.

I look over at Briggs, watching him look out at the water, and I'm not sure why I do it, but I scoot across the foot or so between us, up against the side of him. And like we've been doing this the whole time, like it's natural, he puts his arm around my waist, his hand resting on my hip. I lean into him and turn back toward the water just in time to see two dolphins breach the surface before going under again.

"This is the coolest," I say, my face next to Briggs's, his hand on me feeling warm and comforting.

"I wasn't sure we'd be able to check this one off the list," he says.

I turn to him, my brows pinched. "You put dolphins on our summer activities?"

He turns his head toward me. "I didn't think it would actually happen. I've seen them plenty because I basically grew up here, but . . . it's still always . . . exciting."

His words have slowed, his eyes are searching my face, and there's an intensity in them, like a fire has been lit there. He's so close, I can feel his breath on my face, the way every part of my body touching his feels like it's on fire.

I feel his hand on my hip squeeze me, and ever so slightly, his fingers press into the bare skin just above my bikini bottoms. Something warm grows in my belly, my senses immediately heightened. He smells like sunscreen and salt water. In the distance a seagull squawks.

He leans his face toward mine, erasing some of the small space that's between us. I lean in as well, hovering there, just millimeters away, wanting—no, needing—him to erase all of it.

And then he does.

His lips land on mine, softly and tenderly. My eyes flutter shut and he increases the pressure, the hand not at my hip coming up to my chin as he cups my face, and our bodies instinctively turn toward each other like magnets, drawn together by some irresistible force.

We're knee to knee now, our torsos smashed together, our arms around each other. His kisses go from soft and gentle to heated and needy, and I meet him with equal intensity. His hands are everywhere, at my back, on my neck, tangled in my hair.

One finds the base of my head, just like that first time we kissed outside his apartment, and he angles me back just slightly, giving him more access to my mouth. His tongue sweeps in and touches mine.

Our first kiss was a good one. But like in *Notting Hill*, it was sort of stilted and unexpected. This kiss right now is planned, thought out, desired.

The way Briggs holds me, how he tenderly explores my mouth with his, tells me he's been thinking about doing this just as much as I have.

Kissing scenes in movies are never what they seem when you watch them on a screen. There are repeated takes and a whole room of people watching, making sure the lighting is perfect and that makeup hasn't been removed or smeared. No kissing scene I've ever done has had any feeling behind it except that of a job, a role I was hired to play.

But this kiss with Briggs, out on the ocean with no one watching, no show to put on for cameras, and very much wanted, might just be the best kiss I've ever had.

We spend the next hour on the boat, intermittently talking and laughing and kissing and holding on to each other.

When Briggs fires up the boat to head back to Sunset Harbor, I briefly wonder if maybe we should go in the other direction, just leave and see where life takes us. It's not really an option, even though I wish it were.

It's dark by the time we get to the resort after docking the boat on the other side of the island and taking a leisurely walk back, hand in hand.

He stops us just before the entrance to the resort, our hands swinging between us, a beach bag full of our wet towels and other summer things slung over his shoulder. He looks at me and smiles and I give him one back.

A debate begins in my head. I could invite him up to my room. We just spent the late afternoon making out on a boat, and I would very much like to continue in my suite. To order room service and wear big fluffy white robes and just be together. I don't want this day to be over.

"Do you . . . want to come up?" I ask, my voice sounding a lot like Julia Roberts's character when she asks Hugh Grant's character up to her room.

I know immediately as I say it, as soon as the words exit my mouth, that we shouldn't. It's too much. This is too new, whatever this is. But I want to. Who puts a time constraint on these things anyway? If I were going by what's in the movies, we'd have already hopped into bed together, probably after that very first kiss. But this isn't the movies and I've never been the type to do something like that. I like moving slowly; I always have.

Briggs lets out a breath. "I can't believe I'm saying this, but it's probably not a good idea."

"Yeah." I shake my head. "Totally. You're totally right."

Some hurt feelings settle into my gut, and it's kind of unfounded because I'd just thought the same thing myself.

Briggs pulls me toward him. "You're leaving at the end of the summer, and I don't know what I'm doing with my life, and if I go up there"—he looks up at the resort before looking down at me—"that makes things more complicated."

"I only wanted to kiss you," I say, giving him a little pout.

"And I'd like that, very much." He reaches up and fusses with his hair. I've noticed he does that when he doesn't have his glasses on to fidget with when he gets nervous.

"Yeah," I say. "But it's probably not the best idea."

Briggs stares at me now, and I can see his mind racing with thoughts. "I . . . maybe . . ." He stops and runs his fingers through his hair again. "Maybe not."

"Briggs Barnaby Dalton," I say, leaning toward him, grabbing ahold of the white T-shirt he's wearing. "Why do you have to be so sensible?"

"It's a curse," he says. "Also, Barnaby is not it."

"Crap," I say.

He chuckles as he pulls me into a hug, wrapping his arms around me. I lean fully into him, my face against his chest.

I pull back and look up at him. "Maybe just one more kiss, like one last one."

His answer is to lean in and kiss me softly, our lips locking together.

"Hmm," I say, pretending to ponder after we pull away. "I think I might need one more."

This time I go up on my tiptoes and touch my lips to his a little longer than before.

I pull out of his embrace and take a step back. "Today gets a nine point five."

"Ouch," he says, mimicking being stabbed in the heart. "That hurts."

I smile. "It was a perfect ten until you went and got all sensible on me."

He runs a hand through his hair. "Can I take it back?"

"No," I say, shaking my head. "It's too late."

He hangs his head in mock shame.

"Okay." I turn toward the entrance to the resort, begrudgingly. "I'm going to actually leave now."

"Okay," he says. "Good night, Presley."

"Good night, Briggs Augustus Dalton." I give him hopeful eyes.

He shakes his head. "Nope."

I make a growling sound. "I'm going to figure it out."

"I believe you."

I turn and walk toward the resort on a lighted pathway beneath my flip-flop-clad feet, looking back over my shoulder at Briggs every few steps.

Just as I'm nearing the entrance, I hear footsteps behind me, getting closer.

"Presley, wait," Briggs says, and I turn to see him drop his bag, and then, wrapping his arms around me, he lifts me off the ground and kisses me again. I hold on to his shoulders and let him, our lips moving over each other's like they were always meant to.

He sets me back down and inhales deeply.

"Okay. That's it, then."

"Okay," I say, a little breathless. I almost want to ask him if he's absolutely positive about this, but then he says goodbye and walks away for real this time.

WELCOME TO
SUNSET HARBOR

BELACOURT RESORT
GOLF COURSE
NOAH'S HOUSE
JANE'S HOUSE
NATURE PRESERVE
DAX'S DUPLEX
SEASIDE OASIS RETIREMENT HOME
SUNSET REPAIRS
PHOENIX'S OFFICE
CITY OFFICES
SUNRISE CAFE
SCOOPS AHOY ICE CREAM
KEENE B&B
TOWN SQUARE
BAKERY
GULF OF MEXICO
BRIGGS'S APARTMENT
THE BOOK ISLE
CUTS AND CURLS
TRISTAN & BEAU'S HOUSE
CAPRI'S HOUSE
GEMMA'S HOUSE
HOLLAND'S HOUSE
BEACH BREAK BAR & GRILL
PUBLIC BEACH
N
W
E
S

CHAPTER 14

Briggs

IT'S BEEN A week since I kissed Presley on Dax's boat, and even though it's been packed full of working and doing summer things with her, it's been possibly the most difficult week of my life.

Not really, but having to restrain myself, knowing how good it felt to kiss her and have her in my arms, it's been hard not to want to do that again.

I've tried not to touch her as much, just because it feels like it would be too hard not to take things further if I did. We've gone back to the friend zone, and I've confirmed my suspicions: The friend zone sucks.

"Give it your all!" Scout yells at our mom, who's currently on the other side of a volleyball net from us, getting ready to serve. We're playing two on two at the beach resort. I was more than eager to set up a volleyball net when Presley asked. Presley, in a white tank and running shorts, and my mom, wearing some sort of sweatband like she's from the eighties, are on one team, with Scout and I on the other. And it's possible we should have done this differently because for my mom and Presley, it's like the blind leading the blind.

My mom, with a very focused look on her face, holds the ball up with one hand, and with an underhanded punch from the other, sends the ball sailing, but it hits the net and falls back on their side of the court.

"Oh, come on," Scout yells, stomping her bare foot in the sand.

"Scout," I say, my voice chastising. The kid is competitive. I blame myself for that. I was always telling her winning was the best when she was younger.

"This is the lamest game in history," she whines.

"Go switch sides with Mom," I tell her.

"Yes!" she says, drawing out the word excitedly. "I'm playing with you now, Presley." She jogs over to the other side of the net, her feet kicking up sand as she goes.

My mom comes over to my side of the court, her face red from the late-afternoon heat. We closed the bookshop early when I invited my mom and Scout to come play with us. No one seems to mind around here about the hours we keep, especially during the summer. Off-season hours are always changing for the businesses that stay open during this time of the year.

I serve the ball and it goes over the net, and Scout is right there to send it back to me. It becomes evident pretty quickly that this is turning into a one-on-one game between Scout and me. But my mom gets a few hits in, and so does Presley.

After I've won a game and then let Scout win one (at least that's what I told myself—the kid is really good at volleyball), Presley orders drinks from the resort, and they bring them to us as we sit at a small table in one of the cabanas.

"I've never seen this part of the resort," Scout says as she takes a sip of some kind of frozen drink, a small umbrella hanging out the top.

"I don't think I have either," my mom says.

"Like, this is the most time I've ever spent on this beach," Scout says.

"Me too," mom replies.

I'd spent very little time at this resort growing up because it was mainly for the wealthier people on the island and the tourists. Not for us regular islanders.

But it feels like a regular thing to do now, having spent so much time here these past few weeks with Presley. And now Scout has gotten to spend some time here as well, since I've been bringing her along from time to time, mostly to save me from myself. I'd much rather be alone with Presley, but it's for the best.

We went snorkeling, where Presley panicked about sharks, but we barely even saw any fish. We walked around the small nature preserve, where she spotted a baby alligator and screamed like a little girl. Scout loves to bring this up. We've watched a movie under the stars, using a screen and a projector from the resort, Scout sitting between us. She got to pick the movie and chose *Notting Hill*, but only after some coercion from Presley. We've even flown a kite, which is something I hadn't ever done. And it ended up being a great time. All times with Presley are great times, though, even when Scout is there to babysit us.

Presley is amazing with Scout--answering all her prodding questions and asking her about boys she likes and the things she does with her friends. I sometimes wonder if she's trying to find out what she missed out on, since Scout is the same age Presley was when she started acting.

I turn to Scout, a half-smug, half-teasing expression on my face. "But you have been to this beach before," I say to her.

The apples of her cheeks turn the lightest shade of pink.

Presley looks to me and then to Scout. "What's going on?" she asks suspiciously.

"Remember the teens that—"

"Don't!" Scout yells.

It's too late and Presley is too smart because she easily puts it together. "So, it was you and your friends sneaking onto the beach that day," she says, giving fake-looking accusatory eyes to Scout.

Scout does have the decency to look ashamed. "We were trying to see you and maybe Declan Stone."

"Scout," my mom says, her name sounding like a reprimand, but I don't remember her caring all that much when I told her about it the first time. I believe she said something like *kids will be kids.*

Presley leans toward Scout, a piña colada in her hand. "You know, if you tell me Briggs's middle name, I'll forget about the beach thing and get you an autograph from Declan."

"No way. Are you serious?" Scout asks, her eyes wide as she looks to me. "I'm gonna have to tell her."

"That's cheating," I say to Presley. I'd made my mom and Scout promise they wouldn't tell her, but now it seems Presley is bringing out the big guns. The woman is relentless. She's already offered Scout a hundred dollars to tell her, but luckily money doesn't work on Scout. But an autograph from Declan Stone?

I look over to Presley and catch her pointing V fingers at her eyes and nodding before turning them on Scout, like a secret pact between the two.

"Scout," I say.

"Ugh, fine," she says.

"Briggs Ishmael Dalton, how dare you," Presley says to me, and my mom snorts out a laugh.

"It's definitely not Ishmael," Mom informs her. My mom isn't so easy to bribe, and she loves my middle name. I think she's enjoying this game I've been playing with Presley. I don't think she could be bought, unless Presley were to offer an in-person meeting with Henry Cavill. That would break her, for sure. But so far that hasn't been on the table. Still, I wouldn't put it past Presley.

My sister, on the other hand, is a lot easier to sway.

Presley shoots me a dirty look before turning her attention to Scout. "I'll get you one anyway," she says.

"Really?" Scout jumps up and down in her seat. "You're the best."

"Okay, if you won't tell me his middle name, then how about an embarrassing story?"

My mom rubs her hands together like she's been waiting her entire life for this moment. "Where do I begin?"

"Mom," I say, a mostly fake irritation in my voice. "There aren't that many."

She shakes her head and looks to Presley, and a trickle of unease moves down my back.

"He had a massive crush on Candace from *Phineas and Ferb*."

I chuckle, nodding my head. That wasn't so terrible. "I did," I say.

"He learned how to rewind on the remote and would watch her scenes over and over."

Presley smiles. "That's kind of adorable. Ashley Tisdale, who voiced her, is—"

"Nope," I say, cutting her off and holding out a hand. "Do not ruin her."

"I wasn't," she protests.

"Oh yeah, he had a huge crush on Ashley Tisdale too," my mom says.

"Apparently he still does," Scout says, giggling and pointing at me.

"He made me send an email to her fan club," my mom tells Presley.

"I was ten," I say, but I can feel my cheeks getting warm. Maybe I should just tell her my middle name so we can stop this.

"I need something juicier," Presley says to my mom.

"He slept with a blue stuffed dog until he was thirteen," my mom says.

"This is not fun," I say, swiping a hand down my face.

I was actually fourteen, but I'm not about to admit that, or admit that Blue Doggy—not a very creative name—is packed in a box in the closet of my old bedroom at my mom's house.

"Oh," Scout says, excitedly. "And didn't he need a night-light like forever?"

My mom nods, smiling. "He did need a night-light." She turns to look at me. "Have you ever gotten over that one, Briggsy?"

I cover my face with my hand. “Of course I have,” I say.

But to be honest, sometimes I still consider leaving the bathroom light on and cracking the door. Only because I want to be able to see the face of my assailant should I ever be in that situation.

“Oooh,” my mom says, dragging out the word, her head cocked to the side, her eyes looking mischievous. “And you used to sometimes play dolls with Scout when she was a toddler.”

“I wasn’t playing dolls,” I tell Presley. “I was sixteen, for crap’s sake.”

“But you used to pretend like they were talking to her and do all those little voices.”

“Should I leave?” I ask the table. “I’d like to leave, or for the two of you to leave.” I point to my mom and sister, who seem to enjoy this too much.

“That is the sweetest,” Presley says, her hands pressed to her chest.

“I’d say probably the most embarrassing Briggs story,” my mom keeps going, “was the time he sleepwalked to the neighbor’s house, went in through their back door and ended up on their couch. They were so confused in the morning, and so was Briggs. He thought he’d been kidnapped.”

“What? It was very jarring,” I say, trying to defend myself over the laughter.

"Poor Briggsy," Presley says, reaching over and tapping my hand with hers. I'd hold it there if my family wasn't watching. I miss being able to do that, just hold her hand.

"But you haven't heard the best part," Scout says.

"Hey," I say to Scout. "You weren't even alive when this happened."

My mom shakes her head. "No, I was pregnant with Scout, actually. But the best part is that Briggs was in his tighty-whities."

Presley snorts out a laugh.

"So, imagine our neighbors—the Parkers, who still live next door—waking up to find a sleeping Briggs in his tighty-whities on their formal sitting-room couch."

"Can we be done now?" I ask.

"No way, Briggs Wilbur Dalton," Presley says.

My mom and sister both snicker at that.

"I wish I had named him that," my mom says. "I do love *Charlotte's Web*."

The subject changes from roasting me to favorite childhood books, thankfully, and after another round of drinks, my mom and Scout head home. I stay behind for a bit, chatting with Presley, purposefully sitting across the table from her and not next to her with my hand draped across the back of her seat and fingers playing with the ends of her hair like I'd rather be.

I sort of wish I'd never kissed her, only for the sheer fact that we could be sitting close together right now, holding hands, or back at my place snuggling on my couch. But now that we've crossed that line, we can't go back.

I don't regret it, though. It was everything I thought kissing Presley James would be. And I'd like to do it again. But it's for the best we don't. Even though I catch myself staring at her lips sometimes. Like . . . right now, for instance.

"What are you looking at?" Presley asks, a knowing grin on her face.

Well . . . crap.

"Nothing," I tell her. "Nothing whatsoever."

She leans back in her chair, the half-drunk piña colada on the table in front of her, the condensation on the glass beading and trickling down, leaving winding trails on the surface.

"I think we learned something today," she says.

"And that is?"

"I'm terrible at volleyball."

I chuckle and she smiles. "You're not so bad."

"And you're a terrible liar. Still, I'll give it a six out of ten."

"Really?" My brows move up my forehead. "I'd have expected less."

"I'm feeling generous today," she says. "I'll rate it higher if you tell me your middle name."

I give her a closed-mouth smile, shaking my head. She will never let this go, nor will she probably ever guess it. "I'm honestly surprised you haven't hired private investigators."

She sighs. "I've considered it. But then I'd have to go online, and I'm staying out of that realm."

"Speaking of which, I looked up your name and the movie this morning, and no news."

She nods, an appreciative expression on her face. "That's good."

I weave my fingers together and place them in my lap. "Will it be bad if you lose the role?"

"It won't be good," she says. "It will set a precedent. I'll stand to lose other contracts."

"How many do you have?"

"Right now, I have three. I had four, but I lost one. Because of . . . the *incident*," she says, leaning in and nearly whispering the last word.

"And they all film when?"

She shrugs. "I only have *Cosmic Fury* this year. Another shoot starts in January, and the other possibly next summer."

Next summer. Presley has her whole life mapped out—she already knows what she'll be doing a year from now. And I don't even know what I'll be doing at the end of this summer. I should probably start looking for a job or figuring out my next step. But I sort of feel paralyzed by it. Like I'll make another wrong move or bad choice. Still, my bank account is pretty much demanding it right now.

She sits up, looking like she's about to leave. "Walk with me on the beach?"

"Sure," I say, getting up from my seat.

We walk through the still-hot sand, though the sun is no longer glaring down on it, and onto the wet sand where the waves have been breaking, then farther until our feet touch the water. I tuck my hands into the pockets of the basketball shorts I'm wearing as we start walking along the shore.

"So have there been any more stalkers looking in your room?" I ask as our feet splash in the shallow water, a teasing smile on my face.

A couple of days ago while I was working at the bookshop, Presley called me, frantic because someone was outside her window and she was sure it was paparazzi or a crazed fan. I told her to call the police . . . Well, she called Beau, the one policeman we have on the island. He came over and checked and it happened to be one of the resort's gardeners.

"Shut up," she says, pushing me lightly on the arm. "I thought for sure I'd been found."

"I'm still kind of amazed word hasn't gotten out." I think it's made me realize that word travels fast on this island, but then it just sort of stays here.

"I know," she says. "It's been amazing. This has been the most perfect summer." She does a little spinning thing, hands out toward the sky, water splashing around her ankles.

I want to grab her right now and kiss her perfect pink lips, but I don't.

I tease her instead. "You know that it's only June, right? Today is literally the first day of summer, officially."

"Oh, that's right. Happy first official day of summer to you," she says.

"And to you," I say, with a dip of my head.

She looks out toward the ocean. "Official or not, it's been summer to me. Is it sad that I've been so deprived of the season that only three weeks in and I can already declare this one better than any other summer?"

"No," I say. "I've had regular summers, and I can definitely say this already ranks in the top twenty-eight of them."

She snorts out a laugh. "Well played."

"I give it a six point one out of ten," I say.

"Wow, you're even tougher than I am."

I think about all my past summers; most of them are blurry, or not very memorable. This summer could have possibly been listed under one of the worst ever, having had to return to the island with no plan for what to do with my life, and yet, it's been kind of the best. If I had to base it on the part since meeting Presley, it's a ten for sure. Or maybe a nine point five since I can no longer kiss her. Why am I so sensible, anyway? What a stupid way to be.

"We've packed a lot in already. I've never had a summer like this," I tell her. "In fact, if we keep up this pace, we'll run out of things to do."

"We'll just start the list over again," she says.

"I like that plan," I say, feeling something warm settling along my shoulders that's not from the humid air. It's just, simply, Presley.

I don't want to think about the summer ending and us going our separate ways. I want to think about endless summers and infinite possibilities.

But I know that's not how life works. So, I'll just take what I can get and try not to fall harder than I already have for the woman smiling next to me as we walk along the beach.

CHAPTER 15

Presley

"HOW DARE YOU disrespect me, Falgon. I'm the leader of this team, and you will do as I say," I recite the line to Briggs, who's leaning against the counter, a screenplay in front of him, as I pace around the front part of the bookshop.

It's the next Monday and Briggs had to work all day, so I came over an hour before closing to keep him company. It was a slow day, so he closed the store after I got here and now he's running lines with me, something he offered to do yesterday when we took a bike ride up to the lighthouse on the opposite side of the island. The bike ride was fun and the lighthouse was . . . just a lighthouse. But I was with Briggs, so we could have been looking at a random palm tree or counting blades of grass and I'd have been happy. Okay, maybe not counting blades of grass. Or maybe even that? Briggs can find a way to make me laugh no matter what we're doing.

"But what do you even know of the Syndarians, Callis? They will trample all over us with this plan." Briggs says his line with a strange alien voice that sounds a little like he's sucked on some helium.

"Stop," I say through a laugh. "Falgon is this like massively huge battle warrior."

"Who's playing him?"

"Landon West," I say, picturing the popular Australian actor, with his dark-blond hair and light-blue eyes. He's mainly done superhero movies up until this point. Not that an intergalactic warrior is all that different.

"Oh, right," he says, pushing his glasses up his nose. "Of course. He'll make a great battle warrior."

"And Callis's love interest."

"So, like an enemies-to-lovers sort of thing?"

I cock my head to the side. "Well done, knowing your tropes."

"You can thank Marianne McMannus for that."

"I suppose growing up with a mom who owns a bookstore, it would be a shame if you didn't know at least some literary themes."

"It would," he agrees.

"Impressive, Briggs Cyrano Dalton,"

He snorts out a laugh. "Nope."

"Drat," I say, stomping a foot for added emphasis.

"Okay, let me try the line again," he says, clearing his throat and saying it once more with a deeper baritone this time around.

"Better?" he asks after he's read it.

"Much better," I say.

I'm not even sure why I'm running lines with Briggs right now. I usually do it when I get a script so I can familiarize myself with the character and figure out how much time I'll need to memorize it. But I haven't done it yet, because when I first got this script I was busy shooting another film, and then I went and had a breakdown for all the world to see. So, trying to work on this script right now may be completely pointless.

Briggs looked online for any news when I first arrived at the bookshop, just in case. There was nothing new. No articles saying I'd been dropped. For all the general public knows, I'm still playing Callis Astron. No matter how many petitions have been sent in hopes of that changing.

Not that I know about any petitions in particular, but I can safely assume there are some. There would be, even if I didn't have a viral video of me losing it out there. People always have opinions, especially about such a well-loved story. No one could possibly measure up to how they pictured it in their head.

"Okay," Briggs says. "Next line."

"Give me a hint," I say, giving him my best sheepish grin. I guess it's good I'm prepping now, just in case.

"Listen here, Falgon—"

"Got it," I say, cutting him off before he gives too much away. I take in a big inhale. "Listen here, Falgon. We don't need to know anything about the Syndarians. All we need to do is go in there and obliterate them. And if you don't think I can lead this team, then you can get back on your lunastrider and go back to Arcturus."

"Nailed it," Briggs says, with a sort of proud-looking dip of his chin. Then he scrunches his nose, before pushing his glasses up. "What's a lunastrider?"

"It's like a horse, but bigger and scarier," I say.

"That sounds cool. Do you get to ride one?"

"Of course. But for me it will be riding a mechanical rig against a green screen, and my lunastrider will be done with CGI in postproduction."

"You ruin all the magic."

"You're welcome."

We're smiling at each other now. We've been doing that a lot lately. Especially since we've been on our own the past few days because Scout hasn't been able to babysit us since our afternoon of beach volleyball. So, we had to do the bike ride to the lighthouse and the boogie boarding the day before on our own.

I knew that's why Briggs invited Scout along, even though he didn't tell me so. But after we kissed that last time, suddenly Scout was joining us on our summer activities. I don't mind—

she's a great kid. But I've also enjoyed these past couple of days without her.

Briggs snaps out of our unintentional staring contest first. He looks down at the script.

"Okay," he says. "Where were we?" He scans down the document with a finger until he finds it, tapping on the dialogue where we left off.

He clears his throat. "I don't like your ways, Callis."

I think for a second before the line comes to me. "You don't have to like them; you just have to let me lead."

"Good. Okay, so it says that next Callis takes a step forward and puts her hand on Falgon's chest," Briggs says, reading the direction.

"Right. And then the next line is . . . hold on, don't tell me," I say, holding out a hand and closing my eyes, trying to remember. I open them when the words come to me, and I start pacing again as I recite them.

"I need you to trust me, Falgon. You're second in command, but the team looks to you before me. If you show them you trust me, then they will also trust me."

"I want to trust you," Briggs says, reading Falgon's line, attempting to use the deep baritone voice as he reads.

"I . . ." I stop talking, trying to think of what's next. I only studied it a bit when I first arrived here, so I should cut myself some slack. Still, this is something I'm usually good at.

"What's next?" I ask him.

He looks down at the script. "Then . . . Falgon leans in and kisses Callis."

"Right," I say, with a nod. "And then the next line is . . ." I stop to try to remember what happens after the kiss.

"Do you . . . need to practice that part?" Briggs asks.

"What part?" I say, pinching my brows together.

"The . . . kiss?" He lifts a shoulder, briefly. "I mean, if you need to practice that, we could . . . I could . . ." He stops talking.

"Yes," I say, quickly. "I could definitely use some help with that."

Presley James, you naughty woman.

I'm lying. This is a lie. I've never needed to practice a kiss while running lines in my entire career. But if Briggs is putting a kiss on the table under the guise of practicing for this movie with me, then I'm not passing it up.

He takes a step toward me, and I do the same, until we're standing in front of each other.

"So . . . I guess you should say your line again," he says.

I nod. "Okay. Um . . . If you show them you trust me, then they will also trust me." My voice comes out soft this time, nothing like the warrior I'm supposed to be playing in this movie.

"I want to trust you," Briggs says Falgon's line, his voice also not the one he was doing before. It's just him now.

We stare at each other for just an instant, and then his arms are around me, his hands at my back, and I barely can take in a breath before his lips are on mine and my hands instinctively move up to his face, my fingers curving around his jaw.

It's not soft, it's not timid. It's straight-up passion in lip form as he holds me against him, his mouth moving in time with mine. This kiss is feverish and desperate. His hand moves up my back and into my hair and I feel like I'm on fire, heat moving from my head to my toes.

This is the best practice kiss ever, even though the one we shoot will be nothing like this. Not the way Briggs is running his tongue over my bottom lip, because that's considered bad etiquette when filming. No tongues allowed. But right now, it's good etiquette. The very best kind of etiquette.

His hand has moved from my hair to my neck and he's left my mouth to kiss a path down my jaw, to a spot just below my ear, and I feel like I might melt. My legs feel like JELL-O. I'm barely standing.

A knock on the glass door of the bookstore has us pulling apart from each other like we've just been caught doing something criminal. It takes a second for me on my newborn-calf-like legs to right myself.

We both look over to see who just ruined the second-best kiss of my life (the first being on the boat), and I instantly recognize the bratty Betty lady, her hands on the glass, cupping her face as she looks inside. That massive sun visor is still on her head, even though the sun is setting now.

She yells something through the glass that neither of us can decipher, and Briggs walks over to the door, unlocking it before opening it up.

"You're not supposed to be closed yet," she says, pointing to the open hours sign on the door.

"We had to close early," Briggs tells her.

"Why, so you could lock lips with that gal?" She points to me, and I'm torn between trying not to laugh and also glaring at the woman because she ruined my moment with Briggs. Forget bratty—she's freaking moment-ruining Betty.

"You can come back tomorrow," Briggs offers.

"You can't sell me a book tonight?" She scowls at him.

Briggs looks to me, and I give him a why-not shrug. I kind of hate the woman for interrupting our practice kissing, but she's stubborn, and the sooner he helps her out, the sooner she'll leave.

He opens the door and ushers her in with a wave of his hand. She walks in, her nose lifted upward, like she hates the smell of the place.

"I need some book by Sunny Palmer," she says. "What kind of name is that? I hope it's a pen name, because if it's real, she should change it."

"Let me show you where it is," Briggs says, walking her over to the fiction section where I bantered with him that first day I'd escaped from the resort. What a whirlwind it's been. It feels like so long ago. But it really wasn't. Three weeks, that's all.

And it's only taken me three weeks to realize that I want to keep him. I've had the thought before, but more along the lines that I don't want to lose him when the summer is over. But now I want him for keeps. I know how that sounds, like how I take souvenirs from the set of a movie I worked on.

But he wouldn't be a souvenir—he'd be mine. All mine.

This isn't just a crush, or a summermance; it's full-blown, I'd-like-to-see-where-this-goes, possible feelings of love happening right now.

It could be full-blown love for all I know, since I don't think I've ever been in love before. I thought I was with Zac Efron, but then I got stuck in his trailer window and realized it was totally one sided.

What I'm feeling is very different. It's brain consuming and body snatching. Is that love? I think it might be. And I could be wrong, but I think Briggs feels the same.

I should tell him how I feel. I should just lay it all out there. I know we come from different worlds, and I know Briggs has no desire to be part of what I have to offer, but we could figure it out . . . Couldn't we?

They locate the book, and then mean Betty talks Briggs's ear off as they walk toward the register, saying something about an air freshener, but I'm only half listening because my attention is on Briggs, the half-smile on his face as he helps the crotchety woman, and how handsome he is when he fidgets with his glasses.

Rude Betty pays for her book, and then he walks her to the door.

She turns back to look at me. "Stop slouching," she says, pointing a bony finger at me.

"Yes, ma'am." I say, doing just as she commands. Honestly, I never thought I had bad posture until I met this surly woman.

She makes some sort of harrumph sound as she leaves, and Briggs shuts the door and locks it behind her.

"Well, she's gone," he says when he turns back toward me.

"Yes," I say, weaving my hands behind my back and rocking on my heels. And thank goodness for that because I would very much like to get back to the kissing practice.

Briggs clears his throat. "So, should we run more lines?"

"Yes," I say, a little too quickly. "I was kind of hoping to go over that last scene, just one more time."

He gives me a knowing smile and walks toward me, my body beginning to hum just in anticipation of his nearness.

"Hello! I'm here," Scout yells from the back entrance of the shop, and like we planned it, both Briggs's and my shoulders drop at the same time.

Foiled again.

“We’re up front,” Briggs calls out. He gives me a disappointed-looking smile, probably mirroring the one on my face.

“Oh good,” Scout says as she comes in through the back of the store, her ponytail swishing behind her. “Mom wants to know if you two want to come play games with us tonight.”

Briggs sighs, and it’s long-suffering, like this is the hardest task he’s ever been asked to do.

“Sounds good,” I answer for the both of us.

Thank goodness we have so much more summer to go. There’s plenty of time for me to explore these feelings for Briggs and see if he feels them back. Plenty of time to take this summermance to a full-blown romance. I just hope Briggs feels the same way.

WELCOME TO

SUNSET HARBOR

BELACOURT RESORT

GOLF COURSE

NOAH'S HOUSE

JANE'S HOUSE

NATURE PRESERVE

DAX'S DUPLEX

SEASIDE OASIS RETIREMENT HOME

SUNSET REPAIRS

PHOENIX'S OFFICE

CITY OFFICES

SUNRISE CAFE

SCOOPS AHOY ICE CREAM

KEENE B&B

GULF OF MEXICO

TOWN SQUARE

BAKERY

BRIGGS'S APARTMENT

THE BOOK ISLE

CUTS AND CURLS

N

W

E

S

TRISTAN & BEAU'S HOUSE

CAPRI'S HOUSE

GEMMA'S HOUSE

HOLLAND'S HOUSE

BEACH BREAK BAR & GRILL

PUBLIC BEACH

CHAPTER 16

Briggs

"This is incredible," Presley says, holding binoculars up to her eyes as she looks up at the starry night sky.

We're lying on sleeping bags, which are on top of a beach blanket, all of which I borrowed from my mom. The waves crashing against the shore have been the background soundtrack to what's been a pretty perfect night.

Sleeping under the stars. That's what we're doing tonight. It was one of the things Presley told me she'd never gotten to do when we were first getting to know one another all those days ago. I wasn't sure when we'd get to, since timing and the weather had to cooperate. But everything fell into place for tonight. We're not on the private beach, but one further down the island.

It's been three days since the practice kiss that really wasn't a practice kiss. And what a kiss that was. I really hope Landon West doesn't kiss Presley like that. Maybe I won't watch *Cosmic Fury* when it comes out. I don't think I'd be able to take it.

There's been no other kissing between Presley and me since. Not practice ones or real ones pretending to be practice. I think we've gone back to our unspoken rule of not kissing because of . . . Actually, I don't even know why. Wait, yes I do. She's a famous actress, and I'm a nobody. She works in Hollywood, and I . . . need to find a job and figure out what I'm doing with my life and have a bank account that isn't on the verge of zeroing out.

But somehow all of that seems less insurmountable lately. Like, who really cares about the details? I need to care about them, though, because I have a heart, and it's on a precarious perch right now. One that, with just a small little nudge, could fall hopelessly and desperately for the woman lying next to me. And, if I'm being totally honest with myself, it may already have.

It feels like a bad move for my heart. Like if I were to write it out on paper, there's just no way that I can carry the one and divide it by two to get to the result I'm hoping for. Which is . . . what? I don't even know. Summer doesn't last forever. Well, it kind of does on this island, but that's not what I mean. This summer right now that I'm having with Presley has an ending. And I'd prefer it didn't.

"I feel like I'm hogging the binoculars," Presley says, pulling them away from her face and turning toward me. She's lying on top of a red sleeping bag in a white T-shirt and black leggings.

"You are," I say.

"Briggs Samwise Dalton," she says, her voice mock appalled. "Why didn't you say something?" She tries to hand them to me.

I push them back toward her. "I'm kidding. I can see this anytime." Not that I ever do this kind of thing. It's been over a decade since I slept on the beach.

"Oh my gosh," she says, excitement in her voice, lifting her head up slightly. "Is it Samwise? Did I get it?"

I shake my head in tiny, probably imperceptible, movements since it's pretty dark out here. But she must see it because her head drops back down on the pillow, defeated.

"Do you think I'd hate that one? I'd rock that middle name," I say.

"It does sound pretty cool," she says, turning her face toward the sky and bringing the binoculars up to her eyes again.

"It definitely beats Homer," I say, referring to the name she tried earlier tonight.

"Briggs Homer Dalton has a ring to it, though."

"Not really," I say, thinking my real middle name doesn't sound half as bad as some of the ones Presley's been guessing, but then I think of it and . . . no. I still hate it.

Presley looks up at the sky again through the binoculars that were once Keith's. He loved anything to do with the cosmos and knew so much about constellations and planets. He'd take me out at night to look sometimes. It's one of the fondest memories I have with him. I wish I had told him that before he passed.

"It's kind of funny," Presley says, still looking at the sky, "to think how insignificant things really are when there's this whole universe out there."

"That was deep," I say, my voice teasing.

"I mean it," she says through a chuckle. "Why do people care so much about me?"

I think about that for a few seconds. "Probably because in your profession, you're under a microscope. Like Sirius right there." I point to the brightest star in the sky. "You stand out more than others and so you get the most attention. You're the most studied."

"Now who's being deep?" she asks. She lets out a long exhale. "I think when this all passes, when I have to go back to my acting life, I'm doing things differently."

"How do you plan to do that?" I ask her.

In my peripheral vision, I see her head turn toward me, so I reciprocate.

"I don't want to play any more of the stupid games they make me play," she says, tucking some hair behind her ear. "I think I'm going to take fewer contracts, not put myself out there so much. And no more pretending to be with someone for exposure. Or going places just to be seen and photographed. I just want to be real."

"You seem pretty real to me," I say, reaching over and poking her in the arm, as if she might be an apparition.

She chortles. "I think you've gotten to see the most authentic me I've been in a long time. A part that's felt buried until recently."

"Well then, I like the real Presley Shermerhorn."

"That's Presley Renee Shermerhorn to you. I freely share my middle name, not like some people I know."

"Actually, Google shares your name freely with people."

We're smiling, our heads turned toward each other. Then Presley's smile falters and she looks back at the sky.

"Maybe I want to quit my job and start something new," she says after some silence.

"Quit acting? I thought you loved it."

"I do love it," she says. "But just the acting part. The other parts, like the having to put my best foot forward all the time part, can really suck sometimes. Most times, really. And when I don't do that, for once in my life, it turns into a viral video for all the world to spread and talk about and judge me for."

I don't say anything in response because what is there to say? There are no words to soothe her or to take away the ugliness of people.

"The dumb part is," she continues, "if you don't play the game, then you are forgotten. And if you are forgotten, then you don't get work."

"Who could forget you?" I ask.

She smiles. "Lots of people."

It's on the tip of my tongue to tell her that I could never forget her. That I'll never be able to forget her or this summer. Probably for the rest of my life. Even if it ended tomorrow and she went back to LA, it would still be the best summer I think I've ever had.

But I don't say that. Because it feels like too much, too soon.

"Well, you could always be a heart surgeon," I say, remembering what she told me when we were roasting marshmallows.

"That's way too much school," she says.

"True," I say. "How about something in . . . finance?"

She snorts out a laugh. "No one wants me managing money. That would be a terrible idea."

"A balloon artist?"

She pretends to ponder that. "I'd rock that."

"I'm sure you would."

She looks to the sky, holding the binoculars up to her eyes again.

"Point out some constellations," she says.

We spend the next while identifying star formations, and I tell her some of the lore behind them, at least the parts I can remember from what Keith taught me.

After a bit, she sets the binoculars down next to her and rolls to her side so she's facing me.

"This night gets a ten," she declares.

"Finally," I say, shooting a fist up in the air in triumph. I roll over to face her. "But the night isn't even over yet. Shouldn't you maybe wait until the morning before you decide?"

"I mean right now, like this moment. It's a ten."

"So, if you somehow get eaten by a gator in the middle of the night, then that part won't count?"

"I'll be dead, so I guess the answer is yes? But also, are there alligators out here at night?"

"I don't think so."

"That's not a very confident answer," she says, scooting over toward me on her sleeping bag.

"Are you scared?" I ask, nudging closer to her so we're nearly face to face now.

"Maybe a little," she says.

"I've got you," I say, placing a hand on her hip, my thumb rubbing over the smooth fabric of the leggings she's wearing.

"You'll save me from an alligator?" she asks, placing a hand on my chest, over my heart, which has picked up its pace from being this close to her.

"I'd definitely try," I tell her. "But I'd probably just get eaten too."

She laughs, and it's bright and beautiful, and with the waves in the background, it's a perfect combo of my two favorite sounds.

"I've been thinking," she says, her fingers tapping lightly on my chest. "Or really, I was wondering if maybe you could help me go over a part of the script again."

"What part?" I ask, hoping she's referring to where we left off at the bookshop.

"I really need help with the part where Callis and Falgon . . . kiss," she says, her voice almost a whisper.

My mouth goes dry, instantly. "I think I could possibly be swayed to help you with that again."

She closes the distance, her lips softly touching mine. I close my eyes, the hand at her hip slowly moving up to the curve of her waist, where it rests. I feel her hand, the one that was on my chest, move up to my shoulder. The pressure of her lips on mine intensifies, and I want to personally thank whoever wrote the book that inspired the movie for giving us an excuse, as flimsy as it is, to do this right now. To kiss under the stars, the sound of the ocean waves in the background.

"Okay, yeah," she says while I'm trailing kisses along her cheek and down to her jaw. "This night is definitely a ten."

I pull back and look at her, and we smile at each other.

Her smile falls as she reaches up and runs a hand through my hair. "Can I keep you, when the summer's over?"

"Keep me?" I ask.

"I'm saying I don't want this to be over at the end of the summer, Briggs Huckleberry Dalton."

"Nice try."

"Thwarted again," she says, and I chuckle.

"How do you expect to keep me?" I ask, very interested in her answer.

"I don't know," she says. "It feels like there's almost too much to navigate to make it work. But . . . I'd like to try if you would."

I lean in and kiss her lips. It's a quick kiss, but it's my answer. I would like to try this with Presley. I have no idea what that will look like, what it all even means. But right now, with her snuggling up to me, and my heart fully taking a dive over that edge, I don't need all the answers. Right now, I just need her.

Just as I'm starting to doze off with Presley in my arms, I hear her say, "Hey, Briggs, don't sleepwalk into the ocean, okay?"

I chuckle and pull her even closer to me, and then we fall asleep under a starry sky.

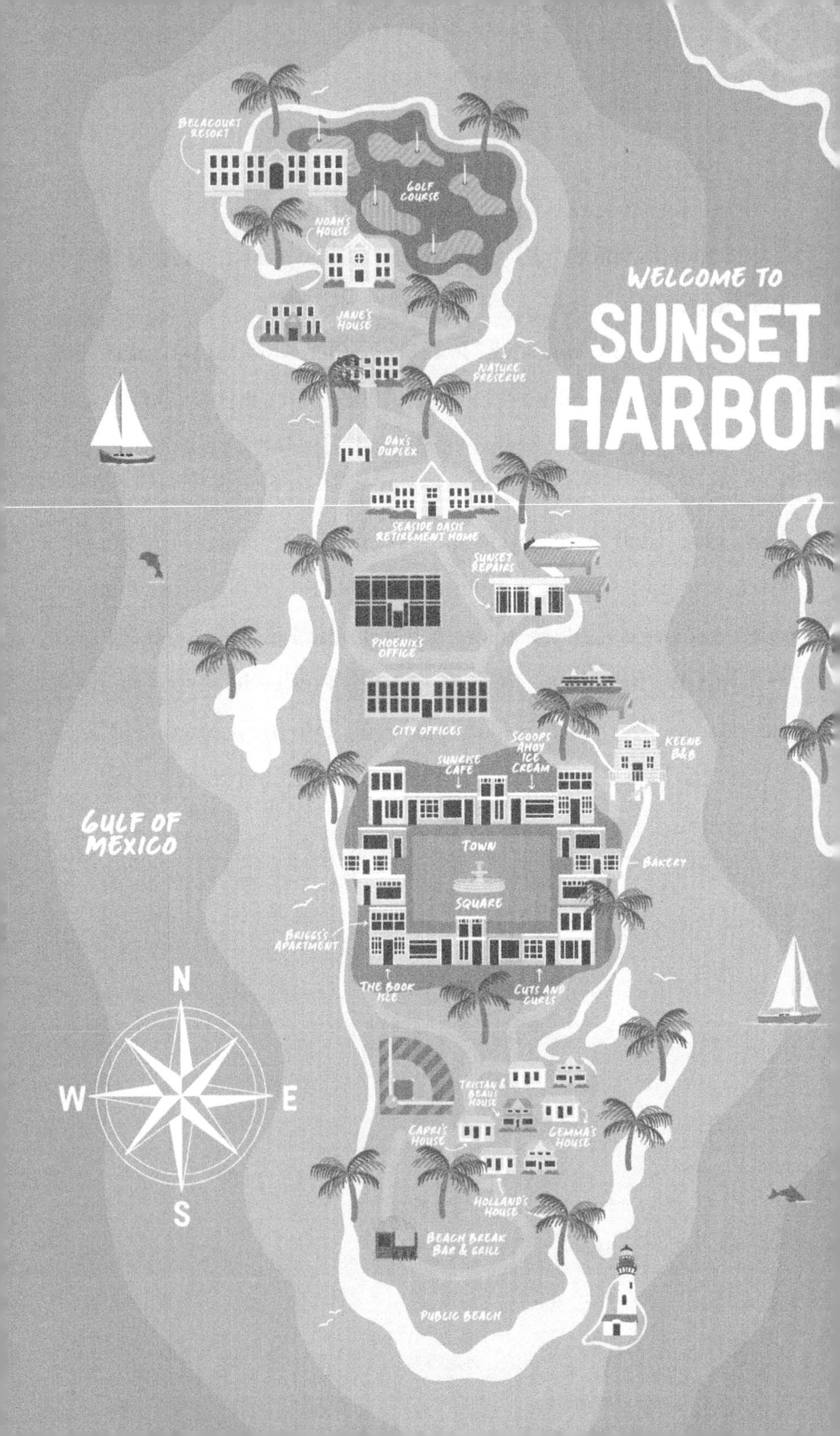

WELCOME TO

SUNSET HARBOR

Belacourt Resort

Golf Course

Noah's House

Jane's House

Nature Preserve

Dax's Duplex

Seaside Oasis Retirement Home

Sunset Repairs

Phoenix's Office

City Offices

Sunrise Cafe

Scoops Ahoy Ice Cream

Keene B&B

Gulf of Mexico

Town Square

Bakery

Briggs's Apartment

The Book Isle

Cuts and Curls

N

W

E

S

Tristan & Beau's House

Capri's House

Gemma's House

Holland's House

Beach Break Bar & Grill

Public Beach

CHAPTER 17

Presley

I WAKE UP to seagulls squawking, Briggs's arms around me, and a familiar, yet annoying, clicking sound.

Blinking my eyes at the morning sun, I wonder what time it is. The clicking sound continues. Is it some sort of crab? The sound an alligator makes before an attack? The mating call of some sort of seabird?

"Briggs," I say, shaking him, worried that we are possibly under attack by some kind of wild animal.

"Hmm?" he says, squinting his eyes against the rising sun.

My gosh, he's adorable. I kind of felt dumb for asking him if I could keep him last night—it was on a whim, really. I hadn't planned to do it. But I meant it. I want to see if we can make this work between us. I don't know what it will be, but I want to try.

"Do you hear that?" I ask him.

"Hear what?" He wipes his eyes.

The clicking noise stops, and I rack my brain trying to figure out what it could be. It sounds so . . . familiar.

Then it hits me.

"A camera," I say, panic quickly moving through my body.

"A what?"

"I heard a camera clicking. A shutter going off," I say. I've gotten very used to the sound. I roll over onto my stomach, and peeking my head around, I try to find whoever it is that's taking pictures. The clicking starts back up.

I spot a photographer, someone hiding behind a palm tree, or trying to, not even ten feet from us, a telescopic zoom lens pointed in our direction.

I swear under my breath. "Briggs, someone's taking pictures of us," I say, before finding the black sweatshirt I brought with me and quickly putting it on, tightening the hood around my face. I didn't bring my sunglasses, because why would I bring them to sleep on the beach? But that was a rookie mistake. In LA, I have sunglasses with me no matter what time of day it is.

Briggs is shuffling around now, trying to find his shoes.

"What should we do?" he asks, the imprint of a pillow on his face.

"Let's go back to my room at the resort," I say.

He nods. "Don't worry, I'm sure it's just an idiot from this island."

"Do you know anyone who happens to own a paparazzi-looking camera?"

"Not that I know of, but there are tons of bird watchers around here—maybe it's one of them?"

"Regardless, they were taking pictures of us, whoever they are. I promise you, I know when I'm being photographed."

"Okay," he says. "Let's get out of here. We'll just leave all this and I can come back later."

I nod my head and he takes me by the hand, and we run in the opposite direction of the cameraman. We run until we get to the resort and then take the stairs up to the second floor where my suite is located.

With shaking hands, I dig the key card out of the pocket of my yoga pants and open the door, Briggs following me into the room. I shut the door behind me and double lock it for no reason, since this is a private resort and they're not about to let someone with a camera on the premises without permission.

"I've never seen a suite at this resort," Briggs says, looking around the entryway. It occurs to me that I've never had him up here. I did invite him up that one night, but other than that, there really hasn't been an opportunity.

I look at the space through his eyes, setting my key card on a whitewashed entry table and flicking on the lights before we walk through a small alcove and into the sitting area, the bedroom just beyond that. There are two sofas and a coffee table in the center of the modest-size room. And a kitchenette in the corner with a small bar and a dining table. The space is decorated in a beachy-modern motif with light-colored wood and different shades of blues with some splashes of orange. Someone has been here—I can tell by the fluffed-up throw pillows, and the blanket I've been using while reading is now folded and placed thoughtfully on the couch.

I feel anxious, wondering if this little world I've been living in for nearly a month is about to collapse. I wrap my arms around myself.

"You okay?" Briggs asks.

"Yeah," I say.

"Should we . . . look online for any news?"

I nod, little rapid movements of my head. "Yes, let's do that."

He pulls his phone out of his front pocket and takes a seat on one of the couches, and I sit next to him. My body feels achy from sleeping outside, and I could use a shower from all the sea air and humidity, but first things first. I say a little prayer that there's nothing and it's just someone here on the island looking at birds but also snapping pictures of two people sleeping on the beach. Which is still weird and violating, but I've been dealing with it for a long time now.

Briggs pulls up the internet on his phone and types my name into the search bar, and I look away, thinking maybe if I can't see it, whatever pops up won't be a reality.

But Briggs curses. The word sounds foreign coming from his mouth, and I realize I haven't heard him swear before.

"What?" I ask him.

He twists his lips to the side before handing me the phone.

I see the headline first: *Where Is Presley James?* Cosmic Fury *Role Up in the Air.*

I scan the article, Briggs leaning in toward me doing the same. I'm reading the words as quickly as possible, trying to ignore the sinking feeling I have in my stomach. The good news is, there's no word about where I am, no mention of the island. Which means I don't have to worry about the photographer, whoever it was. At least not yet.

The bad news is, I have to call my agent. The bubble I've been living in hasn't quite popped, but it definitely has a slow-leaking hole. My days hiding in Sunset Harbor are numbered.

I lean into Briggs for support, and he puts his arm around me, kissing me on top of the head, telling me without words that he's here. It's something that feels like a couple who've been together for a while might do: being able to say things without speaking. Briggs and I do that already, and I don't even know what we are officially. Still, I'm overwhelmingly grateful he's here with me right now.

"So, what's the plan?" he asks, pointing at his phone, which I'm still holding in my hands.

"I need to make some calls," I say, hating the words that are coming out of my mouth right now.

"Okay," he says. "I'll just . . . I can wait downstairs, or you can call me when you're done?"

"No," I say, shaking my head. "Can you . . . I was hoping you could stay."

"Of course," he says. "My mom and Scout have the bookshop taken care of today, so I'm here as long as you need me."

"Thank you," I say, leaning in and kissing him softly on the lips. The fact that he's here, that he wants to stay, eases some of the ache I'm feeling in my heart.

I get up from the couch, go to my bedroom, and grab the phone off the charger on the nightstand. The phone I haven't been carrying with me, because what was the point? No one knows the number, and it really is a piece of junk phone. It was a safety net, something to have just in case. I hate that I have to use it today. I hate what that might mean: This could be over.

I pick up the phone and call my agent.

"How soon do you have to leave?" Briggs asks, his arm around me as we sit on the couch, his thumb rubbing a short path up and down my arm.

It's been an hour of phone calls and feeling very drained and tired as my old life has come crashing back.

"I don't know," I tell him. "My agent, Kara, is getting all the details sorted right now."

It turns out the filming date for *Cosmic Fury* was moved up to next month. Hence the sudden reason to find me, for people to really start worrying. Kara was told by the producers of the movie that she needed to locate me right away or they were going to recast and that I'd be in breach of contract. She thinks that info somehow was leaked to the gossip sites. I didn't say out loud what I'd been thinking—that it was probably leaked by her, or even more likely, by my mom.

I guess it's a good thing it was leaked because had I not seen it, I would just be staying here living my best life, having no idea what was happening behind the scenes.

I didn't anticipate how hard this might be, having to leave. Mostly because I didn't see it coming. I mean, I knew it was going to happen eventually, but I really thought I was going to get the entire summer before I had to go back. That feels like a foolish thought now. I, of all people, should know well that things change all the time in this industry.

I think if there weren't a Briggs on this island, if I hadn't spent these past few weeks with him, getting to know him, falling hard for him, that I'd just pack up and go home, no problem. I probably wouldn't have made it even a full week here if it weren't for Briggs.

"I hope you can stay a few more days," he says. "Just so we can get a few more fun things in. Our last hurrah." He nudges me with his shoulder.

See? This is what I'm talking about. I have to leave soon. My time on this island is ending, and Briggs wants to keep it going as long as possible for me. To keep giving me this amazing summer that I'm so sad is ending.

"What will we do?" I ask him, feeling all kinds of gooey, happy feelings toward this man.

"I was thinking of borrowing the boat again and maybe going fishing tomorrow?"

"Really?" I turn my head up toward him. "I've never done that."

Thinking of the boat conjures up thoughts of kissing Briggs for the first time. Well, not the first time, but the first *real* time. Perhaps we can take a break from fishing to do more of that? Or not even bother fishing at all?

"I figured," he says. "I'll set it up. We could go in the afternoon after I get done working at the bookshop."

I kiss him on the cheek before laying my head against his shoulder once more. "Sounds perfect."

"And maybe if you want to go tubing again, we could make that happen."

I shake my head back and forth against his shoulder. "I have a contract that will be in effect sooner than expected, so I'd better not."

"I guess swimming with sharks is out then too?"

I snort laugh. "No way in hell am I doing that, Briggs Ernest Dalton."

I look up, eyebrows raised, wondering if I got it this time.

"Sorry," he says.

"You know what would cheer me up right now is you telling me your middle name."

"How about I save it until right before you leave," he says.

Right. I'm leaving. Good hell, maybe I should quit this job. I'm miserable right now.

I can't quit, though. Not for a burgeoning relationship or whatever this is between Briggs and me. I love what I do, despite how much it takes over my life. Despite how little of a life it gives me. I will definitely be making some changes when these next contracts are completed.

"You know, you could come with me," I say.

He cocks his head to the side. "Come with you where?"

"Back to my home, to LA?" It sounds ridiculous even as I say it, but if I could bring Briggs with me, I think I'd be less sad about leaving.

Do I even hear myself? Bring Briggs with me, like he's some sort of souvenir.

"Never mind," I say, feeling like an idiot. It would be nice if I could think before I speak. "I'm just being stupid."

He gives me a sad smile. "I'd go with you," he says. "But I just—" He pauses, exhaling through his nose. "I need to figure out what I'm doing with my own future, first."

I nod. "Yeah. I get it."

"I could . . . come visit, though? Maybe next month?"

"Really? Truly?" I say, looking up at him. "That would be so amazing."

Briggs could come for a visit. I could show him around town. Maybe he'll love LA and want to move there. Or he could hate it. Or I could move closer to him at some point.

I'm getting ahead of myself. But I have to hope that it will all work out. It's the only way I'll be able to leave this island.

CHAPTER 18

Briggs

"BRIGGS!" Scout comes running into the bookstore from the back, waving her phone at me.

"Here you go, Mr. Shuman," I say, looking back at the older man who's just purchased some books and handing him his change.

The man waves goodbye before leaving, slowly moving toward the door on old fragile-looking legs, the bells jingling as he walks out into the humid air.

"Briggs!" Scout yells again, now standing in front of me doing some sort of weird jumping thing.

"What, Scout?" I ask, laughing at how ridiculous she's being right now.

"You're famous!" she says, holding up her phone for me to see, but the screen is black.

"I'm . . . what?"

"You're famous," she says again, turning the phone back toward her before muttering, "Oh crap," and putting her passcode in. She hands it to me this time.

I look at her screen, and then feel the color drain from my face. There, under the headline *Presley James Has Been Spotted, and With a New Man*, is a picture of Presley and me, asleep on the beach.

"No," I say, scrolling through the article with the edge of my thumb, feeling a twisting in my gut when I see more pictures. One of Presley and me making a sandcastle, and another of us playing in the water at the resort, our arms wrapped around one another. One of me helping Presley get off the boat after we went tubing, and next to that, a grainy capture of us in a lip-lock in front of the resort. There's another one of us riding bikes and one of us walking down the beach together, Presley smiling, her arms outstretched. The most disconcerting ones, though, are of us roasting marshmallows in my mom's backyard, and one taken through the window of the bookshop, our arms around each other.

Then I read the words.

Presley James has been seen with a new beau, according to sources, while vacationing on an island off the Florida coast. It turns out the mystery man is a local who works at the town bookshop. Could this mean the rumors are true that Presley and

Declan have called it quits for real this time? And did it have anything to do with the viral video?

Having read and seen enough, I hand the phone back to Scout.

"My friends are gonna freak out," Scout says, cradling the phone in her hands like it must be protected. She's got all the proof she needs right there that Presley James is on Sunset Harbor.

"Please don't tell them," I say, back to my old ways of trying to protect Presley, but then I realize it's pointless. This article is from a prominent gossip site, and anyone can see it. Chances are it's spread around the island already, or it will soon enough. I'm just grateful whoever wrote it didn't print my name or the name of the island.

"Actually, Scout," I say, searching the counter for my phone, and when I find it, placing it in the pocket of my shorts. "Can you watch the shop? I need to go talk to Presley."

"Sure," she says. "But hurry back because I'm gonna need to throw this in my friends' faces."

I feel like maybe I should quickly talk to her about bragging and how it's not a good thing, but I don't really have the time right now, so I hurry to the resort, running as fast as I can in flip-flops. I'm winded and sweating by the time I get there.

“Excuse me,” one of the employees says, trying to stop me as I run past her and take the stairs two at a time up to Presley’s suite. I don’t have time to check in with anybody now.

I knock on the door and then take my glasses off, cleaning them with the edge of my shirt while I wait for her to answer.

The door opens after I knock a second time, and I see Presley there, her eyes bloodshot and her face blotchy and red.

“You saw it,” is all I say.

She nods her head as tears well in her eyes, and she opens the door wider, letting me in. I walk inside and shut it behind me. I want to take her into my arms and hold her, let her know we’ll figure this out together, but instead I follow her as she walks toward the sitting area.

“Presley, I—”

“Briggs, this is my mom, Didi Shermerhorn,” she says, holding her hand out toward a woman who looks to be in her late fifties sitting on one of the couches. She’s wearing some sort of blue pantsuit, and her hair is in a very straight, shoulder-length bob. She has the same coloring as Presley, especially in the hair and eyes. She stands up as we approach.

“It’s nice to meet you,” I say, holding out a hand toward her, which she takes and gives a delicate shake.

“Likewise,” she says, before pulling her hand out of mine. “It’s nice to meet the reason why my daughter has been hiding from me.”

I look to Presley, who's rolling her eyes.

"Mom, I told you I came here on my own," Presley says.

"Well, I can see why you stayed," her mom says, looking me up and down. "He's handsome."

"Uh . . . thanks," I say, not sure how to respond to that.

Presley shakes her head at her mom. "Can I have a minute with Briggs, please?"

Yes, we need a minute so we can figure this out. I can't take the heartbroken look on her face right now.

Her mom gives me a closed-mouth smile before going to the bedroom and shutting the door.

"I'm sorry," I start. "I didn't know your mom was here."

"She showed up this morning."

"How did she find you?"

She sniffles. "I'm sure she got it out of my agent or my assistant, since they know now."

I put my hands on her arms and rub them. "Presley, are you okay?"

She shakes her head, the tears starting up again. "No, I'm not," she says. "That article, Briggs . . . it's not good."

"Well, yeah, but they didn't mention my name or the name of the island, so that's good."

"It doesn't look good for me," she says.

"I'm not following," I say, letting go of her arms.

"Those photos in that article," she says, pointing to some random spot in the room, "show me laughing and having a great time, and not looking repentant for my actions captured in that stupid video. I look ungrateful and irresponsible . . . and it's not a good look, Briggs."

"Oh, Presley," I say. "I never thought of that. I'm so sorry. We can fix this."

She shakes her head. "I don't know if we can."

"We can figure something out," I tell her. There's got to be a way.

She pushes some hair behind her ear. "There's a picture of you and me in your mom's backyard," she says, a single tear dropping from her eye and down her face. I want to wipe it away, but somehow, I get the idea she wouldn't want that right now.

"I know," I say. "I have no idea how anyone got that one."

She lets out a breath. "Briggs, it could only be your mom or Scout."

"What?" I say with a confused-sounding laugh. "Presley . . . there's no way."

Her shoulders drop, and she puts her face in her hands. "That's the *only* way, Briggs. Who else would have taken those photos?"

I stare at her, wondering how she could think my family would do something like that. I understand the evidence is damning—it is a picture of us in the backyard, and I did say my mom and sister were both gossips. But they wouldn't do *this.* They're fiercely loyal; they've been going to bat for Presley since we asked them to.

"They didn't do it, Presley. They wouldn't."

She wipes tears away with the back of her hand. "Your mom mentioned the bookshop isn't making a good profit."

"So?" I ask, not understanding where she's going with this.

"People get paid a lot of money for pictures like that," she says.

"Wait," I say, taking a step back from her, feeling shocked by this turn of events, by the words coming out of her mouth. "You think my mom sold pictures of us, for the bookshop?"

"Or maybe she just needed the money? I don't know." She says the last part through a sob.

I shake my head. "I'm telling you right now, my mom and sister did not do this."

"I know you don't want to believe it. And I know you didn't have anything to do with it, Briggs. But . . . there's just no other way."

"It wasn't them," I repeat myself. I feel like if I keep saying it, maybe it will get through to her. "What about whoever was taking pictures of us yesterday?"

"I thought about that, and I'd believe it if it were just the one shot, but there were private, intimate pictures on there, Briggs.

No one else would have known. Do you know how violating that feels?"

"Well, I was in the pictures too," I say, my hackles rising.

"I know, but—"

"But I'm not a ridiculously famous actor," I say, cutting her off. "So, I guess it's not the same."

"It's not the same," she says, her voice rising. "This is my career, Briggs." She points to herself. "I get to deal with the fallout, and you . . . you just get to work in a bookstore."

"Right," I say. "You're right. I'm a nobody."

"That's not what I'm saying." She puts a hand to her forehead.

"Isn't it, though?"

"I'm sorry, I'm just upset," she says.

I don't say anything. I hardly recognize the person standing in front of me right now.

"I have to leave," she says. "I'm going back to LA tonight. I've got to do damage control."

I point at myself. "For me?"

"No," she says, shaking her head. "Or, I guess, yes. For all of it. For leaving, for running away, for that stupid video. And for those photos."

"So . . . then what?" I ask after a few beats of silence.

"Then . . . I start working on the film," she says.

I point to her and then me. "And you . . . and me?"

Another tear falls down her face. "I want to thank you for all the things we did this summer, for all you did for me."

"Oh, got it," I say, taking another step away. So that's it, then.

She shakes her head. "You mean a lot to me, Briggs, but it's just too hard. There's . . . too much. Our lives are too different."

Too hard. Right. I'm starting to see a trend with Presley James. When things get hard, she runs away. Glad I figured that out now and not later when it would have been much worse.

I wait to see if she has anything else to say, and maybe a part of me is sort of hoping she takes it all back. But when she just looks at me, tears running down her face, I know that's not going to happen.

"Goodbye, Presley," I say, before walking away from her and out the door.

WELCOME TO

SUNSET HARBOR

Belacourt Resort
Golf Course
Noah's House
Jane's House
Nature Preserve
Dax's Duplex
Seaside Oasis Retirement Home
Sunset Repairs
Phoenix's Office
City Offices
Scoops Ahoy Ice Cream
Keene B&B
Sunrise Cafe
Town Square
Bakery
Briggs's Apartment
The Book Isle
Cuts and Curls

Public Beach

CHAPTER 19

Presley

MY HOME IN Calabasas feels cold and sterile as I dump my suitcase on the floor of my bedroom with the almost all-white decor and then collapse face-first on my bed.

Usually when I travel for work, I can't wait to get back to my home, to all the creature comforts I'm accustomed to. But this time around, I actually hate being here. I hate what it means. I hate that I decorated this place in so much freaking white. There was so much color in Sunset Harbor. The water, the green foliage, the amazing sunsets. A pair of beautiful green eyes and dirty-blond hair.

I was more colorful there, too. More light in my eyes, more coloring in my face. I hardly recognized myself when I'd look in the mirror, I was so . . . happy.

And now I'm back in LA and it all feels drab and sterile and stupid. I saw myself in the entryway mirror of my two-story

Mediterranean-style home just a few minutes ago, and I look like I've died and been unwillingly brought back to life.

Presley, you colorless fool.

The paparazzi were waiting for me when we landed. No doubt the flight information had been leaked by my mom.

"How could you not even tell your own mom where you were?" she'd asked me on the flight home, riding in first class with tickets I'd purchased.

I hadn't wanted to have this conversation on the plane, but it needed to be said. After earlier that day with Briggs and the way he looked at me before walking away, my own heart breaking into a million freaking pieces, I was not in the best mood.

"You were the last person I wanted to tell," I'd said.

"Why's that?" she'd asked, looking genuinely upset by my answer.

"Because you report my location to the paparazzi all the time."

"I do not," she'd said, the sincerity gone and the facade back and lit up like a marquee board.

"Mom, I needed a break from everything. I had one planned, and I thought we could go together, and then you . . . ruined it."

"I ruined it? I didn't make that video, Presley. Is this because of Declan?"

"No," I'd said emphatically. "He's all yours, that's not the problem. I'm not blaming you for the video; that was on me. But it was the fact that you told people where we were going on that trip, and you wanted to turn it into a publicity thing."

"But I did that all for you," she'd replied. "The world is always watching you, Presley, whether you like it or not. Everything I've done is for you."

"Mom," I'd said, stopping her from the *I gave up my life for your career* speech she often gives me when I push back. She has worked hard, especially when I was younger, and I came out mostly unscathed from an industry that can take some terrible turns if you don't have the right people in your corner, and I'm grateful to her for that.

I looked at her with pleading eyes. "When I say I need a break, I need you to believe me."

She'd looked away then, out the window of the plane. She did apologize later, as we'd started our descent into LAX. And we had a heart-to-heart about everything. It wasn't our first, and it won't be our last, I'm sure.

Now, here on my stupid white bed, I can't stop thinking about how terribly things turned out with Briggs. I can't stop replaying the conversation in my head. I hate the memory of that hurt look on his face, how painful it was to tell him about the pictures. And then I thanked him for all he did for me? Like he was some sort of glorified tour guide?

Oh gosh.

I miss Briggs, and it hasn't even been twenty-four hours. I feel this emptiness without him. I'm sad that he didn't believe me. That he wouldn't even consider that the pictures were taken by his family. How could it possibly be anyone else? I do appreciate how loyal he is. But that's Briggs.

When I saw the pictures, I knew right away he wouldn't believe me. I also knew that we wouldn't be able to get past it. I'd always be worried around his family, not being able to trust them, and he'd be defensive like he was today. I knew when I saw the pictures in that article that we'd been flung up the side of an insurmountable hill. There was no way to get over it.

I hope the way things ended doesn't forever taint my memories. I hope I'll be able to look back on the past few weeks and remember all the fun things I did with Briggs and feel something positive, like the happiness the adventures created. Even cut short, and terribly so, it was still my first real summer.

It's sort of ruined right now, after my exchange with Briggs, those pictures in that article, and the heartbreak I'm feeling, but I hope someday I can move past all that.

I'm still face down on my bed, my tears soaking the duvet underneath me, which is white, of course. I'm changing that tomorrow. I'm ordering myself a bright-blue bed covering. I'm going to brighten up this entire place. My world is no longer white. It's orange, red, blue, and heartbreakingly green.

I should get up and shower off the grime from the flight, but I don't bother doing any of that. I don't even change into my pajamas. I just crawl up my California King bed and under the sheets, and then I cry myself to sleep.

"How was that?" I ask Kara after I've recorded what's to be my apology video, written and directed by my publicist. We picked a drab background with natural lighting to sit in front of, I'm wearing a trusty old sweatshirt, I've got minimal makeup on, and my hair is pulled up in a bun.

And it's all a big show.

It's the first day of July, only fifteen days until we start filming, and the producers of *Cosmic Fury* expect it of me. So, here I am, telling the world I'm sorry about being caught having a very human experience, albeit a pretty awful one. I do feel bad for losing it on set; it was unprofessional of me and inconsiderate. And that's what I say in my apology.

I don't offer excuses, no reasons, no telling the world what had been happening in my life at the time to try to divert the blame away from me. The general public won't know that I hadn't had a real break in fourteen years and that my mom had ruined my first opportunity. Oh, and that she and Declan Stone are a couple. I think my being away actually pushed them closer together.

“I think it was great,” Kara says, giving me a thin smile. I feel bad for my whole team—my agent, Kara, my publicist, Leslie, and Shani, my assistant, who thank goodness is still working for me. They were the ones dealing with this while I was gone, trying to spin stories and manage contracts while I was having the time of my life. I’ve apologized to all of them, repeatedly. I’m not sorry I left them like I did, but I am sorry they’ve had to deal with the fallout.

“I’ll have Leslie watch it and make sure it’s what she wanted, and then I’ll post it on your socials,” she says.

“Thank you,” I reply, sitting on my white couch, my legs curled up under me as I hug a white (ugh) throw pillow.

I placed a massive order for new colorful things for my house and it will be here next week. I can’t wait. I’m no longer the Presley who likes things bright and white and pristine. I want colors and disorder. No, actually, I don’t want that. I’ll keep bright and pristine but get rid of most of the white.

“There’s also the matter of the pictures on the island,” Kara says, tapping the end of a pen to her chin.

“What about them?”

“They’re getting a lot of buzz. I think people like seeing you with someone who’s not in the business.”

“Oh,” I say, not really wanting to talk about this.

"It could be a good spin. Would the man you were seen with—what was his name?"

"Briggs," I say. I don't think I've said his name out loud since I got home, and it makes my heart speed up and my stomach drop at the same time. Briggs Ebenezer Dalton. I was prepared to use that name next, but never got the chance. And now I guess I'll never know. It would be weird to text him out of the blue and ask him, right? He did say he would tell me before I left, but I'm sure that was the last thing on his mind when we said goodbye.

"Yes, Briggs," Kara says. "Do you think he'd be willing to take some better pictures with you? The ones posted were pretty grainy. Leslie thinks it will help things after the backlash from the apology once it's posted."

Ah, yes, it's a damned-if-you-do, damned-if-you-don't type of thing. As soon as my apology goes up on social media, there will be an initial round of *we don't accept your apology* online, with stitches on TikTok of people breaking down my words. But then that will settle and hopefully we can all move on.

"No," I say, answering her question. That won't happen. Because I won't subject him to that, and also because the world doesn't deserve him. And more importantly, Briggs doesn't deserve to be some kind of publicity pawn. Even if things had worked out with him and we were trying to figure it out and see where things might go with us, I wouldn't put him through that.

Although, knowing Briggs, he'd do it for me—or at least he would have, before I accused his family of betraying me.

Good hell. I will never get over him if I keep reminding myself how amazing he is. Not that I'm actually trying to get over him. I think it will take a long time to do that, and also, I don't want to. I don't want to get over him.

"That's not going to happen," I say to Kara, and she gives me one single nod. "Any other ideas?"

She taps the pen again, but this time on the pad of paper in front of her. I kind of love that Kara still uses pen and paper and isn't looking down at her phone, typing it into the Notes app like the rest of us.

"I guess we could have you seen with Declan again," Kara says.

I close my eyes and bury my face into the stupid white pillow I've been holding in my lap. I look back up at her. "You know he's dating my mom, right?"

She keeps her eyes on the pad of paper in front of her. "I'd heard."

I let out a breath. "I guess if you think it'll take any attention from Briggs, then fine."

I want to laugh, or cry, or both. Didn't I just tell Briggs the other night on the beach that I wanted to do things differently this time? Didn't I say I wasn't going to play all the games, that I wanted to be real? And here I am, doing planned apologies and scheduling appearances with Declan. Why can't this job be just about the acting and nothing else? It's so frustrating.

Kara jots something down, her pen scratching along the paper as she writes. "The apology video should do most of that, but a couple of sightings with Declan would probably seal the deal. I'll get that set up."

"Great," I say, the word coming out resigned. I am feeling resigned right now. To a life I both love and hate simultaneously.

Kara leaves after making me put a few other obligations in the phone calendar that I share with Shani, and I'm left alone in my starkly white living room.

Mindlessly, I turn on the television and flick through the channels until I stop on one showing *Notting Hill*, just at the beginning when Julia Roberts's character, Anna Scott, first walks into the travel bookshop.

Because I like to punish myself, to kick myself when I'm down, I watch the whole thing while I cry.

WELCOME TO
SUNSET
HARBOR
BELACOURT RESORT
GOLF COURSE
NOAH'S HOUSE
JANE'S HOUSE
NATURE PRESERVE
DAX'S DUPLEX
SEASIDE OASIS RETIREMENT HOME
SUNSET REPAIRS
PHOENIX'S OFFICE
CITY OFFICES
SUNRISE CAFE
SCOOPS AHOY ICE CREAM
KEENE B&B
GULF OF MEXICO
TOWN
SQUARE
BAKERY
BRIGGS'S APARTMENT
THE BOOK ISLE
CUTS AND CURLS
N
W
E
S
TRISTAN & BEAU'S HOUSE
CAPRI'S HOUSE
GEMMA'S HOUSE
HOLLAND'S HOUSE
BEACH BREAK BAR & GRILL
PUBLIC BEACH

CHAPTER 20

Briggs

THE FOURTH OF July is a big celebration on Sunset Harbor. It's an all-day event. First there's the pancake breakfast, and then the parade, then everyone plays games on the beach, and then at night there's music and dancing with a live band, and once the sun has gone down, there are fireworks, of course. You can't celebrate the holiday without those.

I've missed most of the day, choosing to work at the bookshop so my mom and Scout can enjoy the festivities. We tend to be fairly busy on this holiday, since we get a lot of tourists on the island for the celebration. But things are slowing down at the shop now that the bonfires and dancing are about to start. So, I'll close up the shop and go to some of the evening activities.

Maybe. I'm not really feeling it. I promised Scout I'd go for at least the dance part, but honestly, I'd like to hole up in my apartment and feel sorry for myself like I have been for the last six days since Presley left.

It's not a glamorous life, but it's mine.

The crazy part is, while Presley was here and I was busy every day, it felt like it went by in a flash, but these last few days have felt like an eternity.

I feel a little bit like Hugh Grant's character in *Notting Hill*, walking around in a bit of a fog after Julia Roberts's character left, "Ain't No Sunshine" playing on repeat in my head. Only there's plenty of sunshine on this island. What I wouldn't give for a gloomy and rainy day to match my mood.

I'll just keep going through the motions like I have been, having superficial conversations with people who come into the bookshop, putting on my best fake smile. My mom knows I'm faking it, and she's called me out on it a time or two, or three. I tell her what I tell myself: It'll be fine. *I'll* be fine. And I will. I just need some time. Until then, I might be walking around like a fake-smiling zombie.

At least I know it wasn't my mom or Scout who took those pictures. I never doubted them, but just in case—in case there was a tiny, minuscule chance—I asked them, and they denied it fully. And I believe them. But I guess the biggest piece of evidence is, there hasn't been a mysterious influx of cash appearing out of nowhere.

I didn't tell them that Presley blamed them, mostly to protect their feelings about her. I don't know why I want to salvage their opinion of her, but I do. It would hurt them. Well, my mom would be hurt—Scout would want to exact revenge. As it stands, she's already referring to her as Parsley, which makes me laugh every time. I think it's best to keep all that from them. All they know is that things didn't work out between Presley and me and she went back to LA. I think Scout was mostly upset she never got the promised Declan Stone autograph.

I wish I could find out who was behind the photographs. Not to throw it in Presley's face, but . . . Okay, I would probably throw it in her face a little. But I'd like an answer, for my own peace of mind. It won't fix anything; I'd just like to know.

"There you go, Carl," I say, handing him a bag of refrigerator-repair manuals. They finally arrived after being delayed twice. Honestly, he could have ordered them off Amazon and they would have gotten here faster than they did from our suppliers, even if two-day shipping isn't a thing on the island. But I appreciate the business.

He makes to leave but then turns back to me. "Did you ever find out if your mom is seeing anyone?" he asks me.

I shake my head. "No, I didn't."

"Oh" is all he says.

"You know, Carl, you could ask her yourself."

His cheeks turn a dark shade of red. "Oh no, I don't think I could do that."

"Why not?"

"What if she rejects me?"

I don't know much about Carl, just that he's never been married and has lived on the island for most of his life.

"What if she does?" I ask him. "Better to try and fail than not try at all."

He nods, his head moving up and down slowly as he appears to be taking in my words.

Maybe I've missed my calling, and I could be some sort of matchmaker for older men. I could help them navigate the dating scene.

"Yeah, I don't think I'll do that," he says plainly, before exiting the shop.

Well, that was the shortest career I've ever had.

I do need a career, though. And I've started working on it. During the slow times at the shop, I've been fixing up my résumé and looking at what jobs are out there. I've seen some decent possibilities.

I still need to call Jack and find out why he's trying to get ahold of me. Even if it is to tell me we owe a bunch of money I don't have. I can't keep putting it off. I pull out my phone from the back pocket of my jeans, and search up his name in my contacts, but then I realize it's almost time to close, and it's a holiday. The call can wait one more day.

I don't put the phone back, instead I scroll further down my contacts until I get to one: Presley Shermerhorn. I stop there and stare at it, my thumb just under her name. I put her real name in there because it made her more real to me. And it was real . . . wasn't it? My feelings for her were real. Even though every day that goes by I wonder if I just got caught up in it, in some kind of summer romance. Maybe it was just one sided, but even as I tell myself this, I know it wasn't.

What Presley and I had was a real, tangible thing. And now it's over.

Tucking my phone back in my pocket, I walk over to the door of the bookshop and lock it, turning over the *open* sign, and then I begin working through the task list to shut the place down.

"Briggs!" Scout screams my name and waves, her voice carrying over the crowd and the local band, Mo and the Kokomos, playing a Beach Boys' song. She's always had a loud set of pipes, since the day she was born.

I walk over to her, trying for a genuine smile instead of my well-practiced zombie one, and most likely failing.

I realized something as I walked over here . . . I don't want to be here. It's true I knew that before heading over, but now it's setting in that I really, really don't want to be here. Everyone is smiling and dancing and having a great time, and I feel like I have a permanent rain cloud over my head. All I really feel like doing is kicking something.

But Scout doesn't seem to care, or probably doesn't even notice my hesitation, because she grabs me by the arm and drags me over to her friends, a group of girls dancing together.

"My brother's here," she says to them, a big smile on her face, and her friends all look at me at the same time and then start screaming and asking me questions, talking over themselves.

"What's Presley James like?"

"Are you going to marry her?"

"Did you break her and Declan Stone up?"

"When is she coming back to the island?"

I turn to Scout, who's smiling and watching, loving every minute of this queen bee moment she's having. I give her a look, a nonverbal plea to help me out, but she doesn't do anything to stop the chaos.

This is the first time I've had to field questions. No one else on the island has asked me—not one single person who's come into the bookshop. Either word hasn't spread to everyone yet or everyone still believes my mom. If that's true, she might want to consider running for mayor. She could gaslight this whole community into doing her bidding.

It's also possible she's told people not to talk to me about it, spreading it around the island that I'm heartbroken. I hope that's not the case. Even if it is, it definitely didn't spread to this group of teens currently bombarding me with questions.

"Girls," I say, holding up my hands to get them to stop. They all end their questioning at once. I let out a breath.

"To protect Presley's privacy—"

They all moan at once, cutting me off, their shoulders falling at nearly the same time. Do they practice this?

I turn to Scout, giving her a questioning glare. What can I even say right now?

I clear my throat. "I'll say this: I had a great time with Presley while she was here, and . . ." I pause, racking my brain for more to say, because right now I feel like I'm writing some generic online review. "And I wish her well."

There. It was boring, but it's the truth.

"But like, was she your girlfriend?" a girl with strawberry-blonde hair asks me.

"No, she wasn't. We were just friends," I reply, realizing belatedly that my bland answer wouldn't be enough, because it never works on Scout. She always has too many follow-up questions.

"But did you love her?" another girl with nearly-black hair chimes in.

"I . . . well," I hesitate, adopting a casual stance. "I don't . . . think so." This is a lie. There were definitely love feelings happening. At least for me there were.

"Did you ever hold her hand?" a girl with curly red hair and freckles asks eagerly.

"I did," I confirm, and they sigh in unison. Is there some kind of manual for fourteen-year-olds that gets them all on the same page with this stuff?

"Did your heart feel like it was gonna burst out of your chest when she was around?" the girl with the nearly-black hair asks.

"Well, I—"

"Did you get sweaty palms and butterflies in your stomach?" the strawberry-blonde girl cuts me off.

"I think I probably—"

"Dude, you've got it bad," declares the girl with the dark hair.

I'm not even sure what just happened. I've barely answered their questions and they've already diagnosed me.

"So, what went wrong?" asks the strawberry-blonde girl.

"It was a lot of things. She's famous, and I'm not. And we live very different lives." What am I doing? Why am I even telling them this?

"Those are just details," the girl with the black hair says.

"They're kind of big details, though," I say.

"Just apologize and tell her you're sorry," the redhead says.

"It's not that simple."

"Sure it is," Strawberry Blonde pipes in. "Buy her flowers."

"Oooh." The redhead nods in agreement. "And bring her a gift. Girls love gifts."

Now they're discussing what I should buy for Presley as an apology gift. Okay, this is ridiculous. I'm not taking relationship advice from a bunch of fourteen-year-olds.

And anyway, I don't need to apologize to Presley. If anyone should be apologizing, it's her. She's so . . . stubborn. She refused to look at any other possibilities, any other options for who might have taken those pictures.

I realize that my mom and Scout did make the most sense, from her point of view. But it wasn't them, and I knew it wasn't. Why didn't she believe me? For Presley to not trust me, to not even want to try . . .

I'm so sick of thinking about all this. What Presley and I had is over. And that's really all there is to it.

I've been tuned out, thinking to myself and looking off into the distance, so when I return my focus to my teenage love therapists, I find that like all fickle teens, they've ditched me and are now dancing to Mo and the Kokomos singing a version of "Fun, Fun, Fun" by the Beach Boys.

Well, that's my cue. Time for me to go.

I make my way out from the party and get stopped a couple of times to talk to people and catch up (cue fake zombie smiles), and then I go back to my apartment, where I watch the fireworks from my bedroom window and try to stop myself from wondering what Presley is doing right now.

Happy Fourth of July to me.

WELCOME TO
SUNSET HARBOR
BELACOURT RESORT
GOLF COURSE
NOAH'S HOUSE
JANE'S HOUSE
NATURE PRESERVE
DAX'S DUPLEX
SEASIDE OASIS RETIREMENT HOME
SUNSET REPAIRS
PHOENIX'S OFFICE
CITY OFFICES
SUNRISE CAFE
SCOOPS AHOY ICE CREAM
KEENE B&B
GULF OF MEXICO
TOWN SQUARE
BAKERY
BRIGGS'S APARTMENT
THE BOOK ISLE
CUTS AND CURLS
N
W
E
S
TRISTAN & BEAU'S HOUSE
CAPRI'S HOUSE
GEMMA'S HOUSE
HOLLAND'S HOUSE
BEACH BREAK BAR & GRILL
PUBLIC BEACH

CHAPTER 21

Presley

I HATE THIS so much.

"Presley, over here!" a paparazzo yells.

"Declan! Look this way!" another one says.

We've just exited Nobu, and thanks to my publicist—and I'm sure my mom—there are plenty of photogs here to get my picture with Declan Stone. We are officially back together. Only, we're not. Because he's with my mom now, and also, I don't like Declan like that. I never really did, even when we actually tried to date for that little bit.

My apology video went as expected: Hated the first week, and then all the fuss died down and has pretty much been forgotten about, just like my publicist predicted. I've been too busy to think about it all that much. With meetings, press conferences, and costume fittings, I feel like I haven't had a moment to myself. Filming starts in less than a week, I've got so much to do, and right now I'm having to pretend to be back with Declan.

I'm playing the game again. I'm not being real. In fact, I'm being the most unreal I could possibly be, standing here with this man, his hand on my lower back. He looks like he always does, handsome in a rugged way. Dark hair perfectly coiffed, clean-shaven jaw, in a dark-gray suit and blue shirt that makes his eyes pop, but unbuttoned too low in my opinion.

"Wave and smile," Declan says in my ear, his breath causing creepy little tingles to move down my spine. Mostly because I don't like his breath on my ear, but also what the hell did he eat in there? An entire clove of garlic?

But I do as he says, pulling my lips up into a fake smile, leaning my head away so I don't have to smell his breath. The sun is setting, and the lighting is perfect, we're here to give everyone a show, and a show is what they'll get. But really, what I'd like to do is run away from my mother's boyfriend.

Presley James, get yourself together.

"Lower that hand any farther and I'll cut you," I say through my teeth, keeping the grin bright on my face, posing for the cameras in a little black strapless dress and matching shiny patent leather heels that I had delivered today because I hated everything in my closet. It was after I tried this dress on that I realized I just hated the thought of getting done up for tonight, and it had nothing to do with my clothes.

“You wish,” Declan says, his smile bright and intact.

We’ve gotten so good at communicating through our smiles that it’s like second nature and no one is the wiser.

“Your breath smells like a butt,” I tell him, my cheeks starting to ache from the strain, while turning to my side and wrapping an arm around him from the front.

We are just adorable right now. The picture of love and affection.

“Your face looks like a butt,” he says through his teeth, waving at no one in particular.

“I hate you,” I say through my teeth. I don’t actually hate Declan, I just don’t like him.

We pose and preen, and everyone eats it up. The flashes are going off, and the paps are yelling questions for us to answer, which neither of us do. We just let them speculate like they always do. It’s kind of dumb how easy it is. Show up together for dinner, look cozy as you leave, and voilà, you’re front page on the gossip sites and someone has made a countdown clock for your future wedding and added more pictures to their Presclan fan page.

“Give him a kiss,” one of the paps yells, and at the request I almost upchuck the spicy tuna roll I ate earlier. I’d hate to do that; it was a really good roll.

Declan leans in and gives me his cheek, tapping it with his finger, which makes the photogs all *awwww* together in unison.

My gosh. How have I been putting up with this nonsense for so long?

At least Declan has offered his cheek and not puckered up for our little audience. I'm grateful for the gesture because I absolutely am not kissing him on the lips, especially not after I had to peel him off my mom not even an hour before we came here.

What is my life?

I smile for the cameras and then lean in, giving him a little peck on the cheek. Then I turn my head toward his ear so no one can see my lips and from an angle it looks like I'm telling him something secret and private. But what I really say is, "Seriously, what did you eat?"

Declan, apparently as done with this torture as I am, waves one last time and then takes me by the hand, and we start walking toward the car, another celebrity couple exiting after us and thankfully taking on the attention.

My smile falls as soon as we're out of the limelight, and I tear my hand away from Declan's and follow him to the waiting black SUV at the end of the walkway.

But just as I pass the last of the paparazzi, I see someone who looks familiar and I blink a couple of times, not fully comprehending.

Standing at the edge of the group, a camera in her hand is . . . Betty. Rude Betty? That can't be right. I walk toward her because

I have to know. My mind could be playing tricks on me, or I'm about to have a nervous breakdown and this is the initial warning, but I need to make sure it's her.

"Betty?" I ask as I approach her. There's no massive visor on her head, but it's absolutely her.

"Betty?" she questions, tucking her chin in, one brow lifting high on her forehead. "My name is Deborah."

"Um . . . What are you doing here?"

She gives me a wicked-looking smile. "My job," she says.

"Your . . . job?"

"Presley," Declan yells, and I hold out a finger toward him, the universal signal for *hold on*.

I'm so confused right now, and my brain is attempting to put everything together.

I ask the most obvious thing as I try to parse through all the questions filtering through my mind at once. "You're paparazzi?"

She wobbles her head side to side. "I prefer *media photographer*."

"But you were on the island . . . on Sunset Harbor. Did you follow me?"

"Oh no," she says, waving the idea away with her hand. "It was just luck, really. I was trying to get the scoop on Noah Belacourt. See if I could get anything juicy. But imagine my surprise when I saw you there. Presley James, fallen-from-grace actress, sitting on that bench in the town square."

"You didn't even have a camera," I say, remembering how she lectured me to sit up straight. I thought she was just a crotchety older woman who lived on the island.

"Ah," she says. "But that's how I get all the good pictures, you see. I hide my camera in bushes and use a remote." She gives me a wink and pats her pants pocket, where I see a rectangular shape popping through. "And no one thinks a sweet older lady would be taking secret pictures of them. It's a magic trick. I get you to look one way while I'm doing something else over here." With her finger she points upward and then to the side.

I'm a little taken aback by the sweet older lady thing. Has she met herself?

"Wait, so it was you," I say, pointing a finger at her, my brain finally putting the whole thing together. "You took all those pictures of me with Briggs on the island."

She stands up a little taller then. "And I got paid a pretty penny for it. I've almost got enough to retire to Boca Raton."

"But how did you get the ones in his mom's backyard?"

"Easy," she says. "Especially on an island where everybody talks. It works the same way in small towns. I just got people talking and made some friends, told them I like to go bird-watching, and suddenly I've got easy access."

I hate everything about this, and it was a complete violation, but I'm also slightly impressed.

"Were you the one taking pictures of us that morning on the beach? Hiding behind the tree?" It didn't look like her, but now that I know she's an evil sort of genius, maybe I didn't realize it.

"Oh no," she says, shaking her head. "He hid behind a tree? What an idiot. I'd never do that. I have no idea who that was. I'd already sold the pictures I'd taken and left the island the day before. I think that was just a regular old paparazzo who'd caught wind of you being there. Little bastard jumped on my train."

I'm sort of in shock right now, facing this same woman, clear across the country. And then my stomach does a sort of turning thing, and it's not the spicy tuna from dinner.

"I blamed people for those pictures. Innocent people."

She nods. "I can see how that might have happened."

I blamed Briggs's mom and sister for those pictures.

I'm an idiot. Not that I would have ever suspected that this grouchy woman was taking pictures of me, but why was I so sure it was Briggs's family that I refused to consider there was another option?

I look her in the face. "Betty—"

"Deborah," she corrects.

I breathe out my nose. "Whatever. I'm really glad I ran into you, but I'm probably going to have to get a restraining order against you."

She gives me a shrug like it's no big deal. "It's all in the game, right? You wouldn't be the first, but you just might be the last. And stand up straight. You really do have terrible posture."

I don't know why, but I put my shoulders back and stand a little taller.

"Also, no one is fooled by you and Declan Stone," she says. "Plus, I've got pictures that no one wants to buy of him snogging some older woman."

Oh gosh.

"But that guy on the island," she goes on. "That's the real stuff right there."

Briggs. Oh, Briggs. She's right. This crazy lady is right. And I messed it all up.

With that, Deborah—who will always be Betty to me—gives me a nod of her head, like she didn't just rock my world, and then, lifting her nose up toward the sky, she walks away.

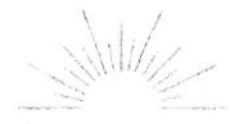

Later that night, I'm sitting on my bed, wearing the white T-shirt that Briggs let me borrow after having spilled iced coffee on me the first time I met him (I never returned it and am not giving it back now; it's my favorite souvenir from the island). I've written approximately five thousand different versions of a text to him. Nothing seems right. I want to tell him what happened and apologize, but the words all look wrong on my screen.

> **Me:** Hey, Briggs, turns out you were right. It wasn't your mom and sister who took the pictures. Hilarious, right?
>
> **Me:** Hey, Briggs, remember when I accused your sister and mom of taking pictures of us and selling them to a gossip site? Turns out I was wrong. It was that weird lady with the big hat instead. Hahahahaha. Anyway, please forgive me. Pleeeeeeease.
>
> **Me:** Hey, Briggs, I feel terrible, but it turns out I was wrong about the pictures. Anyway, hope life is going well for you!
>
> **Me:** Briggs Conrad Dalton, I am miserable without you and I messed up and will you forgive me and can we run away together and I hate hate hate how things turned out between us and can you forgive me please I hate it here nothing feels right and I miss the island and your face and your hands and you were supposed to tell me your middle name and I wish I could see you right now and know if I screwed things up so badly that we can never have a chance and could you please tell me your middle name?

The last one was a bit of an unhinged run-on sentence that I'm super glad I didn't send.

In the end, I don't send him anything. It just feels wrong to text him. I could call him, but would he answer? Is it pointless to even try? He deserves to know that he was right, and I was a stubborn fool who should have believed him, and would he just forgive me and take me out on that boat and make out with me again?

There I go once more with the run-on sentences. I fall back on my pillows, my phone in my hands. He deserves to know, and I'll tell him. I just have to figure out the right way to do it.

CHAPTER 22

Briggs

"HEY, JACK," I say into my phone, feeling anxious as I pace back and forth in the princess living room.

I've finally grown a pair and am doing something I should have done weeks ago. Even if it took me another week to get up the courage. Now I just need him to lay it on me. Are we going to apologize? Will I need to sell a kidney to pay off some remaining debt? It's time to rip the Band-Aid off and find out.

"Briggs," he says, and the way he says my name doesn't sound like he's mad or that he's the bearer of bad news. So that's a good start. "You finally got a chance to call me back, huh?"

"Sorry," I say. "It's been a bit crazy."

"Oh?" he says. "New job?"

I pause, trying to think of what to say. *No, but I spent last month with Presley James and got my heart trampled on; so yeah, crazy, right?*

I clear my throat. "Um, no. Not yet. You?"

"No," he says. "I wanted to apologize to you for how we left things."

"Uh yeah," I say. "Me too."

"I know we probably both said things we didn't mean."

"For sure," I say. "I'm really sorry about all that, Jack."

"Anyway, I just wanted to make sure we're good."

"We're good."

"Well, I'm glad we got that worked out," he says.

"Yeah, me as well."

I've stopped pacing now and am standing in the middle of my mom's childhood-dream living room waiting for the ball to drop, for him to now tell me we owe a butt-load of money, and I'll have to figure out how to come up with it. Maybe I will have to sell a kidney after all.

He takes a breath. "So, now for the real reason I've been trying to get ahold of you."

Ah yes, here it comes. My stomach drops to the floor.

"What's that?" I ask him.

"It's taken me a while, but I've gotten us some investors," he says. "For the software."

My stomach immediately pulls itself off the floor and is now doing a spinning, butterfly kind of thing.

"You . . . got investors?"

"Yeah," he says. "It's a good amount of money too, enough to get things off the ground. Pick up where we left off."

"Are you . . . serious?" I ask, the pacing picking back up as I walk from the kitchen to the living room. Back and forth, adrenaline coursing through me.

"Totally serious," he says. "So, what do you say, Dalton? Should we get the band back together?"

I'm feeling sky high when I make it down to the bookstore where my mom and Scout are working, my mind still reeling from the conversation with Jack.

It turns out that he never gave up on the project. He's been working this whole time to try to fund the company, and he did it. We have enough to make it really work this time and to pay ourselves a decent salary for now. It seems almost too good to be true. My kidneys are happy I get to keep them.

This whole time, Jack was working, making things happen, even after all the things we said to one another before walking away from the business, and I was just . . . sulking on an island. Of course, there was the distraction of Presley there for a while, but the job thing and the nearly empty bank account were always in the back of my mind, looming there.

It makes me wonder what that says about me. I didn't even think of what else I could have done when we used up the money. I just walked away. Do I give up too easily? Did I . . . do the same thing with Presley?

I guess it doesn't matter now, not for the work thing at least, because thanks to Jack, I've got a job. I'm working again. We don't have offices yet, so for now I'll stay on the island and work from the apartment while we iron things out. But I'm getting paid, and I get to do something I love and hopefully finish what we started this time.

"Check this out," Scout says, shoving her phone in my face the second I walk into the shop. She's got a feather duster in her hand and not her hair this time.

I look down at the phone and see a picture of Presley kissing Declan Stone on the cheek. She looks beautiful in a black dress, and the way the camera captures her, it looks like a genuinely happy picture of two people in love. Even the caption above it says, "Back Together at Last."

"Looks like Parsley has moved on already," Scout says, giving rolling eyes and duck lips to the image on her phone. "How could she go back to gross Declan Stone?"

"Gross? Didn't you beg her for his autograph?"

"Ew," she says. "Don't remind me. I'm over him."

I'm not sure I believe her, nor do I think she'll be taking his picture off her screen saver anytime soon.

"Maybe they're together?" I feign nonchalance. "It doesn't really matter."

Does it hurt to see a picture of Presley with another guy? Not really. Not when it's Declan Stone and I know there's nothing going on there. It's the picture of the game she told me she didn't want to play anymore that bothers me the most. Was anything

Presley said to me true? Does she go around telling every guy she spends time with that she wants to "keep" them?

"Well, I think she looks terrible in that dress," Scout says.

I give her a side hug, which she squirms out of. "Thanks for having my back."

"Enjoy it. It'll probably be the last time." She gives me a teasing grin.

"Last time for what?" my mom asks as she walks toward us. She'd been in the back of the store, organizing shelves for a shipment of books arriving later today.

I shake my head. "Nothing. But … I do have some news."

"Oh?" my mom asks, her eyebrows moving up her forehead.

I tell her and Scout about my old job, and Scout gets bored about two seconds in and begins pretend sword fighting with the feather duster.

"Briggs, that's amazing news," my mom says, giving me a hug.

"So, I'll be here for a bit longer, if that's okay with you," I ask her when she pulls away, already knowing what her answer will be.

"Of course," she says. "I love having both my babies near me."

"Mom, I'm not a baby," Scout says, sounding irritated.

"It's a figure of speech," my mom says. "And you'll always be my baby."

"Whatever," she says.

"So . . . ," I start. "I won't be able to work at the bookshop as much. I can still help, but I need to devote some time to working on AssistGen."

"Ass what?" Scout asks.

"Scout," our mom says, her voice a reprimand.

"Sorry, I didn't hear what he said." She holds her hands out by her sides, the picture of innocence.

I chuckle. "It's the name of the company I started with some friends."

She crinkles her nose. "It's a dumb name."

"Thanks," I say.

"Don't listen to her—it's a great name," my mom says, patting me on the shoulder. "And of course, Briggsy. You need to work on your company, and I'll keep things afloat here. To be honest, I've been a little bored, not having to work as much."

"I'll still help out as much as I can," I say.

She waves my words away with her hand. "We were fine before you came back, and we'll be just fine again."

"Ouch," I say, pretending to be hurt.

"You know what I mean."

"Well, I won't be starting until next week, so put me to work," I tell her.

"Perfect," she says. "We just need to make room for all the books I ordered."

We get to work, and for the first time since Presley left, I feel lighter and happy to be here working at the bookshop.

WELCOME TO
SUNSET HARBOR
Belacourt Resort
Golf Course
Noah's House
Jane's House
Nature Preserve
Dax's Duplex
Seaside Oasis Retirement Home
Sunset Repairs
Phoenix's Office
City Offices
Scoops Ahoy Ice Cream
Sunrise Cafe
Keene B&B
Gulf of Mexico
Town Square
Bakery
Briggs's Apartment
The Book Isle
Cuts and Curls
N
W
E
S
Tristan & Beau's House
Capri's House
Gemma's House
Holland's House
Beach Break Bar & Grill
Public Beach

CHAPTER 23

Presley

IT'S THE FIRST day on the set of *Cosmic Fury*, it's hotter than hell, and I'm in full costume, which is stifling futuristic armor and tactical gear, and a blonde wig—the thing that's causing the most discomfort in this heat—braided tightly away from my face. I stand in front of a fan—they have a bunch around to help stave off the heat—lifting the heavy hair off my neck to try to cool off because I can't stop sweating.

I'm having a hard time remembering why I like this job as I've sat for two hours in makeup (in an air-conditioned trailer, thank goodness), where they added dirt and scratches to my face and arms, making it look like I've been through countless battles when I haven't yet even been through one.

The crew is bustling around, setting up cameras and adjusting the lighting to capture the next shot. Massive rigs and cranes hoist the cameras high above us, with some below, making sure they get every possible angle.

I never know how a movie will turn out until I get to see it from start to finish—since we film scenes out of order, and today we're at the midway point, about to canoe our way through the swamps of the fictional planet of Ayrndor (which right now is Ocala National Forest, with its crystal-blue water and cypress trees draped with Spanish moss) to sneak attack the Syndarians. Very little will need to be done in postproduction to transform this setting into an alien world teeming with danger and intrigue; it's pretty perfect looking as is. It would be even more stunning if it didn't feel like a sauna.

The director, Jason Orson, likes to film things in realistic settings more than on sound stages, and luckily the United States is full of places that can be manipulated to look otherworldly.

I usually love working with directors like this, getting to be out in nature and seeing places I might not otherwise. But today, with the possibility of getting eaten by an alligator in these spring waters, and with sweat dripping down my back, I'm not loving it.

I am, however, in the same state as Briggs. Even if he's a couple hundred miles and a quick ferry ride away from me. And for some reason, that gives me comfort. I still haven't told him about Betty, who's actually Deborah. I've picked up my phone countless times, and drafted more texts, and nothing is right. He needs to know, though. I need to tell him.

"All departments, prepare for a take. Actors to their marks, please," the first assistant director, a guy named Brock, says through a bullhorn.

I walk away from the fan and miss its cooling effect almost immediately. Approaching the director, I find him discussing the scene with Landon West, who's dressed in similar garb to mine.

"Okay, Presley," he says when he sees me approach. "You and Landon are going to film your scene right here." He points to a spot of land near the water. "Your teams will be waiting in the water on the canoes. You'll say the line, do the kiss, and then you'll jump into the canoes afterward. Got it?"

That's right, the first scene we're filming for *Cosmic Fury* is the one Briggs and I practiced all those nights ago. I honestly thought the universe was playing a prank on me when I saw it on the call sheet. As if Briggs Dalton isn't on my mind enough already.

"Yeah," I say, nodding my head, the wig feeling heavy and itchy. I'm still not exactly sure I'll be able to just jump into a canoe, but we did practice it earlier and I think I've got it.

"Okay, let's go, people," Brock yells through the bullhorn.

I take my spot with Landon and someone from makeup comes over and quickly dabs the sweat off our foreheads. Landon and I are standing across from each other, our crew of misfit aliens in full costume in the canoes on the water just behind him.

Jason approaches us. "Presley, I need you to look like you're frustrated with Falgon in this scene because he doesn't trust you. And Landon, I want you to really sell your anger that Callis has been tasked with taking on the team over you, okay?" We both nod, and as Jason walks back to the camera, I try to get into character.

All right, Presley, you can do this. You will not think about Briggs and his green eyes and sandy-blond hair and how it felt to run your fingers . . .

Presley James, stop this right now.

"Action," yells Brock.

I do what he says, quickly taking on the character of Callis. I'm not a lovesick woman—I'm a freaking warrior.

"How dare you disrespect me, Falgon. I'm the leader of this team, and you will do as I say," I say to Landon, my words curt, my eyes focused on him, my lips pulled into a straight line.

"But what do you even know of the Syndarians, Callis? They will trample all over us with this plan," Landon says, his voice gruff and nothing like the one Briggs used when he said the line.

Crap. I'm thinking about Briggs again, and now I've forgotten my line.

"Cut," Brock yells.

The script supervisor, a woman named Dawn, comes over to me. "Do you need the line?"

"Just give me a couple of words."

Dawn holds the script up in front of her, peering down at it through her glasses. "Listen here, Falgon—"

"Got it," I say with a nod.

I've got to get my head in the game. I will not think about Briggs anymore. I must focus on the task at hand. I am Callis, not Presley. Callis.

"You ready?" Jason asks from behind the camera, and I give him a thumbs-up.

Brock yells action, and we roll again.

"Listen here, Falgon. We don't need to know anything about the Syndarians. All we need to do is go in there and obliterate them. And if you don't think I can lead this team, then you can get back on your lunastrider and go back to Arcturus."

Landon gives me an Oscar-worthy scowl. "I don't like your ways, Callis."

"You don't have to like them; you just have to let me lead." I take a step forward and put a hand on Landon's armored chest.

"I need you to trust me, Falgon," I tell him. "You're second in command, but the team looks to you before me. If you show them you trust me, then they will also trust me."

"I want to trust you," Landon says his line, his tone low, his chest moving up and down. For a second I see Briggs in the armor, looking at me through those black rectangle glasses, pushing them up his nose because he feels uncomfortable.

I miss him so much. Why haven't I told him that? Why haven't I called him or gotten on a plane and just gone to him? I've been so busy. But also, I'm an idiot—that's why. A chicken. I need to tell him about Betty/Deborah and apologize for everything. I need to tell him that I think I'm in love with him.

My mind is conjuring up thoughts of Briggs so rapidly, each of them tumbling over the other, that I'm not ready when Landon leans in to do the kiss, his handsome face inches from mine, and I end up taking a step back from him, making him trip a little on his feet.

"Cut," Brock yells through the bullhorn.

Okay, yes, I need to tell Briggs all those things, but right now I really need to concentrate on this film.

Dawn comes over, and I hold out a hand. "I've got it," I tell her. It's not even a line—it's a freaking kiss.

"You ready, Presley?" Jason asks. "Let's take it from the top, okay?"

I give him a nod and turn back to Landon. Brock yells *action*, and we go again.

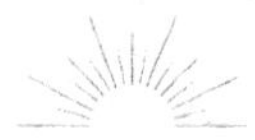

In the end, I finally get fully into my part and we get the scene done in a couple more takes, including the kiss, which made me miss Briggs even more. At least the jumping-into-the-canoe part went better than expected. I also didn't get eaten by an alligator, and thankfully, didn't even see one.

I decide, after we finish the scene, that I'm calling Briggs when I get back to my hotel. But by the time we wrap and have dinner, and I've showered off my makeup and the sweat and gone over the call sheet for tomorrow, it's too late, and I commit to calling him in the morning.

Maybe I'm too late anyway. Maybe he won't want to hear what I have to say. It's possible I've done too much damage—being so certain like I was, and then not reaching out to him in the aftermath—that we might not be able to come back from it.

I have to try, though. Don't I? I just don't know what to do, exactly. Send him flowers? That sounds like a stupid idea. If only I could see him in person, then he could see my eyes, see the sincerity in them. But I don't have time off in the foreseeable future to make a trip to the island. After filming wraps here, we immediately head to the Badlands in South Dakota.

I go to bed feeling frustrated and lost. But when I wake up to a call from the assistant director telling me we've had to delay shooting for a day because of some unexpected rainy weather and I have the day off, I know what I'll be doing.

My assistant, Shani, makes all the arrangements, and before I can really think it through fully, what I'm going to say, how I'm going to feel when I see him, I'm on a plane to Fort Myers. It's a one-hour flight, and from there a car will take me to the ferry.

I'll go to the bookstore and if he's not there, I'll knock on the door of the princess apartment. I'll search the entire island until I find him. And then . . . who knows. But I have to try. Briggs might be mad and he may not want to see me. But I have to try, or I'll regret it. If I don't, I'll always wonder what could have been.

CHAPTER 24

Briggs

"OH, YOU LOOK so pretty, Mom," Scout says when my mom walks into the bookstore from the back entrance.

"Thank you, Scout," she says, doing a little spin in a summer dress with a red floral print.

"You do look great, Mom," I say, standing next to the register.

"But ew," Scout says from the other side of the counter. "You're going on a date with Carl." She scrunches up her face like she just drank straight lemon juice.

My mom rolls her eyes. "Nothing will come of it, but it's kind of fun to be noticed."

I refrain from reminding her that those were the same words she said to me when she went on her first date with Keith. But I don't want to freak out Scout. Plus, I don't think anything *will* actually come of her and Carl—I've seen them together, and Carl cannot hold his own with the likes of Marianne McMannus.

Keith, on the other hand, was a great match for my mom, and even my eleven-year-old self could see that.

"Where's he taking you?" I ask.

"The restaurant at the Belacourt Resort," she says, holding up a pinkie finger like she's fancy.

"Gross," Scout says, not impressed.

"I expect you home at ten thirty," I say, making a joke. But honestly, she really does need to be back by then. There are not a lot of lights on this island. What if she falls into a ditch?

Wow. I'm going to nail parenthood.

Not that I'm going to be a dad anytime soon. But parenthood makes me think of marriage, which makes me think of Presley. I don't know why, but that's where my brain goes. Maybe it's because how I feel about her is how I hope I'll feel someday about whomever I marry: Happy to see her, always wanting to be around her, thinking of her every waking moment, and dreaming of her when I go to sleep.

Trying to get over Presley has been hard. Especially when Scout keeps shoving pictures of her in my face. Mostly paparazzi shots of her walking down a street, sunglasses on, her hands in the pocket of a hoodie.

I keep telling myself it all worked out how it was supposed to with Presley, that it wasn't meant to be. Maybe if I say it enough, someday I'll believe it.

I started working yesterday, which has been a much-needed distraction. I met with Jack first, and the two others we were previously working with are on board as well, but won't be joining us until next month. So, we discussed our plan of attack, and then I spent the rest of the day coding some of the features for the software, fixing bugs that were never fixed the first time around, and testing the program to make sure it runs smoothly. It felt incredible to be working again. To be doing something I enjoy.

"Okay, Carl will be here any minute," my mom says, coming out from behind the counter to the main area of the shop. "How do I look?"

"Mom," Scout says, her voice annoyed. "We already said you look pretty."

"I know, but tell me again." She fans herself with her hand. "Ahhh, I'm nervous."

"For Carl?" Scout asks, sounding appalled.

"Just to be doing this again," my mom says, looking from Scout to me. "I never thought I'd be dating again."

She gives Scout a sad smile, and Scout gives her one back, a moment of grief moving through the room like it often does, popping up in an instant.

My mom clears her throat. "What will we even talk about?"

"I bet he could go on and on about refrigerator-repair manuals," I say, offering a bit of levity to the moment.

"Stop," she says, but she's laughing. She turns to my sister. "Scout, you be home by nine, okay?"

"Nine?" Scout protests. "I'm fourteen, not ten. Everyone at the party will make fun of me."

"Fine," our mom says. "Nine thirty."

"That's not much better."

"Or you could not go to the party at all," Mom says, a stern look on her face that both Scout and I know well.

"Fine," says Scout. "I'll be home by nine thirty."

The bells on the door ring as it opens, and as a family, we all turn our heads toward it, expecting to see Carl, but instead we see . . .

"Presley," my mom says, greeting her with a sort of wobbly smile—like she's not sure if she should be smiling, but also doesn't want to be impolite.

"Hi," Presley says, giving us all a little wave. She's wearing a pink summer dress, a small purse over her shoulder. No hoodie covering her head, just sunglasses, which she slides up to rest on top of her head.

She looks amazing and I'm staring. I blink my eyes and look away, but they move right back to her.

"What brings you back to the island?" my mom asks her.

"I'm just here for today. Right now . . . this evening," she stammers. "It took me longer to get here than I thought it would, and I have to take the ferry back tonight. I just came to talk to

Briggs," she says, before giving me a closed-mouth smile full of so much meaning.

"Well, okay," my mom says, looking around for something. When she spots her purse on the counter, she grabs it and puts the strap over her shoulder. "Come on, Scout, let's give Briggs and Presley some space." She walks toward the door, waving at us before she opens it.

Scout has her arms folded as she follows my mom out the door, but as she passes by Presley, she gives her a dip of her head and says, "Parsley," before walking out the door after my mom.

The door shuts behind them, and Presley turns to me. "Did . . . she call me Parsley?"

I nod, just once. "She did. She's . . . protective."

Presley smiles, but then her face falls. "You told them what I said . . . about the pictures." She says this as a statement, not a question.

"Would it bother you if I did?" I ask, confused.

She wraps her arms around herself, rubbing her upper arms with her hands. "No, I did say it, after all. It just doesn't seem like something you'd tell them."

I look away then. "Well, you're right. I . . . didn't tell them," I admit, and then push my glasses up the bridge of my nose.

She gives me a rueful grin. "I'm glad you didn't, because I was wrong," she says.

"You were . . . wrong?"

"Yes." She nods. "I was incorrect in my assumptions."

"How could you know that?" I ask her.

"It's sort of a funny story, actually. I ran into a mutual friend of ours. Or, not really a friend."

I pinch my brows together, not following.

"The woman—the strange, demanding one that we'd see around town. The one with the big hat." Presley mimes a large hat on her head with both hands.

"I don't . . . understand," I say. What does that strange woman with the strong sense of smell have to do with the pictures?

"I know this is weird," she says. "But as it turns out, she's a paparazzo."

"What?" I say, not believing her.

"Apparently she came to the island to check up on Noah Belacourt and then happened to run into me."

"How . . . but . . . what?"

"I know," she says. "I didn't believe it either. But I saw her in LA, snapping pictures, and she admitted to it."

I twist my lips to the side. "But how did she get the pictures of us in my mom's backyard?"

Presley nods. "I had the same question. She said she's been doing this awhile and it's easy to make friends with people, so I'm guessing it was from a neighbor's yard?"

"But she was never carrying a camera with her."

"She hides it and uses a remote. It's a magic trick."

"Whoa," I say. "That's . . . really weird."

"It is. Anyway, her name is Deborah Voss, and I've filed a restraining order against her."

I tilt my head. "That sounds like a smart plan."

"So, she was the one who took the pictures, all of them except the ones of us on the beach that morning. She doesn't know who that was. She made a pretty penny and plans to retire in Boca Raton."

Presley smiles as she looks down, but then she looks up at me.

I chuckle. "That's . . . wow."

"I know."

There's silence in the room now, both of us looking anywhere but at each other. Presley hugs herself again, and I fiddle with my glasses.

"So, that's what you came to tell me?"

She nods.

"You . . . could have just called," I tell her. "You didn't need to come all the way out here to tell me."

"I'm working in Florida right now, actually. On *Cosmic Fury*."

"Really? Where?"

"Ocala," she says. "And we had the day off because of rain, so I thought I'd come tell you in person."

"Well, I'm glad you did," I tell her, and I mean it. "It's good to see you, Presley."

It's actually heart-achingly hard to see her, to be honest. I know I missed her, but I don't think I realized how much until right now. How sort of painful it feels to be in the same room and not be able to touch her or wrap my arms around her. Or kiss her.

"I also was hoping that maybe—" She stops talking, a hand now fiddling with the strap of her purse.

"Yeah?" I ask, wanting her to keep going, dying to know what she has to say.

"I was hoping you'd forgive me?" Her eyes fill with tears.

"Of course," I say. "Done."

She laughs then, a sad-sounding one, and a single tear falls down her cheek and onto her chin.

"I appreciate it," she says. "I also kind of hoped maybe we could see each other again, sometime?"

"Absolutely," I tell her, honestly. "I'd love that."

She takes a tentative step toward me. "I'm saying this all wrong. I don't just want to see you once in a while. I would like to see you on a regular basis."

"Oh," I reply, realizing what she said, realizing what she's really trying to tell me. I run a hand through my hair.

"I've missed you a lot," she says. "More than I've ever missed anyone, actually. And had I not messed everything up so badly, my hope was that we would try this out. Try *us* out. And maybe see where it goes."

"I saw pictures of you with Declan Stone," I tell her.

"Yes," she says.

"I thought you didn't want to do that kind of stuff anymore."

"I don't," she says. "That was to keep the paparazzi away from you."

"Because you didn't want them to see me?"

"No." She shakes her head. "I didn't think you'd want it."

"You're probably right," I say.

She takes another step toward me, and I stay still, standing by the counter.

"So, do you think maybe we could try?"

I stare at her for a beat before looking away, toward the bookshelves. I picture her standing there wearing her glasses, in that tank top and shorts all those days ago, smiling at my stupid jokes.

I look back at her. "You're amazing, Presley, and I loved spending time with you."

"Loved?" she says, shaking her head.

In the movie *Notting Hill*, I was annoyed with Hugh Grant's character when he turned Julia Roberts away. But now that I'm having my own version of that moment, Presley with me in a bookstore, telling me she wants to be with me, I sort of get it. It feels . . . hard. Like too many insurmountable things in our way.

And like Hugh Grant, I, too, feel like my heart couldn't take another round of breaking from Presley James.

"I can't believe I'm saying this," I finally reply, running a hand through my hair. "But . . . maybe it's not a good idea."

"Oh," she says, her eyebrows moving up her forehead. She wasn't expecting that answer from me.

"No, I mean—" I let out a breath. "The company I started, AssistGen, we have some investors and we've just started things back up. I'm going to be really busy with that for the foreseeable future, and you, well, you've got to get back to your big, career-making movie. Callis the warrior."

"Ye-yeah," she stumbles, her eyes brimming with tears again. "You're right. But you know, Briggs, those are just details."

"They're kind of big ones," I say. "You're a big movie star, and I'm a software engineer."

She takes another step toward me. "Don't forget, though, I'm just a girl, standing in front a boy, asking him to love her."

I cock my head to the side. "Did . . . did you just use the line from *Notting Hill* on me?"

"I'm sorry," she says on a sob, more tears falling down her face. "I didn't know what to say. I don't like your answer, Briggs. I don't want to accept it."

"I don't like it either," I say. "But I think we have to."

The next morning, it's so quiet you could hear a pin drop as I sit at the dining room table at my mom's house, Scout and my mom sitting with me. I've just told them what Presley said yesterday evening after they left the shop, and how I turned her down. I still can't believe I did. And I wish I had some settled feelings in my gut, like I made the right decision, but I don't feel them at all.

I didn't feel them after I told her it wouldn't work, and I didn't feel them when, before she left, she walked over to me and lifted up on her tiptoes and kissed me on the cheek, and I definitely didn't feel them when she walked out the door, the bells jingling as she did. Nor did I feel them as I tried to sleep last night and failed.

Which is why I came here this morning before the shop opened to have my mom and Scout confirm that I made the right choice.

"Briggs, you moron," Scout says loudly, as if she couldn't take the silence any longer. "You should have said yes."

"You only want me to so you can meet Declan Stone," I say.

"No," she says. "He's gross, remember? Well, I'd still meet him if I could. But you can't say no to Presley James."

"But I did say no," I remind her, those feelings of unease swimming around again in my stomach.

"Well take it back," she says. "That was a mistake."

"Was it, though?" I ask my mom.

"Do you think it was?" she asks, doing that mom thing where you answer a question with a question.

"I don't know," I say.

"You do know, you moron," Scout says.

"Scout," my mom chides.

Scout looks to my mom, holding a hand out toward me. "Well, he is. He's clearly in love with her."

"What do you know about love?" I ask. "You're fourteen." But then I think back to her group of friends asking me questions at the dance. Maybe she knows more than I think.

"Do you love her?" my mom asks.

I put a hand through my hair. "I think I do."

"See?" Scout says. "And then he went and messed it all up."

I stare at her and then my eyes move to my mom as my brain begins to process what I've done.

"I think Scout's right. I messed it up," I finally say.

My mom shakes her head. "Briggsy, you can fix this."

"How?" I ask her.

"Don't you have her number? Call her," she says.

"Should I call her?"

"Yes," they say in unison.

"Or," Scout says, "you could find out where she's filming her movie and go tell her yourself."

"Oh yeah," my mom says, pointing to Scout. "I like that plan. Do you know where she's filming?"

I rack my brain. "It's in Florida," I say.

"That's perfect," Scout says.

"Ocala," I say, suddenly remembering.

"Where in Ocala, though?" my mom asks.

I fall back against my seat. "I have no idea. Maybe I should just call her."

"No," Scout says. "Leave it to me."

A few hours later, after getting some work done because I couldn't exactly skip out when we're only a few days in, I'm on the ferry toward the mainland.

Scout found out the filming location by cross-referencing social media with permits that were pulled in Ocala. I did have a quick but stern conversation with her about stalking, but it's thanks to her that I'm heading there today.

I have no idea how I'll find Presley once I get there, or if I'll even be able to get onto the set, but I'm going to try my best.

Scout was right about not calling her. I need to chase her, especially after having turned her down so terribly last night. She needs to see that I'm going to work at this, however I can.

Maybe she's changed her mind since she left yesterday. Maybe I'm too late. But I have to try.

WELCOME TO

SUNSET HARBOR

BELACOURT RESORT

GOLF COURSE

NOAH'S HOUSE

JANE'S HOUSE

NATURE PRESERVE

DAX'S DUPLEX

SEASIDE OASIS RETIREMENT HOME

SUNSET REPAIRS

PHOENIX'S OFFICE

CITY OFFICES

SUNRISE CAFE

SCOOPS AHOY ICE CREAM

KEENE B&B

GULF OF MEXICO

TOWN SQUARE

BAKERY

BRIGGS'S APARTMENT

THE BOOK ISLE

CUTS AND CURLS

TRISTAN & BEAU'S HOUSE

CAPRI'S HOUSE

GEMMA'S HOUSE

HOLLAND'S HOUSE

BEACH BREAK BAR & GRILL

PUBLIC BEACH

CHAPTER 25

Presley

I'M MISERABLE ON set the next day. First of all, because of the rain yesterday, the air is even more hot and stifling, if that's even possible . . . which I guess it is since I'm currently suffering in it.

But it's horrible, and the woman doing hair has had to resecure this blonde wig to my head twice already, and someone from makeup has had to reapply most of mine because it has literally been melting off my face. I did say I like these on-location shoots, didn't I? I think I've changed my mind. I'd prefer air-conditioned sound stages to this.

The other reason I'm struggling today is because of Briggs. How could I not be? I'm heartbroken. I love him. I'm in love with Briggs Mortimer Dalton. I don't know if that's his middle name—I was too devastated to ask him before I left the bookshop yesterday. And I guess now I'll never know. I guess I could text him, and maybe I will when the sting of this has gotten less . . . sting-y. If that ever happens.

At least I tried. At least I won't have regrets where Briggs is concerned. I tried, and I failed. But the important part here is that I did try. Who are we kidding? I will always have regrets about Briggs. Always.

"Do you think they're trying to kill us?" Landon asks in that Australian accent of his as he sidles up to me, but not too close because we all have an unspoken rule about sharing unnecessary body heat. "I'm dying out here."

"I've never wanted air-conditioning so badly," I tell him.

I think about Sunset Harbor and the sea breeze that makes summer so much more tolerable—pleasant, even. This landlocked part of Florida is basically torture right now.

"Actors to their marks, please," Brock yells through the bullhorn.

Landon and I walk over to the waiting canoes, already filled with our teams. We're about to embark down the waterways of the springs, until we meet the Syndarians and have an epic battle where, spoiler alert, we are the victors. Because this is a happily-ever-after kind of film. Or, sort of, I guess, after our team kills a bunch of evil otherworldly beings. So, not happy for them. But the good guy wins in this story, so hooray.

At least it'll be easy to have a scowl on my face and hatred in my eyes today. Maybe I should thank Briggs for breaking my heart. Had it gone the other way—the way I was hoping—I might not have been able to stop myself from smiling through my scenes like a lovesick fool. I'm just not that good of an actress. The jig would be up.

"Quiet on the set," Brock yells through the bullhorn.

"I guess it's time to do our job," Landon says.

"Let's do this," I tell him. My words sound like I'm ready to go, but my actual physical body wants to lie down on the patchy crabgrass and maybe just cry for an hour or two.

But I don't, I get to work and after filming for a few hours, we take a break while Jason goes through what's been shot to make sure he has all he needs. If he has, then there's just one more scene to film and we'll be done. My time in Florida will be over.

I'll leave this state behind, and Briggs too. It'll be a fresh start. On to wherever life takes me next. And that's South Dakota for our next shoot. Which, to be honest, doesn't sound all that exciting.

I walk over to craft services to get some water and possibly a snack, when one of the assistants, Jan, approaches me.

"Hey, Presley, there's some guy at security asking to talk to you," she says. "Do you want me to get rid of him? He says he knows you." She looks down at a scrap of paper in her hands. "His name is Briggs Gatsby Dalton. He said you'd only know him by his full name."

"What?" I say, my eyes immediately tearing up. I grab the paper from her and read the handwritten words. "It's Gatsby?" I look at Jan, who gives me a confused shrug.

Could it be? His middle name is Gatsby? I never even thought of that as an option. But yet, that's what it is. I just know it.

"What should I tell security?" Jan asks.

I don't even answer her. I just take off running, pulling the blonde wig off my head as I go, and the cap as well. There's nothing I can do about the armor, and I'm sure I look ridiculous right now, but I don't care.

"Briggs!" I shout when I see him standing there, just outside the guard's station. I run toward him, passing security, and stop right in front of him.

"Hi," he says, his lips—his beautiful lips—pulled up into a smile.

"Your middle name is Gatsby," I say, my words breathy from running.

He nods. "It is."

"I love it," I tell him.

"Well, you and my mom have something in common, then. I used to hate it, but now I think I kind of love it, too." He takes a step toward me, and I take one toward him.

"You're here," I say, and then furrow my brow. "How did you find me?"

"Scout," he says, chuckling.

"You came all the way here to tell me your middle name?"

He looks me in the eyes, a smile on his face. "That, and I also wanted to tell you I love you."

I blink, rapidly. The tears are back again. Makeup and hair are going to hate me today.

"You love me?" I ask him.

He nods, moving even closer. "I'm not sure what got into me yesterday when you came to see me, but it was the wrong choice and I'd like to try this thing with you and see where it goes."

I'm struggling for words right now, still not believing he's here, standing in front of me.

"I'm prepared to use the daft prick line from *Notting Hill* if necessary," he says.

I laugh amidst the tears streaming down my face. "You don't need to," I say. "Because I love you too, Briggs Gatsby Dalton."

And then he's kissing me; his hands are in my hair and then on my face, and this stupid armor I'm wearing is a ridiculous barrier, but I don't care. Briggs is here. Briggs Gatsby Dalton is here, and he loves me and I love him.

The beginning of this summer started out as possibly one of the worst in my entire life, but it's somehow morphed into my best summer ever, and I have the man who currently has his arms wrapped around me, his lips moving against mine, to thank for it.

I know we'll have some things to work through, different sorts of barriers in our way, but after we've kissed properly and we walk hand in hand back onto the set, I know I'll do whatever it takes to make it work, whatever I have to do.

Because he's worth it.

EPILOGUE

Briggs

THE NEXT COUPLE of months go like this: I visit Presley as much as I can while she films *Cosmic Fury*, and we go to a few places in the United States I've never seen before. Places like the Badlands in South Dakota, with its unique rock formations and barren expanses, and White Sands National Park in New Mexico, where the endless white sands will end up looking like a desolate, icy planet in post-production.

I feel bad for the cast, who have to wear winter clothes in the high temperatures, but not bad enough to come out of Presley's air-conditioned trailer.

The Redwoods in California are probably my favorite thing so far—all those towering, monstrous trees and the morning fog weaving through them like a ghostly blanket. We go on walks during her breaks, enjoying the cooler weather, and talking about future plans, which right now seem distant since Presley won't be done with this shoot until next March, at the earliest.

"I think I should buy a place on Sunset Harbor," she says, wearing a light jacket and a black knit cap over her dark hair. Her arm is linked through mine and she leans against me as we walk, pine needles and leaves crunching under our feet.

"I bet my mom would sell you the princess apartment," I tell her.

She looks up at me, her eyes widening. "Really?"

"I was kidding," I say, reaching up and fiddling with my glasses. "You'd actually want to buy it?"

She nods. "I have a lot of fond memories in that apartment."

I chuckle. "So do I."

I'm still living in my mother's childhood dream above the bookshop, at least for another couple of months while Jack and I try to figure out office space. It looks like it will most likely be back in Fort Lauderdale. For now, we've been working on our own and having meetings on Zoom. Things are going well and moving quickly, so I don't anticipate our current setup lasting much longer. If we want to grow this business—and that's the plan—we'll be better off in the same office.

Until then, I'll continue to work from wherever Presley is, using her breaks from filming to help her run lines and getting in trouble when I mess up her hair and makeup after kissing her soundly.

Getting to see her in her element has been captivating. I knew she was a great actress because I saw her perform on screen, but to watch her live, to see her fall into the role of Callis like it's something she's been doing for years, is incredible. And I get a front-row seat for all of it. I don't love that front-row seat as much when she has to kiss Landon West, though. I'd prefer a back-row seat. Something very far back. Another time zone would be preferable.

She rarely has downtime long enough to go anywhere, but when she does, we take advantage of it. One weekend in August, Presley went back to Sunset Harbor with me for a wedding, and a couple of weeks later, I attended a charity gala and an awards show with her.

Being by her side on the red carpet is not my favorite thing. Don't get me wrong—I love being there with her and enjoy watching her pose for cameras and answer questions with ease, but I also feel a bit like a cat at a dog show. I'm awkward, and it's obvious in the pictures. Jack has made a computer screensaver out of a particular shot of me with wide eyes and triple chins. What a jerk.

I'll keep taking terrible pictures by Presley's side for as long as I can. Once we get the office up and running, I won't have as much opportunity, and I'm savoring every moment I get to spend with her.

Presley

WHEN BRIGGS HAS to go back to the office for AssistGen, I become a stage-five clinger. A long-distance one, but that doesn't stop me from texting and calling and wishing every waking hour that I was with him instead of on this stupid movie set. A month goes by without seeing him in person, and all I want to do is kiss his face off, but I have to wait until our break for Thanksgiving to get the opportunity. When the holiday finally comes around and he's there waiting for me at the Fort Myers airport so we can take the ferry to Sunset Harbor together, I not only kiss his face off, I also cry like a big idiot.

Thanksgiving is perfect, just Briggs and me with his mom and sister. Marianne usually likes to invite other Sunset Harbor residents to join them, but she keeps it small for me, which I adore her for doing. She makes the most incredible turkey with a white gravy that I'd honestly like to drink, but I hold myself back since I'm still having to dress up like Callis and those costumes are not that forgiving.

For the short duration we're on the island, I find time to close on the house I bought. It's right on the beach and has a wraparound porch where I plan to spend as much time snuggled up with Briggs as I can, once our schedules slow down. Which won't be until February for me, and for Briggs . . . well, we don't know when that will happen. I try not to think about it or I get twitchy with anxiety.

A month later, production takes a longer break for Christmas, and I spend every minute of it with Briggs. I introduce him to my dad, who, like everyone who meets Briggs, likes him instantly. We have dinner on Christmas night with my dad and my grandparents. Rounding out the party like some weird Hollywood dramedy, my mom and Declan Stone join us. They're still going strong, which is just . . . great. But having them there was not as weird as I was anticipating, even if on paper it all sounds very strange.

When February rolls around and filming wraps, I don't bother going to my house in Calabasas; I head to Florida to be with Briggs. He takes some time off from work and we head to Sunset Harbor, lying on the beach and soaking up the sun, and of course snuggling up on the porch at my new home.

"Do you know what I think?" I ask him as we sit tangled together on a two-person swing that I purchased for this exact purpose, listening to the waves as they crash against the shore and gazing at the moon lighting up the night.

"What's that?" Briggs asks, his hand making lazy patterns on my arm as he holds me close.

"I think we should quit our jobs and just do this for the rest of our lives."

He sighs. "That's a great idea. Maybe the best one you've ever had."

"I agree, I'm a genius," I say.

"You are. But . . . you've got contracts and I've—"

"Contracts, shmontracts," I cut him off. "Stop ruining my dreams, Briggs Gatsby Dalton."

I don't want to think about the next movie, which starts shooting in three months. This one, a spy thriller set in the 1940s called *Operation Dark Horizon*, won't be as long of a shoot as *Cosmic Fury*—or as intense, thank goodness.

But filming another movie means being away from Briggs, and I hate the thought of it. I have to deal with it though, because my time off, which I spend soaking up every moment with the love of my life while bouncing back and forth between Fort Lauderdale and Sunset Harbor, flies by. Before I know it, it's time to go back to work.

Briggs

"YOU LOOK MISERABLE," Jack declares as we finish a planning meeting on a hot summer day the following August. We're sitting in his office, the only one with floor-to-ceiling windows, which I lost in a game of rock, paper, scissors.

"What makes you say that?" I ask him, a light, modern-style desk between us.

"It's pretty obvious, Dalton," he says. "It's the puffy eyes that really give it away."

With the time difference between here and Burbank and Presley's schedule for the movie she's working on, I've been staying up late to FaceTime her. Often, it will be three in the morning for me when we finally say goodbye. It's not ideal, but it's what we're doing to make this work.

I let out a breath, swiping a hand down my face. "Long-distance relationships suck," I tell him.

Jack looks at me, his elbows on the desk, fingers steepled. "So don't do the long-distance thing," he says.

"Yeah," I say, sarcastically. "Wouldn't that be great."

Great, but not really possible. We're definitely on an upward trend with AssistGen, bringing on more and more clients and making a steady income, but we have a long way to go before I can just pick up and go where I want.

Jack has taken on the role of CEO and I'm the COO, and it works, especially with the team of ten we have working for us now. Except for the few hiccups you'd expect from a startup, things have been running smoothly for the most part. The luxury of not being here for the day-to-day seems like a far-off dream.

Jack lifts a shoulder and lets it drop. "I've been thinking about it, and with the time difference between Fort Lauderdale and the companies we've been working with in Tokyo and Shanghai, having you in California would be beneficial."

I furrow my brow at him. "Okay, but what about the other work I do?"

"You can do it from there," Jack says. "We'd miss your pretty face, of course. But I think we could make it work. And if we don't, you can always come back."

"Have I been that miserable?" I ask.

"The worst," he says, giving me a solemn-looking nod before his lips break into a smile.

I don't jump on the idea right away, but after plenty of discussions working out the logistics, I go to California, back to working in Presley's trailer while she's on set, running lines with her and ruining her makeup when she has a break.

I've never been happier.

Presley

"WHAT ARE YOU thinking about?" Briggs asks me as we snuggle up on the couch at my house in Calabasas—the one that will no longer be my permanent residence come November when shooting for *Operation Dark Horizon* is done. Just one month from now.

The house on Sunset Harbor is where I'll call home for the foreseeable future, especially when I take a much-needed break.

Thanks to my own planning and some contract cancellations resulting from the viral video that has finally died down quite a bit, I have no upcoming projects and I'm going to keep it that way for a while. I just want to be where Briggs is; that's my plan. I'll have to do some press tours when these last two movies I've worked on are released, but I'm hoping to drag him with me for all of that.

I can't wait to make the island my home. The residents of Sunset Harbor have been so great to me. Protective, even. Somehow—I'm guessing probably because of the workings of Marianne and Scout—no one leaks anything to the gossip sites or the paparazzi when I'm there. Some of them have also taken to keeping an eye out for any suspicious-looking visitors and reporting them to me. Most of them have been false alarms, but I do appreciate it. I'm amazed at how I can walk around almost freely. It might be the most normal my life has ever been.

"I'm thinking about how happy I am to be here with you," I tell Briggs. He's been gone for the past two weeks, back to Fort Lauderdale for meetings, and I've hated every minute of it. I turn my head just slightly to give him a light kiss, which quickly morphs into something not so light.

"I guess there is something else I've been thinking about," I say, once we come up for air from all the kissing. I'm now wrapped in his arms, his nose nuzzling into my neck.

"What's that?" he asks.

"Marrying you," I say bluntly. I hadn't been thinking of that exactly, but it has been on my mind. A lot. I'd like to keep Briggs in a permanent way.

He pulls away from my neck so he can see my face. "Marrying me?"

I smile and give him one quick nod. "Have you never thought of it?"

The hypothetical subject has come up, of course, but more like possibilities and not something that's a foregone conclusion. He doesn't know it's been that way for me ever since he showed up on the set of *Cosmic Fury*—I was done for from that moment on.

He leans in and kisses me on the lips. "Every day," he says.

"You have not," I say with a giggle.

"You don't believe me?"

I shake my head. I guess I do believe him, though, since I've thought about it every day as well.

"I have proof," he says, pushing up from the couch and getting to his feet. He quickly jogs over to his computer bag, which is sitting by the front door.

Butterflies dance around in my stomach as I sit up, running my fingers through my tousled hair, anticipating what his proof might be. They multiply when he walks back toward me with a nervous smile.

"Let's see this proof," I say, standing up from the couch as he approaches.

He swallows. "I've had this for three months," he says, reaching into his pocket and pulling out a black, velvet box.

"Oh," I say breathily, reaching a finger out and touching the soft material of the case. It's real proof. I thought he was going to show me a text he sent to his mom or something. But this is the real thing.

He snatches it back like I was about to grab it, and we both laugh.

"You've had it for three months?"

"Yes, but I've been looking for nearly a year."

"You have?"

He nods. "I had different plans for this," he admits, looking down at the box in his hand before he bends down on one knee in front of me.

I start to tear up. I wasn't expecting this. I didn't even mean to say that I was thinking about marrying Briggs; it just came out, and now here he is in front of me, about to propose.

"Wait, what were the plans?" I ask, wanting to know what he had in mind for this moment.

"I was thinking of doing it on the beach under the stars," he says, looking up at me.

"On a sleeping bag with Keith's binoculars?" I ask, remembering that night almost a year and a half ago.

"Yes," he says.

"Well, what if I want that? The whole stars-and-beach thing?" I ask him.

"You want to wait?" he asks, standing back up.

I nibble on my bottom lip. I so badly want to see what's in that box. I mean, I know what it is, but I want to see what he picked out. I want to see it and then I want to say yes and put it on my left hand and never take it off. But I also want what Briggs has envisioned.

"Yes," I tell him. "I want what you were planning."

"Okay," he says, putting the velvet box back into his pocket.

"Don't make me wait too long," I say.

"I'll do my best," he promises, before pulling me in for a kiss.

Briggs

I DO HAVE TO make Presley wait longer than I'd intended, but by the time she's finished filming and is settled in her house on the island, we have a week of on-and-off rain. This isn't uncommon for December, but it's not conducive to a night on the beach under the stars.

When things finally align—the weather is good, and we're both available—I enlist Scout to help me bring Presley to the beach, which she is more than happy to do.

"I've always wanted a sister. And especially one who can introduce me to Timothée Chalamet," she says before I shoo her off to go get Presley.

It takes Scout a bit longer than I was anticipating, which gives me enough time to work up a bunch of nervous energy. But when I see Presley walking toward me, a smile on her face, all my anxiety falls away.

"Hello there," she says as she walks up to me. I'm standing at the edge of the setup I've put together—the beach blanket with the sleeping bags on top. I've placed lanterns around to give us some light and I've also thrown some rose petals on top of the bedding, as well as some on the sand around us. My mom sent me with a basket of goodies, some snacks, and some champagne and glasses to celebrate.

That is, if Presley says yes. Which I'm pretty sure she will. But who knows, maybe she's changed her mind in the last six weeks.

"Hi," I say, now feeling slightly nervous that we might not be on the same wavelength. I grab her by the hand, giving it a little squeeze.

"So," she says, looking around at my setup. "What's all this for?" She gives me a broad smile.

"Well, I thought we could sleep under the stars again," I say. "With no paparazzi this time."

"Are you sure?"

I shrug. "I'm never sure about that."

"It comes with the job," she says.

We haven't seen much of the paps around here, not for a while. But you never know.

"So, you have me here, on the beach," she says, the smile on her face morphing into something more coy. "What do you plan to do next?"

I grin, any nervous feelings I had dissipating.

"I don't know," I say, pulling her toward me, snaking an arm around her waist. "I figured we'd sleep on the beach, maybe look at the stars."

"And?"

"And . . . that's it."

"Briggs," she chides.

"Okay, fine. I did have something else in mind."

I pull away from her, taking a step back and giving myself enough room for what I'm about to do.

"Are you ready?" I ask her.

"I am," she nervously replies.

"Should we look at the stars first?"

"Briggs Gatsby Dalton."

"Okay, fine," I tell her, and then push my glasses up my nose. Time to be serious.

Slowly, I get down on one knee, still holding her hand. "Presley," I start. "I think I fell for you that first day when I dumped iced coffee all over you."

She lets out a laugh, tears brimming in her eyes.

"And I'm pretty sure I knew I was falling in love with you after you jumped into my arms in the ocean when you were scared by some seaweed."

"It was a fish," she interjects.

"Shhh," I say, tugging on her hand. "I'm trying to propose here."

"Oh right," she says. "Carry on."

"I love your determination, your unwavering drive, and your tenacity in the face of challenges. I love your humor and the sound of your laughter. I love how you care for others, how you make me feel valued and appreciated. I want to be worthy to be by your side, and promise to work every day to be so."

She's crying now, and I can't help but feel choked up myself. I reach into my pocket and pull out the black velvet box that I've been holding on to for four-and-a-half months now.

"So, Presley Renee Shermerhorn," I say, opening the box and holding it out toward her. "Will you marry me?"

She doesn't look down at the ring, but keeps her eyes on me instead.

"Yes," she says, a single tear falling down her face.

"Yes?" I ask, making sure I heard her right. I don't even know why I ask; it just feels like the thing to do.

"Yes," she says, laughter in her voice. "I want to marry you right now, Briggs Gatsby Dalton."

"Do you want to see the ring?" I ask, still holding it in my hand.

"Oh," she says, sniffling. "Yes, the ring. I almost forgot about that part."

I stand up, holding it out toward her, and when she looks at it, her lips pull into a huge smile.

"It's a sun," she says, looking up at me, another tear falling down her cheek.

I nod. I knew it was perfect when I saw it in the store—a round center diamond surrounded by smaller ones, arranged like rays. A sunburst is what it's called.

"Since we met in the summer, in Sunset Harbor, I figured it was kind of perfect."

She nods. "It's the most perfect ring ever."

"It's for all the happy summers we get to have together," I say.

She reaches up on her toes and kisses me. "I can't wait."

Thank you for reading! Do you want more of Briggs and Presley? Visit https://BookHip.com/ZHHDQCV to read a bonus chapter!

Read the next book in the Falling for Summer series

Every good summer has a little bad...

I wasn't supposed to be in Sunset Harbor for more than a weekend. But thanks to, let's just call it—an unforeseen act of stupidity on my part—I'm here for the whole summer. And for the first time in my life, I'm in a whole lot of trouble.

The sentence? Community service paid toward the person I accidentally wronged.

The problem? That person happens to be Dax Miller. The guy who always spent more time fighting the law than obeying it. Also the guy I once told to have a nice life amounting to nothing.

So…it's been fun being court ordered to serve him now.

Except the more time I spend with Dax fighting and fixing what was broken, the more I remember that sizzling…something…that's always been between us. Or that smile of his that can get me to do just about anything. Let me be clear, with a politician for a father, I don't do trouble. But what happens when the temptation to embrace that inner rebel becomes too strong to resist?

And what do I do when the guy who has only dated trouble his entire life, has his sights set on me?

FALLING FOR SUMMER

Summer Ever After by Kortney Keisel
Walker & Jane

Beachy Keen by Kasey Stockton
Noah & Cat

Plotting Summer by Jess Heileman
Tristan & Capri

Summer Tease by Martha Keyes
Beau & Gemma

Beauty and the Beach by Gracie Ruth Mitchell
Phoenix & Holland

One Happy Summer by Becky Monson
Briggs & Presley

Rebel Summer by Cindy Steel
Dax & Ivy

ABOUT THE AUTHOR

BECKY MONSON is a mother of three and a wife to one but would ditch them all for Henry Cavill. She used to write at night but now she's too dang tired, so she fits in writing between driving kids around to activities and running a household. With a talent for procrastination, Becky finds if she doesn't watch herself, she can waste an entire afternoon binge-watching Netflix. She's a USA Today bestseller and an award-winning author, and when she does actually get off Netflix to write, she uses humor and true life experiences to bring her characters to life.

Becky wishes she had a British accent and a magic spell to do her laundry. She has been trying to give up Diet Coke for the past ten years but has failed miserably.

Connect with Becky at www.beckymonson.com

Made in the USA
Monee, IL
28 April 2025

16518439R00204